THE MUSGRAVE SOLUTION

Also by John Henderson

*A Blind Eye*

*Anchor Man*

*Murder Scams and Gravy Trains*

*The Taipan Club*

# THE MUSGRAVE SOLUTION

## SIMON WEBSTER'S FOURTH FIASCO

## JOHN HENDERSON

The Musgrave Solution

eBook ISBN: 978-0-9875769-5-8

Book ISBN: 978-0-9875769-4-1

Publisher: John Henderson, Canberra, Australia

Publication Date: 15th August 2016

❀ Created with Vellum

## ACKNOWLEDGMENTS

To my wife Jill Paterson whose support and encouragement, in light of her own successes as a novelist, has been the inspiration to continue the Webster series.

# CHAPTER 1

*H*enry Haynes sat in a quiet corner of the sparsely populated bar and finished off his hamburger and hot potato chips. It was dark outside as it was late, well, late for Henry who firmly believed a nine to five job meant just that. If it hadn't been for the fact that his boss, Ralph Glover, had appealed to Henry for assistance in the scrutiny of some council documents, Henry would have been happily ensconced in his Bondi Beach home watching telly and sipping the occasional beer.

Under normal circumstances Henry would have provided Ralph with any excuse not to be involved with council paperwork. But this was different. Ralph had received documents relating to the redevelopment of a piece of real estate known as The Grovel located in the Sydney harbourside suburb of Elizabeth Bay. Henry was well aware of the history and ultimate disaster involving the property in question. In fact, the family feud concerning the future of The Grovel, the stately Glover family mansion for some generations, had resulted in the brutal murder of Ralph's brother, Bruce. Following an extensive police investigation, the perpetrator of the dastardly deed turned out to be none other than one of Ralph's brothers, Paul, ably assisted in the commission of the said crime by Ralph's uncle, Andrew. Oddly enough, although both men were clearly guilty of the brutal bashing to death of Bruce, the presiding judge ruled that the attack amounted to no more than minor misdemeanours, namely fratricide and parricide. As a consequence, in passing judgement on the two homicidal maniacs, the judge deemed the duo to be pillars of virtue and sentenced them accordingly; three years in the lockup.

With it getting near to Henry's bedtime and still having to walk some distance to his home, he drained his second schooner of beer, dropped off the empty plate and glass at the bar, gave the barman a friendly wave and headed for home. The two drinks consumed with his hamburger and chips had little, or at least little deleterious, effect on Henry's faculties as he was a big man, tall and muscular and who now, albeit in his forties, sported a crew cut hair style, not that his hair style ever had anything to do with his sobriety. He had worked for a property development company, Dayman Brothers, until it went broke only to be bought out by Glover Property Development at a very attractive price. Fortunately for Henry, Ralph Glover took him on as Andrew Glover, the previous boss of Glover Property Development, or GPD as it was referred to, was currently cooling his heels along with his nephew, Paul, as guests of the state in the town's lock-up.

The shambles of the Dayman Brothers' collapse and subsequent events at Glover Property Development had done nothing for Henry's sense of humour, or lack thereof. He steadfastly refused to partake in any social event organised by the GPD staff and appeared to be perfectly happy to persevere with the pain of carrying a giant chip on his shoulder. As it was, this particular night was a rare occasion for Henry as the couple of beers at the pub had induced a sense of peaceful tranquillity, a condition he seldom experienced, especially after the fall of Daymans. To be able to actually enjoy the cool night air and breathe the salty tang of the nearby ocean was something Henry had not been able to appreciate for far too long. So it was late, but somehow he now didn't really care as he slowly made his way along Campbell Drive to Lamrock Avenue where he lived alone in a small brick bungalow. Henry felt good knowing his boss would not have requested his assistance with the paperwork unless it was serious, and Ralph did appreciate Henry's assistance. In fact, Ralph had shown his appreciation by giving him the following morning off work.

But Henry didn't go to work next morning, nor that afternoon. In fact, the last thing Henry was able to recall on regaining consciousness in the hospital ward a few days later was eating a hamburger and chips at the local pub. Whoever wielded the weapon had done a pretty good job on Henry who, according to the hospital medical staff, was extremely lucky to be alive.

Unable to recall anything regarding the brutal attack, Henry couldn't help but think that if he had been killed, he would have been totally unaware of the incident. However, as he was not dead, he was able to acknowledge the peacefulness of the experience and the fact that there had been no sensation of time, or a sensation of anything, for that matter. How very strange. There was no doubt the assailant had both the means and opportunity to kill Henry. There was also no doubt the assailant had every intention to do away with Henry Haynes on a permanent basis, the severity of the wounds inflicted the unmistakable proof of such intent. Henry had been a marked man. However, the problem now was, would the assailant try to complete the job and, more to the point, why?

Detective Chief Inspector Simon Webster was oblivious to the world as he made his way along George Street. Simon was a troubled man with more than the usual mundane and aggravating day to day things on his mind. A significant factor influencing Simon's current discomposure had been a phone call from, as he recalled, a very pretty young lady, Cheryl Drake. While Cheryl herself had not necessarily been totally responsible for Simon's unease, it was her mention of the name Glover that had sent Simon into a state of near apoplexy. To Simon, Glover was what Moriarty was to Holmes and a name he hoped he would never hear again.

As the tall, athletic, detective chief inspector with the receding blond hair made his way along George Street to meet Ms Drake, his troubles were exacerbated by the dawning recognition that he was surrounded by an army of either androids or idiots. The replicant army, a description Simon finally decided far more befitting, was in the process of meekly surrendering to the rapid development of technology at the expense of accepted social norms exercised since creatures crawled out of the ocean and started to communicate with each other. No, Simon wasn't pushing buttons on one of the new high-tech gizmos that every other human being on good old planet Earth seemed to have become addicted; he had a mobile phone for use in an emergency, and that was the limit to this technological dinosaur's knowledge of communicative modernism.

Simon was under no illusion that the art of face to face verbal communication between humans was rapidly heading in the same direction the dodo had taken. The English language, as spoken back in the old days, was undergoing a metamorphosis and destined to quickly pass into the realms of history. Maybe, with a lot of luck, some astute history academic might retain a short vocabulary of essential words and phrases similar to those Simon had committed to memory prior to departing for an overseas trip to Outer Mongolia.

Displaying total disregard for traffic lights, or the vehicle driving lunatics out to emulate the latest computer road rage game, the army maintained its inexorable march along the street.

In fact, the rhythmic procession took on what Simon viewed as possessing an alarming similarity to the march of the living dead he had once seen in some B grade horror movie. *God help us, Cheryl Drake. I hope you're still in the land of the living.*

Having arrived at the Queen Victoria Building coffee shop where he and his sergeant, Noel Elliott, had first met Miss Drake, Simon had plenty of time to muster what thoughts he could recall of the specific events involved. The gist of the problem had been a family feud over a will which included some mansion in the exclusive harbourside suburb of Elizabeth Bay, and the bludgeoning to death of one of the beneficiaries.

*Ah, yes, that's it, the Glovers,* Simon thought. *And it was Paul Glover, not looking at all well, who came up out of the harbour secured to the anchor of Graham Lee's good ship "Gemini". No, I tell a lie, it was Bruce. That's right, it was Bruce, deader than a temperance party wine tasting, who had to destroy our days outing on the harbour, the rotten sod. Paul was the guilty peabrain who did him in, with a little help from Uncle Andrew, both now doing time in the jail. And if I have it right, Cheryl had been Paul's girlfriend, not that she knew Paul was a homicidal maniac, well, not then anyway.*

Lost in his thoughts, Simon was into his second cup of cappuccino before the tall brunette with shoulder length hair approached. Impeccably dressed in a dark grey corporate suit, Simon stood in welcome while acknowledging Ms Drake would probably make a boiler suit look fashionable.

'Sorry I'm late, but it's always the same. As soon as you're in a hurry to get somewhere, someone with all the time in the world on their hands rings and wants to have a social chit-chat.'

'No, that's quite alright,' Simon replied. In fact, it wasn't "quite alright". Simon was well aware of the fact that whenever Georgie, his wife, put the mobile phone to her ear, the chances were it would be Sue, Noel's wife. Unfortunately, Simon was also aware that the conversation would take on the characteristics of a parliamentary filibuster, and with a similar lack of substance. 'I believe, from what you have told me, there are storm clouds on the horizon? But before you explain, coffee?'

'Yes, a latte would be nice, thank you.' Simon excused himself and made his way to the counter to place the order. Ignoring the fact that he had just finished his second cappuccino, Simon decided to join Cheryl with a latte knowing full well his copious caffeine intake would result in a dramatic increase in visits to available conveniences.

'Now, getting back to these storm clouds,' Simon said after regaining his seat.

Cheryl shifted uncomfortably, her expression taking on a mixture of concern and embarrassment. 'Look Chief Inspector, I don't know if there is anything going on now, but I have this funny feeling something will in the near future.'

'Well, that's a good start as I'm sure something will definitely be going on in the future,' Simon remarked. 'Come to think of it, it would be a pretty dull place if there wasn't. It's probably more to the point whether this something, whatever it might be, will involve you.'

'And that's just what I'm trying to tell you. Maybe I should start at the beginning which would be at the end of the Bruce Glover incident.' It was fortunate for Simon that the coffees arrived just as Cheryl mentioned the dreaded name as it provided him with time to take a deep breath and prepare for the forthcoming narrative.

After taking a sip of her latte, Cheryl commenced her sordid tale of murder, imposture, drug dealings and malevolent family gatherings. 'I have no doubt you will recall the events leading up to the murder of Bruce, a little case of fratricide being perpetrated by that, that creature who was once my boyfriend, Paul. Following the death of Bruce, Paul became an imposter by taking on the persona of Bruce with the real Bruce, dead as he was, becoming Paul. As they were identical twins it was not too difficult for Paul to carry out the subterfuge, at least for a while. I think the only recognizable difference between the two was that Bruce was a bit on the gay side while Paul's as straight as an arrow. Anyway, I learnt I was to be the next victim as Bruce, who was really Paul, knew I would eventually spot the deception being perpetrated. Fortunately for me, you and Sergeant Noel Thingummyjig came along and cleaned up the mess before I was dead. Hopefully, all this is of no consequence to what's going on now, and if it's not going on right at this moment, it probably will sometime in the future.'

Simon frowned. 'Elliott, Noel Elliott and no, I hadn't forgotten. In fact, I happened to find the body. Obviously you are unaware there is another Glover hiding in the closet, and that's Ralph. He's taken over the property development business previously run by the uncle and co-murderer, Andrew.'

'Of course I know Ralph,' Cheryl acknowledged. 'He's a lovely man and we get on very well together, nothing at all like his despicable brother. In fact, Ralph is my problem. You see, Ralph is a pretty lay-back sort of bloke who has this idiotic view that all people are good unless they should prove otherwise while I tend to view people the other way round. By the way, do you know of a Henry Haynes?'

'You mean that cantankerous bugger who works for Ralph?'

'Yes, that's the man, and he is, isn't he?' Cheryl said with a smile. 'I don't know if you are aware of it, but someone tried to bash Henry to death recently. He was in a really bad way and is still in hospital recovering. Although he is a surly sod, it seems a bit over the top to try and bash his brains in.'

'No, I didn't know. But what's Henry's bashing got to do with the Glovers and the storm clouds, quite apart from the fact that he works for a Glover and probably has good grounds for his grumpy attitude?'

'Yes, Henry works for Ralph and, as you said, Ralph has taken over Glover Property Development which was run by

Andrew and Paul Glover. And I suppose you know they're due to be released from jail within the next couple of months?'

'No, I thought they were put away for a lot longer. And you think Paul and Andrew will want to regain control of the business and hired someone to do a job on Henry as a sort of example of what may be expected?'

Cheryl shrugged. 'I'd say definitely to the first question and more than likely to the second. Paul and Andrew are in the right spot to find some knucklehead willing to earn a few bob by bashing the brains out of any person they think may deserve a good going over. And I wouldn't mind betting they want The Grovel, for any number of reasons.'

'But who owns The Grovel now? I haven't any idea as to the legal implications involved, not with Bruce being murdered intestate, and Paul doing a stretch in prison.'

'And that's just it,' Cheryl said in exasperation. 'I don't know where Ralph stands at the moment, and I would bet pounds to peanuts Paul and Andrew will try and take over the Company.'

'And you think Henry's bashing might be the opening gambit?'

'Well, I'm a tad apprehensive. If they are responsible, and I think they must be, they could easily have organised someone to beat the tripe out of him from within jail. And just think what those two imbeciles will get up to once they're released. No, I'm sorry to say I've grave fears for Ralph's life.' Cheryl looked pensive for a moment and then, as an afterthought said, 'Let's just say I wouldn't go around pulling any anchors out of the harbour if I were you.'

Simon drained the last of his latte, sat back, folded his arms and considered Cheryl's storm clouds prediction. Could it be that the lady doth protest too much?

# CHAPTER 2

*T*he walk back to the Day Street Police Station, located within the city precinct, was not hurried. The details surrounding the murder of Bruce Glover were somewhat hazy to Simon, regardless of the fact it had been Simon who had found Bruce's body. In preparation for a day's outing on the harbour, Simon had hauled up the anchor of a luxury cruiser from the bottom of Rushcutters Bay only to find the very dead Bruce firmly attached. The anchor belonged to his good friend Graham Lee, the notorious operator of the illegal casino, The Taipan Club. At the time, Graham had been shacked up with Louisa Porter, the wife, or ex-wife, of the deceased politician, Robert Porter, MP, who had been found stabbed to death on Bondi Beach.

The investigative team assigned to both the Porter and Glover murders had been headed by Simon and comprised Detective Sergeant Noel Elliott and Ron Lange. Ron was not a policeman but an informant with the uncanny knack of knowing where to find the odd snippet of information that usually turned out to be critical to whatever case Simon was working on. Of course, there were many others involved in the death of Bruce

Glover who was referred to and as the case became known, The Anchor Man. The murder of Robert Porter was still an open case despite the abundance of finger pointing and accusations being tossed around. However, the evidence so far uncovered was insufficient to draw any definite conclusion and no-one had been charged, yet.

The police's prime suspect of Robert's murder fell to Monica Sainsbury Ackerman, head of a property development company in Sydney and wife of Walter, the previous deputy Premier of the state. As Monica had disappeared while touring the Amazon Basin with her husband, Simon had come to the conclusion Mr Ackerman had done away with his wife and left her body to float off down the Amazon or, being guilty of Robert's murder, she had gone to ground in some Central American country.

Simon entered the same drab office he and Noel had now shared for several years, the same old office with a venetian blind that didn't work and the same historical ubiquitous green linoleum that must have arrived from England as cargo when the first fleet arrived in 1788. Simon found Noel engrossed in a game of solitaire on his newly supplied computer, the only piece of technological enhancement the office had received since the replacement of a blackboard with a whiteboard a couple of years ago. Simon had also been provided with a new, you beaut IBM which, according to a weasely looking young man, was connected to something called a main train, or something or other, that could access information before you knew you wanted it. How nice.

'Hey Noel, can you dig out the Anchor Man file after you put the red five on the black six?'

Noel was short, barely making it into the police force as a result of his limited vertical attributes. But what Noel lacked in height was more than compensated for with a pugnacious attitude and a nuggetty physique to back up the attitude; built like a tank with broad shoulders, a dark complexion and a nose that had been broken on more than one occasion on the football field.

'Sure thing, boss, but you could look it up on the computer; that's what they're here for.'

'Noel, I don't care if the file is etched on two tablets of granite, I want the file with all those bits of paper we created, now.'

Noel looked hurt. 'Strewth, boss, isn't that taking the hard copy thing to extremes?'

'Now!' After finally getting the requirement through to Noel, who departed the office in search of the file, Simon sat back on his dilapidated chair, locked his hands behind his head and swivelled his seat from side to side. Anchor Man. Aah, yes. The body on the anchor of Graham Lee's boat, Simon recalled. And that place over at Elizabeth Bay, The Ghetto, no, The Grovel, that's it, The Grovel and that stupid Glover family fighting over their mummy's will. Now, what on earth are we dragging all that up for? Simon stopped his swivelling, folded his arms, shut his eyes and hoped it would all go away. "To raise a past mischief is to draw the new mischief on," or words to that effect, he thought. Simon's expertise in the recall of appropriate lines, despite his love of Shakespeare, left much to be desired and was an accurate reflection of his success, or unsuccess, in English Lit at high school.

After about a ten minute absence, Noel returned. 'Here we are, boss,' he said and handed Simon a thick manila folder secured with a pretty pink ribbon tied in a neat bow. 'The registry clerk was a bit put out when I asked him for it. He went to great pains to inform me that all the files are now on computer, so we should look it up ourselves.'

'The registry clerk can just get knotted as I'm sticking to the old ways. Now, can you recall what it was all about, Bruce Glover's murder, I mean?'

Noel shrugged. 'Not much, although I was wondering who owns The Grovel. It was willed to Paul and Bruce so I haven't a clue as to who actually owns it now. I don't know if the Rule of Forfeiture has been applied where a murderer can't benefit from a will, or from his intestate victim. I bet that bloke Darnley over at the local council could tell us.'

'You mean that birdbrain Boswell,' Simon said with a shake of the head. 'No, before we do anything, just let me have a look through the file. And I think your history is a lot worse than my Shakespeare as it was Bothwell, not Boswell mixed up with Darnley.'

'I'll ignore that comment, boss, as there's nothing wrong with my history. Anyway, I thought Anchor Man was done and dusted. Good grief, what's piqued your interest after so long? Don't tell me they're still fighting over The Grovel? And while we're talking about the dead, can you explain why on TV they're always saying "we're now crossing live to" for an interview with someone or other. The only alternative would be to say "we're crossing dead to" which would probably be politically incorrect. As we already know the person the TV is "crossing live to" must be alive, or they'd be dead, why do they say we're "crossing live to" and not just "crossing to"?'

'Crikey, Noel, do you lie awake at night dreaming up these problems? Who knows and who cares?' Simon replied as if he couldn't care less, and didn't. 'My problem, which is far more important than yours, is that I've just had a coffee with Cheryl Drake, you know, Paul Glover's girlfriend, or ex-girlfriend. She told me Henry Haynes, that cranky sod who works for Ralph Glover over at Glover Property Development, was subjected to an unprovoked attack outside his home at Bondi recently. Apparently he's lucky to be alive. Cheryl seems to think it could be the start of a vendetta involving Glover's company.'

Noel looked surprised. 'And what's Henry got to do with Drake?'

'Seems like Cheryl prefers to keep it in the family. After the Anchor thing she hooked up with little brother Ralphie, who probably possesses slightly more scruples than the elder brother, Paul.'

'Yeah, I s'pose we all have to move on, and Bruce has been dead for some time. Still, it's a small world, isn't it? Here we had Henry and Ralph both involved in that Robert Porter murder, and not a whisper from either about Ms Drake. You don't think they did have something to do with his murder, do you? After all, as he was a politician, there were any number of people queued up to stab him in the back, both literally and metaphorically, and no-one's been charged with his murder yet.'

'No, I believe Cheryl Drake's interest in Henry is based solely on her association with Ralph Glover. I don't think she would care two hoots if Henry hadn't survived his bashing if there wasn't that connection. And let's face it, the combined IQ of our felonious freaks, Paul and Andrew, struggles to make double figures. With them due out of jail and running loose, we have all the ingredients needed for some pretty stupid activity. And you can bet Ralph and The Grovel will be involved some-where along the line. Although Henry's bashing took place out of our bailiwick, I think we might go and see what DI Francis over at Waverly knows on the subject.'

The attack on Henry Haynes had been conducted outside Henry's residence at Bondi Beach, hence falling within the police's Eastern Suburbs Local Area Command, or LAC as the various Commands are referred. As a consequence, the investi-gation into the attack was being conducted by Detective Inspector Ian Francis from the Waverly police station, a detective known to both Simon and Noel following the recent investiga-tion into the brutal stabbing of Robert Porter, MP, on Bondi Beach. That investigation had ultimately been conducted by Simon as he had known Robert Porter and his wife, Louisa, for some time. With such a highly regarded member of society being eliminated under somewhat suspicious circumstances, the police hierarchy reasoned Simon was probably better placed to do the investigation than DI Francis who, quite happily, palmed the investigation off onto Simon.

Dressed in mufti and with a welcoming smile, DI Ian Francis rose from behind his desk and greeted Simon and Noel to his office. 'Welcome gentlemen. Good to see you again. Please, take a seat. I believe you're here for some info on the Henry Haynes bashing?'

'Yes,' said Simon as he settled into a comfy lounge chair. Cripes, I outrank this tosser and he has an office as classy as Chief Superintendent Paxton's. 'We would like to have some idea as to just what's going on, especially in light of Henry's connection with Ralph Glover, and the fact that both Ralph's brother and uncle will be released from the town jail in the not too distant future.'

Regaining his seat behind his desk, Francis picked up a buff coloured file from his "In" tray and dropped it in front of him. 'You wouldn't be interested in some information on another case, would you? We're a bit short of anything regarding poor old Henry's bashing. Come to think of it, I think it's safe to say we have stuff all to go on. Sure, he mightn't have had the personality of Happy, but just because he was Grumpy shouldn't provoke the hiding he received.'

'So, if you haven't a clue as to the identity of the perpetrator, you must be Dopey,' Noel blurted, having settled back into a lounge chair with his notebook and pen at the ready.

'I'll ignore that, Sergeant, but no, we have absolutely no idea who is responsible,' DI Francis said with a shake of the head. 'The only thing we have to go on is his involvement in the Porter murder, and from what I hear that involvement was negligible. One other thing I heard relating to that investigation, which doesn't have any bearing on the Hayne's case, was that you irritated a few people when you uncovered the shonkies and scams the politicians would have preferred not to have been uncovered.'

'Good grief, and ain't that the truth,' replied Simon. The investigation into the death of the prominent polly had led to the exposure of systematic exploitation and defrauding of legitimate benefits payable to parliamentarians, along with the gross moral misbehavior of certain members. While Simon had never regarded politicians with any great approbation, by the end of the investigation the used car salesman had rocketed over the politician in the climb up the integrity ladder.

DI Francis heaved a sigh, placed one hand on his hip, scratched the back of his head with the other and said, 'And you now think that when these two Glover ratbags are released there could be some feathers flying?'

'Hell knows, but at least it will be interesting to see what does eventuate,' Simon replied with some apprehension. 'I don't know who holds what position in government now, but I'd expect nothing to have changed since we uncovered the previous scams involving kickbacks paid by shonky developers to compliant politicians. Although we have no idea if there is anything going on at the moment, you can't help but view any redevelopment scheme, especially if it involves the Glovers, without a touch of scepticism. And you can bet the release of our murderous reprobates, Andrew and Paul Glover, is nothing but a harbinger of trouble, and that trouble is sure to involve The Grovel.'

DI Francis frowned and slowly shook his head. 'I'm sorry, Simon, but I seem to be a bit remiss as I haven't been following the Glover's proposed schemes or plans for The Grovel. Care to enlighten me?'

Simon settled himself back in his chair and folded his arms. 'You see, The Grovel is now zoned as a medium density residential site by the council's planning authority, thanks to Paul's ambition for his townhouse redevelopment scheme, and there's nothing illegal about that. However, we have heard on the grapevine that there is a push for the property to become a gambling casino and, while we have nothing to suggest who's pushing this proposal, a couple of names come to mind. These include our old mate Andy Crawford who has made known his interest in the place. Although not an insurmountable problem, anybody wanting to turn the place into a casino would need to get the place rezoned again, but this time as a commercial site, depending on whatever plans are submitted to council.

'While we could see a contest for the casino option, we also have a swag of people lined up wishing to make The Grovel their private home, which would mean council having to revert their rezoning decision back from medium to low density housing, which The Grovel was before Paul's plan was accepted. I'd hazard a guess and say that any approach to the council for a further rezoning would require a bit of heavy-weight support. Strangely enough, I doubt if Paul Glover is in any position to ask support from the tooth fairy, being a murderer and all. But that's neither here nor there as the place has been rezoned to accommodate his townhouse scheme.'

'And you think whatever is going on, or might go on, will involve Paul Glover,' Francis remarked rhetorically. 'I've already spoken to Ralph and he thinks Paul and Andrew would have to be suspects behind Henry's bashing, even if they are still in jail. Henry's a pretty solid bloke so the idea of a random attack seems a bit farfetched. But, come to think of it, there are a lot of nutters out there who wouldn't think twice before having a go at anyone, irrespective of size. No, I think Ralph is on the right track with Henry being targeted by those two loonies, only we haven't any evidence to support the theory.'

'Well, I agree with you there. Ralph is probably right when he says the bashing is somehow tied up with the Glovers, and maybe even Porter's death,' Simon conceded. 'While we have absolutely no intention of encroaching into your investigation, it might be an idea if we keep each other informed of any developments we may come across.'

Francis nodded his agreement. 'Yes, that makes sense. Nothing has happened, yet, apart from Henry being belted up, and that may still turn out to have been a random attack. In light of what you have told me, I've no doubt once those Glover imbeciles are turned out of the town jail, they'll try to pick up where they left off, specifically in regard to that Elizabeth Bay mansion.'

'Just one last question. What was the date Henry got himself into strife?' Noel asked almost as an afterthought.

'We believe the attack was committed around nine on the evening of September fifteen, which was a Tuesday.'

'Well, thanks for your time, Ian. We'll keep in touch if anything develops,' Simon said as the two detectives prepared to leave the office.

# CHAPTER 3

*N*oel, who sat at a very basic four drawer desk at one end of the rectangular office, rolled a sheet of paper into a ball and had a three-point shot at the waste paper basket located next to Simon's similar four drawer desk at the other end of the office. Noel had persisted in his endeavours to emulate Michael Jordan but, so far, his shooting average at around ten percent was not helped in his latest attempt, which came as no surprise to either Noel or Simon.

'Right, boss, seeing nothing has happened to involve us, do you plan on doing anything?' Noel asked, hands now locked behind his head, his legs stretched out in front of him in a relaxed lay-back manner.

'What, you mean about Henry Haynes?' Simon asked, seeking clarification of Noel's vague question.

'Considering what Cheryl Drake had to say, and in view of Henry getting himself belted up, I thought you might make some discrete enquiries somewhere.'

'Yeah, and just who did you have in mind, anyone in particular?'

'Well, for starters I would like to determine who is running

The Grovel over at Elizabeth Bay, but that may mean speaking to that pelican Boswell at the local council. And, come to think of it, maybe it might be an idea to see what the Glover gang has been getting up to while in jail.'

Simon shrugged and pursed his lips as he considered Noel's layout for some discrete enquiries. 'Yes, at least it's somewhere to start. In the meantime, I suppose we should tell the boss what we propose doing. As everything is pure speculation at the moment, quite apart from Haynes that is, if Paxton should happen to find out we're investigating a possible future felony, he'll go ballistic. And while we're at it, it might be an idea to go and have a chat with the Honourable Buckmaster, MP. At least we may learn who's getting the developer's kickbacks since Porter's death.'

The "boss" was Superintendent Nigel Fisher who had returned to Day Street, and back into uniform, after a stint of undercover work involving the drug trade. His clandestine sojourn into the murky criminal underworld had been taken, by those short on the facts of the story, voluntary. If the truth be known, Chief Superintendent Paxton had given Fisher an ultimatum; undercover or jail for the blackmail of Graham Lee. Being somewhat of a realist, Fisher had considered the only option providing him with any chance of seeing his pension was to go undercover.

Superintendent Thomas Musgrave was a big man. As he rose from his high-backed leather chair behind a majestic cedar table, he immediately conveyed the impression of authority and tenacity; definitely not one to be easily intimidated. With his stern look and piercing brown eyes complimenting his physical stature, the air of hostility and belligerence presented Superintendent Thomas Musgrave as the quintessential chief inquisitor or, in this case, the chief jailer of the Sydney City Jail and Corrective Centre.

'Detective Chief Inspector Webster and Detective Sergeant Elliott, I believe. Welcome to the town jail,' Musgrave said with a friendly smile and a handshake that put paid to Simon's initial impression of the man. The two detectives were ushered into the somewhat imposing office, the walls adorned with the plaques of various custodial institutions throughout the world, along with photos of previous superintendents of the establishment. Three large lounge chairs and a glass topped coffee table occupied the centre of the office, while a well stocked cocktail cabinet was set against one wall. It was the legs of the coffee table that took Noel's attention having come across a similar shaped object somewhere before. Unable to recall where he had seen whatever he was reminded of, he and Simon accepted the superintendent's gracious invitation, he having indicated to the lounge chairs. 'Before we start, coffee, gentleman?'

'Yes thanks,' replied Simon taking upon himself to reply on Noel's behalf. 'It's quite a drive out this way.'

Musgrave strode to his desk where he pressed the button of a small intercom system. 'Jessie, three coffees ASP.'

'No problems, sir, on its way,' came Jessie's melodious voice with a characteristic American accent over the intercom.

On returning, Musgrave settled into the remaining lounge chair and folded his arms. 'Right, DCI Webster, I believe you want to have a chat about a couple of our inmates?'

'Yes, that's right,' Simon replied. 'You have two inmates due for release in the not too distant future. As a consequence, we'd like to have an idea as to what they've been up to while in here and what we might expect from them once they rejoin society.'

Before Musgrave could speak there came a knock at the door before a pretty young woman, probably in her early twenties according to Noel's estimation, entered carrying a tray with all the stuff needed for a morning coffee break. Jessie was a brunette and, on reflection, Noel decided "pretty" was not quite the word; maybe elegant was more appropriate. After she had placed the tray on the coffee table and departed, Noel couldn't constrain his curiosity. 'If it's not a rude question, sir, as Jessie is obviously an American, is she part of the establishment?'

'No, we met when I last visited San Francisco. She was working as a tour guide at Alcatraz and I asked her if she'd like to come to Australia and work as my personal assistant for a while. You know, the chance for Jessie to broaden her knowledge. Anyhow, back to your question, DCI Webster. And just who are the two inmates you want to know about?'

'Paul and Andrew Glover. They're both in for murder at the moment but, as I said, they're getting out sooner than later, unfortunately.'

'Well, now why doesn't that surprise me?' came Musgrave's unexpected rhetorical response. 'I suppose they've been incarcerated for, what, one or two years. It was for murder, you say?'

'Yes, that's right. They murdered the brother of Paul and nephew of Andrew. There was only one victim and that was Bruce, the brother of Paul. Andrew happened to be Bruce's uncle so it was only Bruce who was murdered,' Noel replied trying to demystify his initial ambiguous response to a simple question. It was at that point Noel suddenly recalled where he had seen the legs of the coffee table; although somewhat smaller, they had been fashioned in the shape of the beheading block at the Tower of London.

'Yes, yes, I quite understand. Okay, just let me have a look on my computer to see what they're up to,' Musgrave replied as he made his way back to his grandiose cedar table and high back leather chair. 'Ahh yes, here they are. Convicted of first degree murder and sentenced to two years full time jail with no parole. Gee, that seems a bit stiff.'

'What do you mean, "a bit stiff"?' Simon asked, a little nonplussed.

'Well, it looks like they've had no previous convictions,' Superintendent Musgrave replied as he scanned down the page. 'Usually murderers get the longest sentences, but that can depend on a number of factors, previous convictions, the brutality involved, premeditation and motif, just for example. The length of a sentence can also be influenced by our occupancy rate. We let the judiciary know how many beds we have available and for how long we expect those beds to be vacant. If someone is due for sentencing and the occupancy rate here is high, the judge will probably sentence the guilty party, be it a murderer or a jay walker, to a couple of weeks community work or weekend detention.'

Simon couldn't hide his bewilderment. 'You mean to say we go to all the trouble of getting a conviction against some thug for a brutal murder and the presiding judge looks up the vacancy list to see if he can put the felonious freak away, and for how long?'

Musgrave threw his hands up in a gesture to signify the inevitability of the situation. 'Yes, that's how it must appear, but obviously we can't foresee who'll be convicted in the future. All we can do is estimate the number of residents we have in jail at a particular time, together with how many are on leave and on what day they'll be returning. Of course, we usually have a large number of guests returning on a Friday evening for their imposed weekend detention. Depending on how many new fulltime inmates we've received during the week, we'll turf a lot of them out on the Friday, whether they want to go or not, just so we can accommodate the weekenders. In fact, sometimes we get so many fulltime inmates checking in that we have to ask them if they wouldn't mind coming back later when there are vacancies available.'

'You're kidding me? You say there are convicted criminals out in the community at the moment who are supposed to be locked up in jail?' Simon, perplexed by Musgrave's revelation, queried.

'Yeah, that's the normal practice. As I said, we have far too many criminals sent down so we try to work on a shift basis, a sort of rotation scheme where we can let half the population out for a stretch while a corresponding number can come in and get a few days knocked off their period of incarceration,' Musgrave replied as if there was nothing to get excited about. 'Of course, we don't provide to the really bad ones with such facilities, like those guilty of treason.'

Simon's state of perplexity had rapidly changed to one of anger. 'And how many really bad ones do you have at the moment?'

'None.'

'So, just because a murder, which isn't considered to be a really bad crime, is committed somewhere out in society, we shouldn't discount the possibility that the murderer may already be a convicted compulsive murderer and is out in the community, on rotational leave, just waiting for a bed to become available in the jail?'

'Oohh no, you should never discount that possibility. And personally, I consider murder to be a really bad case. It's just that the judiciary doesn't appear to share my sentiments, and the sentences being imposed appear to bear this out. Even when they're in, here, I mean, they can get out for a day or two depending on the excuse. As I said, there's usually someone wanting to take up the accommodation in order to work off a few extra days of his sentence. We're always looking for inmates who want a day outside so we can accommodate part-timers and blokes wanting to cut a few days off their incarceration. If some inmate wants a specific day out, it has to be something pretty important, like a good game of footy somewhere, horse races, a wedding or a distant relative's funeral. A good movie in town is admissible, if I think the movie is okay, that is. So, you see DCI Webster,' Musgrave explained, his hands locked behind his head, 'it's not as simple as it sounds. We do keep a tight rein on the program's administrative arrangements, and the inmates are required to give us notice of when they'll be going out and coming back.'

'Okay, so I take it that as you keep records of who's in and who's out, you can tell us if the two Glovers have been out recently?' Noel asked, just as miffed as Simon.

'Of course. All the inmates are given a card and they have to bundy on and off whenever they enter or leave the place. Here, you can see where Paul and Andrew have been coming and going. In fact, they're pretty regular outers, but they're probably setting up work for when they're released,' Musgrave said as he swung the computer display towards the detectives.

'Outers?' Noel queried, not having heard the expression before.

Musgrave nodded. 'Yes, the term is used in conjunction with inners. The knowledge of these terms and their application is restricted to the staff of the jail, for obvious reasons. An inmate is either an outer, meaning he's not in jail but out somewhere in the community...'

'And don't tell me. An inner is an inmate who has been out but has returned and is now deemed to be an inner,' Simon interjected with a sense of despondency. 'Okay, from your bundy clock records, can you tell me if the Glovers were inners or outers on the night of September fifteen?'

'No problems,' but, mind you, I would prefer it if the arrangements we have been forced to implement here at the jail are kept confidential. Generally, few people outside are aware of our overcrowding problem and those who are just ignore it.'

'And the politicians are aware of the situation?' Noel asked.

'Of course, well, the overcrowding situation but, obviously, not the system we have imposed in an effort to deal with the problem. You see, by letting criminals become outers, it doesn't matter to us if they commit further crimes while out; administratively they're still regarded as being an inmate. As a consequence, an outer convicted of a further crime doesn't pose an increase to the prison population; it just alters the time they'll be staying with us. Anyway, getting back to your question,' Musgrave replied as he tapped out something on the keyboard. 'Ahh yes. The gentlemen to whom you refer were outers on the night in question, Paul came back at nine twenty-seven in the evening. Andrew didn't come back until eleven fifty-one that night.'

'Come on, boss, you'd better let me drive. You claim I suffer from road rage, but crikey, I have an idea the temper you're in might be directed towards other motorists, and that could create a few problems,' implored Noel as they returned to their car after their little chat with the superintendent of the Sydney City Jail and Correction Centre.

'Well, did you expect me to be in anything but some deranged state of mind after that little revelation? Come on, Noel, I've heard of the Bangkok Hilton and the one down at Circular Quay, but I didn't know we had another five-star hotel providing low cost accommodation for a selected clientele. And the way the place is being run, it could take an inmate years to work off a six-month sentence, if he didn't die of old age first. Here, take the keys. You're right, I'm too cranky to drive.'

The two detectives sat in silence as Noel negotiated the suburban traffic along Linton Parade and headed for the city. 'Okay, boss, what's next on the agenda?'

Simon shrugged, his shaken state of mind in the process of returning to something like normality. 'I know it sounds bloody stupid, but here we are chasing up information relating to an event that may or may not happen. Okay, so Henry gets himself into a pickle that may or may not be related to what we think it could be related. On top of that, I have an idea Ian Francis fails to share our concern over the matter, that's if we decide we are concerned. And honestly, Noel, after that chat with Musgrave, I really couldn't give a proverbial as to who does what to who.'

Noel, displaying far more prudence than usual, refrained from getting into a grammatical argument with his boss over the use of "who" or "whom". 'So, it's back to Day Street then?'

'Yes, I'll arrange a couple more stops once we're back in the office. Obviously, I would like to have a chat with Ralph Glover and I'd also like to see who's who up in Macquarie Street.'

'So, you think there maybe something in what Cheryl Drake had to say?' Noel asked.

'That, and the spanner Mr Musgrave threw into the works. Who would ever believe they'd let Jack the Ripper out of clink just to go watch Gunners play Spurs? As someone once said, "But that I am forbidden to tell secrets about my jail", or words to that effect.'

'Don't tell me. Shakespeare?'

'Probably, but whoever it was, it doesn't seem to bother Musgrave. Anyway, let's go and get ourselves organised. I'll let Fisher know we may have a problem and ask him if he can keep in under wraps for a while, at least until we know if there is a problem.'

'Aah, Detective Chief Constable Webster. This is a surprise,' Ralph Glover said in his usual indulgent manner as Simon and Noel entered the office occupied by the boss of Glover Property Development. 'No, on second thoughts, maybe it's not. I suppose you're here to talk about Henry getting himself done over, just as that other copper, Francis, did?'

'Well, yes we are, but before we start, it's Detective Chief Inspector Webster and Detective Sergeant Noel Elliott, and you don't mind if we take a seat?' Simon asked and sat on a collapsible steel chair before Ralph could reply.

'So, what makes you think I know any more than what I've already told the other detective plod?' Ralph asked as he stretched back in his seat behind the very untidy paper strewn table of his Bondi office.

'We just thought you may have overcome your bout of amnesia and might have something more to add, especially as we've uncovered some disturbing facts you may wish to consider. I know it's only a vague possibility, but knowledge of these facts may jog your memory, or at least give you cause to consider your longevity,' Simon replied in a trivial manner. 'Of course, you may be aware that your brother and uncle are already walking the city streets and are probably ready to take over where they left off with Glover Property Development. But as I said, you're probably aware of this and couldn't care less what they're up to.'

'Hey, hang on. First up, what's with this longevity bit?' Ralph asked not quite au fait with the word.

'Your life span, you dodo. You know, it is within the realms of possibility Andrew and Paul might have plans to take back the business, and you might be seen as some sort of an impediment to them realizing those plans. Who knows, Henry might have been the first step in some form of reckoning.'

Ralph sat bolt upright, a look of both incredulity and anxiety etched across his face. 'You mean they're both out of jail? I thought they got three or four years. Hell, it wasn't that long ago I sent Henry over to have a talk with them about that property over at Elizabeth Bay.'

'Oops,' Noel sounded. 'So, they are aware you have an interest in the place?'

'Of course they are, and really Sergeant, I couldn't give a

damn', Ralph replied with an enmity akin to that displayed by the notable southern gentleman. 'Every man and his dog know the place is worth zillions as it is, and could be worth a lot more if the property was to be redeveloped. By the same token, I'm often told I possess delusions of grandeur and living in a harbourside mansion might satisfy my desire for one of the finer things in life. And it's for sure, I didn't expect to see those two idiots running loose for a few more years.'

'So, what did Henry have to say after his little discussion with your family members?' Simon asked.

'Not much. Paul claims he's the legal owner of the house and can do what he wants with it. I'll leave the question of ownership alone for the moment and see what happens. As a last resort, I could take a case of the Forfeiture Rule to the Supreme Court, but it might not come to that. Taking any case that far would probably cost more than The Grovel is worth, developed or undeveloped. Anyway, local council has already rezoned the property from low to medium density residential to accommo- date Paul's townhouse scheme. I believe most, if not all, of the necessary paperwork has already been approved. The only thing left is the demolition and construction work. However, with things as they are, the whole shooting match is stuck in limbo as Paul and Uncle Andy do their time. I suppose the two jailbirds believe the first thing on the list when they get out will be to seek tender applications.'

Simon frowned in deep concentration. 'Okay, so as Paul thinks he's currently the legal owner, what makes you think he and Andrew shouldn't continue to believe everything is hunky- dory?'

'Let's just call it collateral damage brought on by their conviction for murder. The way I see it, and correct me if I'm wrong, both Andrew and Paul have forfeited their trading rights to operate as Glover Property Development. As I was employed by the company and directly involved with its operation, I, by default, became the head honcho. I'm fully aware Paul's idea for redeveloping the property at Elizabeth Bay is purely a scam set up by himself and Andrew, using the cover of Glover Property Development, to obtain the necessary council approvals, which he now has. I don't know if Paul has got around to it, but I somehow think he's overlooking the fact that I now hold the trading rights for Glover Property Development.'

Simon paused to digest Ralph's explanation. 'Now, let me get this straight. What you're saying is that, under current arrangements, any profit made from the redevelopment would go to Paul and Andrew, not GPD?'

'In a nutshell,' replied Ralph. 'And you can bet your life that if the scheme turns out to be a financial blunder, GPD will have to foot the bills.'

'So, you're saying Paul can't redevelop the property because, not having a licence, he can't call for tenders under the GPD banner, but you can as everything under the GPD banner has already been approved by council, and you're the boss of GPD and hold the necessary license?' Noel ventured, the situation from his point of view still veiled in a shroud of incomprehensible bureaucratic hogwash.

'That's about it,' Ralph replied. 'The major stumbling block is Paul, who just happens to be the legal owner, at least for the moment. The only way he'll be able to make anything out of any redevelopment would be to enter into an agreement with GPD, which I doubt he'll do. He's a greedy bloke and wouldn't want to share the profits with anyone. But, unfortunately for Paul, I hold the aces as all the approvals are in the name of GPD.'

Unperturbed at encountering some difficulty in understanding just what was going on, Noel plunged ahead. 'And have you approached Paul and Andrew with any kind of offer, or scheme, that might be amenable to all concerned?'

Ralph harrumphed before replying. 'We offered an eighty twenty split which I thought quite reasonable seeing I was the only member of GPD, apart from Henry, with a current trading licence.'

'Yeah, eighty for who?' Simon asked, secure in the knowledge that it was a stupid question.

'Me, or should I say GPD, of course. As I said, I hold all the aces. If The Grovel is to be knocked down and a bunch of yuppie townhouses erected, for which GPD already has the council approvals, I'm the person, along with my good mate Henry, who'll be doing it,' Ralph proclaimed with an air of supreme confidence.

Simon contemplated the situation and scratched his right earlobe, 'And Henry, you're expecting him back at work in the not too distant future?'

Ralph smiled. 'Yeah, they tell me he's making good progress so I expect him back within the next couple of days. He really took a beating, poor bloke.'

'And obviously, you have no idea who the beater was?' Noel asked.

'None whatsoever, and who am I to slander a family member?'

After digesting Ralph's veiled insinuation, Simon stood having decided there was little to be gained in continuing the conversation. 'Come on Noel, I think we have taken up too much of Mr Glover's valuable time. Oh, yes, and just how are you and Miss Drake getting on?'

Ralph looked up, a trifle surprised by the question. 'Just fine, I hope. Paul didn't treat Cheryl too well and, as far as I'm concerned, he can just buzz off and leave us and GPD alone.'

# CHAPTER 5

*N*oel negotiated the police car through the traffic of Oxford Street in silence, happy to let Simon ponder a situation Noel didn't quite understand. Based on his estimation, Ralph Glover didn't appear to be over the moon with the news that his brother and uncle were permitted to roam the streets of Sydney at their leisure. Any presumption Ralph may have entertained regarding the family's two murdering miscreants, and their expected prolonged incarceration in the town jail, had been well and truly blown out of the water by Superintendent Musgrave's simple solution to prisoner overcrowding.

That the jail had a walk in, walk out policy, where a six months sentence might take years to complete depending on how much time the inmate chose to be either in the walk in or walk out mode, was totally contrary to Noel's understanding of the penal system. But then, Noel's job was to get a conviction, not be concerned whether the jail had the capacity to provide the guilty miscreant with accommodation; that was a job for someone else, least of all the judge's, or so one would think. Regrettably, it was only if a vacancy was available could a judge hand down a custodial sentence and incarcerate a convicted villain, even one of the Jack the Ripper ilk. The alternative; release the monsters back into society on a good behaviour bond or, if the judge was having a bad day and felt vindictive, order the fiendish sod to undergo so many hours of community work. Naturally, such community work could only be conducted under the strict condition that it was not in conflict with the prisoner's principles and did not impinge on his ethical, moral or religious codes.

'So, what's on your mind, boss?' Noel asked his contemplative passenger.

'Not much. I'm beginning to think this is all a waste of time and, to be honest, I don't really care if I never hear the name Glover again,' Simon replied with an air of abject despondency. ' '

'Come on boss, you're not thinking of joining the other side again, are you?'

'No, I'm definitely not cut out to be a crook. And we've already been down that track and decided it wasn't for us. Still, today hasn't been one of the brightest days of my policing career.'

The track, as Simon referred to it, happened some years ago when both hapless junior police officers, driven to despair by an overweight bully of a sergeant, decided to change sides and join the dark side of the law. Simon and Noel, together with Georgie and Sue, the respective spouses of the detectives, had robbed a bank in the centre of the city. Although the robbery had been successful and no-one charged with the offence, it had been decided the dark side wasn't exactly the exciting career envisaged.

'Yeah, it's been one of those days alright,' Noel replied. 'But to change the subject, how's Judy's new house going?' Judy, Ron Lange's partner had, through a convoluted set of circumstances, become the owner of the property next-door to Simon in the seaside suburb of Collaroy. Because Georgie had stuck her nose into someone else's business, Judy's original house had been burnt to the ground, thought to be arsonated by two deranged bikie gang members. Fortunately, Judy was not residing on the premises at the time, but had been leasing it to a young couple who Georgie believed were into the hydroponic cultivation of marijuana. Needless to say, Georgie had the wrong end of the stick, not that the couple weren't into hydroponics.

'The builders were in to finish off last week. I have an idea Judy and Ron will lease the place while they continue to live in Ron's unit over in the Eastern Suburbs. It's more convenient for him as he seems to be drawn to The Cross and Darlinghurst districts,' Simon responded somewhat unenthusiastically.

'Well, I reckon it would be great if someone like Lucrezia Borgia or Vlad the Impaler took up residency. At least you could take a break from being bored to death by watching the TV and, instead, view the excitement going on next-door, which there's bound on be. With all the spooky people who have lived there, they should get the place exercised before another person decides to take up residency. Bloody hell, you stupid moron,' Noel yelled in fury while giving a two finger salute to a brainless young "P" plate car driver who had forced his way into Noel's lane without using a traffic indicator.

Simon closed his eyes and slowly shook his head trying, with some difficulty, not to make comment on Noel's display of road rage, or his use of the English language. Finally, after deciding it wasn't worth the effort, he said, 'Yeah, no doubt some little old lady with the personality of Dorothy will rent the place. That should keep Georgie preoccupied for a while.' On the downside, at least for Simon and Georgie, Dorothy had been a real pain in the butt. On the upside, it was fortunate that Dorothy suffered from acute arachnophobia, a condition Georgie had exploited with unintentional fatal results, for dear Dorothy.

It was following Dorothy's demise, the odd murder or two, and much tortuous domestic wrangling, Judy became the owner of Dorothy's property. While choosing not to live in the house, Judy's visitations to Collaroy had resulted in the establishment of a friendly relationship with both the Websters and Elliotts, and her ultimate introduction to Ron Lange.

Ron, a short middle-aged man with a receding hairline and a not too discrete paunch, probably symptomatic of his partiality to the light amber fluid, came from Brisbane where he and his wife, Ellen, had been employed in the mundane job of conducting petty robberies. It was during one such robbery that Ellen had been fatally shot resulting in a dramatic career change for Ron. Having turned informer on his criminal colleagues, the Queensland police suggested he might like to consider a move to Sydney, taking into account that to grass on criminal colleagues has its own inherent dangers. As Ron was well aware of the precarious predicament he had placed himself, the decision to move south was not a difficult one, a move he was even happy to make in light of his recent bereavement.

With Ron's professional relationship with the two detectives firmly established, it was inevitable that Ron and Judy would eventually cross paths and it was at an afternoon social gathering on Simon's back lawn where their eventual meeting heralded the start of a successful relationship.

'And do you think Andrew and or Paul had anything to do with Henry's injuries?' Noel asked, knowing Simon had his mind on the subject. 'Both had the time to bash him and get back to jail. Even Paul could have made it back in half an hour and that would still fit the time of bashing and his return to the jail by nine thirty. And Ralph obviously thinks Paul is Henry's basher.'

Simon shrugged his shoulders, pursed his lips for a moment and considered the question. 'Well, no doubt they'd have to be on our list of suspects, bearing in mind they weren't locked up on that particular night. It could be that Cheryl Drake is spot on with her ideas on the matter. But then again, someone once wrote about someone being done to death by a slanderous tongue.'

Noel dared to hazard a guess, 'Shakespeare?'

'Probably.'

'Well, I can't see that there's anything we can do as the only crime committed, so far, is the assault on Henry. Even if Francis finds the villainous culprit, he'll probably be charged with committing GBH and spend the next six months doing community work. I must admit, the property over at Elizabeth Bay is interesting and I reckon there's a good chance it'll be responsible for a few more dastardly deeds being committed,' Noel said as they arrived back at the Day Street police parking lot.

Detective Superintendent Nigel Fisher sat behind a paper strewn desk, his chair pushed back, his legs outstretched and crossed at the ankles, hands interlocked together on his stomach, thumbs arched. While displaying his predilection for the best in office furnishings, Fisher also strived valiantly to look the suave sophisticated man about town, whether in uniform or dressed in mufti, as he now was. Unfortunately, his sophisticatedness had suffered a minor, but permanent, setback with the onset of age. His once strapping muscular body had finally conceded defeat to the inexorable force of gravity, the rippling torso once found above the belt line now comfortably settled substantially lower than in his younger days.

Fisher's frosty gaze rested initially on Simon, leaving Simon more than a little uneasy, before he turned his attention to Noel where the detective superintendent achieved the same unsettling result, which was probably the aim of the exercise. 'Okay, boys, I haven't told Paxton anything about your little hunch that there may be problems in the offing. However, I want to remind you, your job is to catch the baddies, not go after potential baddies who you think may become real baddies sometime in the future.'

Simon, having tried unsuccessfully to give the impression of a relaxed detective chief inspector by lounging back in a comfortable office lounge chair, sat bolt upright ready to defend himself against Fisher's disturbing observation. Somewhere in Simon's early police training he had heard the phrase "crime prevention", or "mitigation". As a consequence, he now believed that, given the option, it was preferable not to investigate the crime but prevent it from happening in the first place. Before he could speak, Fisher held up his hand.

'Don't say anything Simon. I know all about the Glover clan and I expect they'll cause more trouble than they're worth. I'm also appalled with the system of housing our criminals. However, that is beyond our control and something we can't change.' Fisher paused for reflection before he added, 'Of course, that's unless our charter is changed and we don't arrest anyone until we've been advised if a jail vacancy exists for any felon a judge might like to put away. Anyway, if you gentlemen would be so kind, I would really appreciate it if you would get out there and investigate the here and now. And just as a foot-note, seeing I have your undivided attention, it seems that while you were off chatting to Superintendent Musgrave and gazing into your crystal balls for something that might happen, Ian Francis over at Waverly rang with a piece of information you might find of interest and which is certainly of the here and now stuff.'

'Nothing to do with the Glover family, I trust?' Noel asked, a sudden feeling of emptiness in his stomach.

'Hell no. Well, I don't think so, but it might be,' Fisher folded his arms, raised his eyes to the ceiling and gave Noel's question some more thought. 'Francis rang to say that the bloke who got himself pulverized and admitted to hospital isn't improving as well as expected.'

'Cripes,' Simon muttered and cast his gaze to Noel with raised eyebrows. 'I thought poor old Henry was on the mend. And now we're verging on a murder case, I've got this funny feeling Francis will be on the blower to see if he can palm the investigation off onto us.'

Fisher shrugged and gestured with his arms, hands upward indicating the accuracy of Simon's presumption. 'No, I don't think he will. He's already been on the phone and asked if we'd take it on, and guess what; I've accepted on your behalf. He's of the belief you're miles in front as a result of the last couple of cases you've dealt with, especially that last one and the killing of that politician bloke. Of course, there's always your previous association with the Glover clan. And let's face it, Henry Haynes works for Ralph Glover and he's into property development, which is as crooked as a dog's hind leg.'

'So, we take on the investigation even though it's not in our bailiwick?' Noel asked.

'Sergeant, I really don't care whose bailiwick it's in. You two seem to know more than anyone else in regards to the Glover group and the shenanigans they get up to. So, the answer to your question, and the answer I've already given Francis, is yes. Go find out what this is all about and I'll go tell Paxton you're working on a real live, or dead, case.'

CHAPTER 6

'You know, Noel,' Simon said wistfully, 'all of a sudden I'm overcome by a sense of déjà vu. Here we are at Day Street and we get lumbered with another probable murder committed nowhere near our area of responsibility. Still, Fisher has made the decision so we're off on another wild goose chase. If the bashing is related to Glover Property Development, or any other property development for that matter, you can bet it will be like the Porter murder with politicians and bureaucrats ducking for cover. I suppose we should get the ball rolling and see how far Francis had progressed with the assault investigation, then go have a chat with that mental giant, Boswell, to see if anything's happening with The Grovel.'

Noel sat back in his chair at the other end of the office, rested one leg on his desk, and clasped his hands behind his head. 'Yeah, okay. But right at the moment I have the distinct impression you couldn't care less as to who bashed Henry. In the first place, it's not Henry's fault he got himself spiflicated and ended up being hospitalized, and I have no doubt he would have preferred not to have ended up in the infirmary trying his best not to die.'

Simon harrumphed. 'No, but for some reason hospitals give me the jitters; they're full of sick or injured people. My only hospital experience was when I was laid up with appendicitis. I knew I was going to die when I found the hospital food was worse than that served up to cattle class passengers on a 747. As for Henry, he may be a cranky sod but he certainly didn't deserve the beating he got and I, for one, hope to hell he pulls through okay. Poor bloke survives the initial belting only to suffer a set-back when we all thought he was coming good. And let's face it, the only people he had anything to do with was in the property development business. I don't think I have to tell you just how rough that can get, especially when they're dealing with egocentric politicians not averse to taking the occasional kickback from a developer seeking a favourable decision.'

Noel removed his foot from the table, sank lower in his chair and shook his head. 'Geeze, not bloody politicians, their snob-bish hoity-toity wives, or mistresses, along with megalomaniacal public servants again? Now I understand why you aren't over-awed by events.'

'And don't forget to add in the Glovers. Anyway, let's cut out all this procrastination and get on with it. We'll go and see Francis then stop off at the local council chambers and have a talk to Boswell.'

Detective Inspector Ian Francis slowly shook his head as he sat back into his seat. 'I'm sorry, Simon, but I didn't like the situa-tion, hence my call to Superintendent Fisher. If there was going to be any violence, I would have thought it would be Henry bumping off some bureaucrat involved with the demise of Dayman Brothers. I take it you know the story; the politicians and local government conspired to renege on a residential rede-velopment plan over at Rose Bay after Daymans had spent a fortune buying up property. Obviously, it cost Henry and a lot of other people their job.'

'Yes,' Simon replied, 'although we still don't know the who or why Henry was bashed in the first place. It may have absolutely nothing to do with the industry. I believe you've spoken to Ralph Glover?'

'Yep, I have a couple of times, both since Henry's hospitalization. He seems pretty sure Henry's assault is property development related as he can't think of anything that would provide anyone from outside the industry with a motive for perpetrating such an act. Sure, Henry has an awful bad temper, but don't we all when given a good enough excuse, and let's face it, Henry certainly had an excuse. Anyway, it's all there on the file,' Francis replied indicating to a buff file prominently marked with the letters "Police CIB".

'And have you spoken to Paul and Andrew Glover?' Noel asked.

'No, I've been out to the jail a couple of times to see if they had any idea who might have assaulted Henry but they never seem to be at home. Strange that.'

'No, not really,' Simon responded, somewhat reluctant to educate those living in ignorant bliss of the accommodation arrangements of Sydney's principal jail. 'You have a copy of the medical report?'

'Yes, and Graham Gallymore, you know, the pathologist who did Robert Porter. He's seen it. There's a copy of the report on the file but the short story is a cerebral aneurysm ruptured, quite apart from the severe head injuries received during the assault. I've spoken to the doctor at the hospital who says the situation is critical, but they're hopeful. Apparently it was totally unexpected, but when an aneurysm ruptures, you're in trouble.'

'But can they categorically state whether Henry's current condition is a result of the bashing, or did he have an existing disorder?' Noel asked as he reached for the file resting on Francis's desk.

'That's something you'll have to take up with the hospital or with Gallymore,' Francis replied.

Noel looked at Simon and slowly shook his head. 'Geeze, boss, and you say you don't like hospitals. 'I certainly wouldn't have the patients to work in one.' DI Francis scowled and slowly shook his head at Noel's very poor attempt of a pun.

Simon's look to Noel was interpreted correctly; the conversation with Francis was over. All in all, the time spent in discussion with Francis had achieved very little. As far as Simon was concerned, the information Francis had contributed relating to the identity of the person responsible for the vicious assault on Henry Haynes amounted to zero. Still, it was early days.

# CHAPTER 7

*A*s both detectives entered the council chambers for the first time in almost two years, Simon couldn't suppress the thought that nothing had changed. Then, as now, Simon felt the uncomfortable gut feeling usually experienced whenever he had the need to enter a government office building; full of aspiring bureaucrats, and generally charged with the exhilarating atmosphere of a Franciscan monastery. Naturally, Simon endeavoured to avoid such establishments whenever possible.

Now, confronted by a grumpy, uniformed, old gentleman who Simon took to be a pensioned off security guard, the two visitors were unequivocally informed that access to the person currently the subject of enquiries necessitated the correct administrative procedures. The sour old codger left Simon and Noel in no doubt that The Book containing the correct administrative procedures, Chapter One para 24, sub-para b. to be precise, categorically stated that all visitors to the chambers must present themselves to the information counter for direction to the officer dealing with the appropriate subject matter, in this case Mr Stuart Boswell. However, Simon was adequately conversant with council policy, more specifically that pertaining to coffee, smoko and any other break the staff were entitled, to accept that the now unattended information counter may not be attended until the arrival of the next ice age.

Unfortunately for the council, on this occasion the expiration of the mandatory inordinately long waiting period failed to achieve its desired effect, in most cases the departure from the chambers by the council's very peeved customers. After a display of resolute perseverance by the two detectives, some signs of life behind the counter heralded the arrival of someone Simon had, unfortunately, the displeasure of meeting before; TBones.

'Aah, Mr Jones. I see you're still in charge of the information desk,' Simon remarked as Trevor Jones, or TBones as he was known, tucked his shirt into his trousers in an unsuccessful bid to look like the well-heeled bureaucrat.

'Yes, I've been here for a while now. My boss is happy with my work, so I'm happy to stay here. Anyway, what can I do for you gentlemen?'

'We'd like to see Mr Boswell, if he's available,' Noel replied. 'In fact, we'd like to see Mr Boswell even if he's not available.'

'And just so we don't confuse the issue, we've spent just about enough time-wasting here already,' Simon growled 'As we are in the middle of an investigation, I would warn you that any more delay will result in you being hauled in for wasting our time and failing to co-operate with police when asked to do so. So, do we understand the situation, Mr Jones?'

'Yes, of course, but there's no need to get stroppy about it. I'm sure Mr Boswell will be delighted to see you.' After making a very brief phone call, obviously to Mr Boswell, TBones moved to the side of the counter and opened a small door. 'If you would like to come this way, gentlemen?'

After leading the detectives down a long corridor, TBones stopped outside an office, the sign on the door indicating they had reached the office of Mr Stuart Boswell, Executive Officer for the Property and Commercial Development Group. After two deft raps on the door the voice from inside, undoubtedly Mr Boswell's, permitted entrance with a curt 'Yes you may enter,' response.

'Well, well, well, two policemen here to upset my day, no doubt. Inspector Barnaby and Sergeant Jones, as I live and breathe,' expressed Mr Boswell as the detectives entered the office. For some strange reason both detectives didn't like Boswell, their views unaltered by the passage of time since they had last met the man. Boswell was short and thin, a pimply face and long black hair. Noel thought that if he ever tackled this bloke on the Rugby field, he would break in half. However, it was clearly evident that whatever Boswell lacked in manly physical attributes was more than compensated by an abundance of conceit, arrogance and egotism.

'Try Chief Inspector Webster and Sergeant Elliott,' Simon corrected as Mr Boswell offered the two men a seat in front of his desk. 'You've come up in the world,' he continued as he withdrew his notebook and pen from his coat pocket, crossed his legs and sat back in anticipation of a stimulating discussion with this intellectual bureaucratic giant.

'Yes, I have, haven't I?' Boswell gloated as he settled himself back in his high-backed executive chair with a look of pompous satisfaction. 'From dogsbody to executive officer is quite a feat, but nothing less than I deserve.'

'Undoubtedly, but just what does the Property and Commercial Development Group do for the council?' Noel replied.

'Before I answer that, I was just about to have a coffee. Care to join me?'

'May as well,' replied Simon. 'I think I need a caffeine fix.' Noel just nodded his acceptance. Boswell strode to a small bar fridge on top of which was a coffee percolator and a supply of paper cups.

'Milk, sugar?' Boswell asked.

'One black, one white, no sugar,' replied Noel.

'Right gentlemen,' Boswell said as he handed the two detectives their coffee and returned to his desk, 'getting back to your question, Sergeant. The responsibility of the Group is, among other things, to procure and dispose of property in accordance with current legislation, notably the Local Government Amendments Act 1980. Obviously, there are many considerations needed to be addressed before any procurement or disposal action is taken by council and the Property and Development Group is the arbiter of such action. I hope that satisfies your curiosity, Sergeant?'

'Yes, quite admirably thank you, Mr Boswell,' Noel replied with more than a touch of rancour. Noel couldn't help but have a vehement dislike for this conceited upstart, quite apart from the fact that he had found the coffee far too strong for his liking.

In an effort to quell the growing enmity, Simon quickly butted in. 'And how many are on the staff of The Group, Mr Boswell?'

'Just me.'

'Yes, just you and who else comprises the Group?'

Mr Boswell's head sank, then slowly shook from side to side. 'No, no, Inspector Barnaby. The Group consists of me, and only me, with any decision made by the Group expressed in the singular, "I". Naturally, I am well remunerated for the onerous position for which I am entrusted, given the value of assets involved, and the fact that I alone am held responsible and accountable for any decision I make.'

'Then to whom are you accountable?' Noel asked, clearly recognizing the fact that this dunderhead could not possibly be left to make any decision more complex than whether to have sugar in his coffee.

'Look, gentlemen, you certainly didn't come here to review my job statement, so let's cut to the chase,' Mr Boswell said, avoiding Noels question with a surprising display of mental dexterity.

'The crux of the matter is, we want to know exactly what's going on with the Glover place, The Grovel, over at Elizabeth Bay,' Simon said.

Mr Boswell sat back and folded his arms. 'That, gentlemen, is confidential as the future of the property is currently under review. However, I am able to say that the current owner of the property is presently unable to meet certain statutory financial obligations which could place the legal ownership of the property in question. Any action by council in regards to the property will be taken in accordance with the recommendations made after an extensive examination of available facts. Irrespective of the recommendations, any, and all, action taken by council will be in strict accordance with the "Local Government Amendments Act of 1980".'

'And I take it you're doing the investigation, or review or whatever you like to call it?' Simon asked expectant of the obvious response.

'Yes. As I have absolutely no interest whatsoever in the said property, I am free to make an objective and unbiased decision on the matter. So, you see, I'm perfectly placed to do the review of The Grovel even if there were others available to do it, which of course there isn't,' came Mr Boswell's smug reply.

Simon grimaced. I can smell a very fishy-like smell here, he thought. Bloody bureaucrats. 'And have you heard Henry Haynes from Glover Property Development was the victim of a brutal bashing which has placed him on the hospital's critical list?'

'Of course. I take a vested interest in the goings on of both companies and personalities who have received council approvals for one thing or another. Fortunately, I have to distance myself from this particular case as any knowledge that comes to hand, irrespective how that knowledge is acquired, may compromise the integrity of my review.'

Noel leaned forward and pinched the bridge of his nose with thumb and forefinger, his other hand resting on his hip. After a few second of total bemusement, he glanced at Simon who, obviously sharing Noel's perplexed state of mind, sat with eyes firmly set on the ceiling, his arms crossed. To break the impasse, Simon finally said, 'So, apart from knowing he's nearly dead, you know nothing of the circumstances of Henry's bashing. I also have an idea you're not interested in the fact that Paul Glover can't pay his bills because he's doing time in the slammer, while Ralph Glover continues his efforts to keep Glover Property Development afloat. And you tell us everything is on the backburners until you finally decide what you're going to do with this multi-million-dollar asset, and that any decision you make will be final?'

'Yep. Exciting, isn't it?'

Simon refrained to say what he was thinking; Boswell had been promoted to the ranks of the council's hierarchy having displayed the personal qualities deemed necessary for such advancement. Knowing full well such personal qualities included arrogance and a good dose of megalomania, Simon was also mindful that a general display of gross incompetence could, invariably, overshadow all such attributes and catapult the incompetent on his way up the bureaucratic ladder. In all, our Mr Boswell was only reaping the rewards he so richly deserved, or believed he deserved. Simon was not amused.

'So, right at the moment all the council approved Glover Property Development plans for The Grovel are void?' Noel asked.

'No, not at all. All the paperwork in that regard is hunky-dory,' replied Boswell. 'However, as there are some minor glitches of a legal nature, which I won't go into, everything has been put on hold pending the results of the review currently being conducted.'

'Okay,' Simon said, his dander rising to the extreme, 'forgetting for a moment as to who owns the place, the approval to knock down The Grovel and build some townhouses was granted to Glover Property Development with Paul and Andrew Glover being the signatories to the plans. Once released from jail, can they carry on as if nothing has happened?'

Mr Boswell closed his eyes and slowly nodded. So, this is what it's all about, he thought. 'The answer to your question, Chief Inspector Webster, is an emphatic no. As the two individuals to whom you have referred have been convicted of murder, they have lost their license to trade. Whether Glover Property Development will be permitted to trade with Ralph Glover at the helm is a matter of conjecture and will be considered by council, i.e. me.'

Simon glanced at Noel who made a significant display of looking at his watch before tapping the watch's face with his forefinger. Simon read the unmistakable message; the meeting had gone on for too long. With their car parked in a limited time parking zone, the detectives would most likely find an authoritative brown envelope attached to the windscreen containing advice that the fine may be paid at any police station or council office.

# CHAPTER 8

*S*pring had sprung and the first hint of warmth in the September sunshine was tempered with a gentle noreaster blowing in off the ocean. For the six people sitting on director's chairs placed in a circular arrangement around a small garden table, upon which an assortment of nibblies had been placed, this particular Sunday afternoon was not so different to many others spent on the back lawn of Simon and Georgie's Collaroy bungalow. Though not strictly ethical, such get-togethers provided Simon and Noel the opportunity to float ideas relating to events under investigation, ideas that could be considered from a perspective using the annoying and infallible attributes of female intuition and logic.

Georgie was tall and slim, her olive complexion complimenting dark brown eyes that peered from under a fringe of dark hair cut in a pageboy style. 'So, both Paul and Andrew had the opportunity to assault Henry?' she asked as she stretched her long, tanned legs out in front of herself before taking another sip of Chardonnay.

'Well, if our head jailer is to be believed, half his inmates had the opportunity,' Simon replied, the memory of Musgrave's revelations still a cause for annoyance. Turning to Ron Lange, Simon asked, 'Ron, can you have a chat to one of your buddies on the inside so we can get an idea of just what's going on from an inmate's perspective?'

'No problem,' Ron replied, 'and you're right on that score. From what you've told me, I can't help thinking this Musgrave bloke must be on the wrong planet. I know for a fact that a lot of inmates are laughing their heads off; free accommodation, all meals and come and go as you please.'

'Yeah, but the thing I want to know specifically is if the Glovers were accommodated on the night of September fifteen, somewhere around nine. According to Musgrave's info, they were out,' Simon said as he lobbed an empty tinny into the metal garbage bin with a hollow clunk, a fair indication that the afternoon proceedings had just begun.

Sue, a blue-eyed blond with the long hair, who just happened to tower over her spouse, gave Simon a troubled look. 'Okay, Simon, if Paul and Andrew did king-hit Henry, what could possibly have been the motive? Henry was just one of the drones and had no influence in the company. If anyone was up to getting thumped, I thought it would have been Ralph. After all, it's not as though Paul doesn't mind a bit of brotherly sacrifice.'

It was Judy, the freckles on her nose and under her eyes accentuated by her grimace, who decided to voice her objection. 'Hey, hang on. No-one has any idea as to the motive behind Henry's injuries, and he's not dead – yet. His attack might have absolutely nothing to do with the Glovers and property development. And while I'm at it, yes, I will have another Chardonnay, thanks Ron.'

'No-one is saying it has, my sweet,' Ron replied as he topped up Judy's glass before offering to Sue and Georgie. 'The only way Simon and Noel will be able to tell if it is related is if, or should I say when, someone else gets belted over the head. At least then we'll be able to form a connection, if there is any connection to be found.'

'Gee, thanks, Ron,' Simon mocked. 'All Noel and I have to do is sit back on our tooshies and see who's the next unsuspecting mortal to get their block knocked off. Ian Francis couldn't work out who belted Henry so, expecting it to become a murder investigation, he palmed the case off onto us. And we don't appear to be making inroads on that score either. Let's suppose, just for argument sake, that Henry's circumstances are Glover related, not that there's anything to suggest they are, at the moment. If, and I use the word loosely, if there happens to be a murder, you can bet your bottom dollar it will be related to the Elizabeth Bay property. I can't help thinking that if I was a Glover, the first victim on my hit list would be that idiot Boswell; trumped up little upstart. If that was to happen, the only thing we could charge the villainous scoundrel with would be justifiable homicide.'

'Yeah, well as far as The Grovel goes, even Boswell seems to think there may be some question as to who actually owns the place,' Noel said dryly. 'Apparently the current owner, who would be Paul Glover, hasn't been paying the bills, which I expect would include the council's rates.'

'That could be true.' replied Georgie, exhibiting her knowledge gained with the experience of having worked in a solicitor's office which, among other things, involved land titles and conveyancing. 'There are circumstances where the council can take possession of a property if certain financial obligations are not met by the title holder.'

'So, the council can just swipe the place, if they so desire?' Simon asked, a little perplexed with the idea that The Grovel might be hijacked by Boswell.

Georgie nodded. 'The circumstances would have to be extreme, but yes, the council giveth and the council taketh away. It wouldn't be the first time a bit of skulduggery has gone on to secure whatever is wanted, irrespective of who holds the legal title. And believe me, that skulduggery can happen at any level of government. But getting right off the subject for a moment, has anyone heard from Graham and Louisa?' Georgie asked of the recently married Louisa Porter and Graham Lee. Notwithstanding Graham's dubious occupation, he and Louisa were close friends to all those sipping wine or beer on Simon's back lawn, both having been involved in several investigations conducted by the two detectives.

Noel harrumphed. 'You've got to be joking? They flew off into the wide blue yonder on their honeymoon and right now probably shacked up in some erotic, oops, I mean exotic hotel as far away from here as possible. And as Graham isn't short a quid, you can bet they turned left at the door and got a good night's sleep, not corralled down the back in cattle class.'

'Seems a bit late for the honeymoon now,' remarked Sue, 'they've been shacked up for God knows how long. Anyway, it's about time Graham did something legal, so I say good luck to them.'

'Well, let's hope the attack against Henry doesn't turn out to be murder, not forgetting the last couple of murders we investigated where every man and his dog happened to be involved,' Noel remarked as he dug another can from the Esky.

# CHAPTER 9

'*D*CI Webster, get in here, now,' roared Detective Superintendent Nigel Fisher from the adjoining office. 'And bring your sergeant with you.'

'Uh-oh, something tells me we're not the flavour of the month,' Simon said, his look to Noel expressing a combination of doubt, fear and guilt for whatever had evidently gone wrong; and something was definitely wrong. Regardless of whatever the wrong was, the two detectives were obviously responsible, the blame soon to be laid squarely at their feet. 'Come on, Noel, if I'm to get a bollocking, you can come and receive your share.'

A tap on the door elicited a very curt response leaving no doubt that Fisher was a tad upset. 'Come in, sit down and not a word until I have finished,' Fisher directed from behind his mahogany desk, his arms folded in a definite confrontational manner. 'Alright gentlemen, now I have your undivided attention, I'll fill you in on events.

'I'm fully aware of the problems relating to the shortage of accommodation for criminals in the town jail, just as I am aware of the walk-in, walk-out system imposed by that block-head, Musgrave. The credibility of his system is based on the supposedly complete honesty and goodwill of the inmates who can avail themselves of the opportunity to leave jail to be with family, pursue future employment opportunities for when they are released, or to enjoy social and sporting events that will help with their rehabilitation. But surprise, surprise, it seems not all the inmates are as honest as they would have you believe. The system of inmates using a bundy card to log in and out is being abused, the extent of this abuse unknown at this stage. Fortunately, Superintendent Musgrave is right onto it, or says he is, and should be able to come up with some sort of remedial action in the not too distant future.

'However, at this point of time, Musgrave is unable to say if this abuse is widespread or whether it is limited to a particular group of inmates taking advantage of a system designed to make jail life a little easier for the unfortunate criminals undergoing penal servitude. Irrespective of the number of prisoners taking advantage of the situation, we are now faced with a small problem. It seems an inmate who was recorded as "In" was found horribly dead last night. That in itself is not so very strange, these things do happen in a jail. But the particular dead inmate wasn't found in jail, he was found floating in the harbour over at Elizabeth Bay with a neat little bullet hole in the back of his head. Seems a bloke doing a spot of fishing off the wharf dragged him in. Funny thing that,' Fisher said and paused for reflection. 'Maybe this one's mixed up with Henry Haynes.'

'Come on, sir, that's a very long bow to draw. Not knowing anything about this recent murder, apart from the fact that the body was recovered at Elizabeth Bay, I'd say it was coincidence. And what's so significant about a dead inmate of the city jail being found murdered somewhere when the records show he was supposed to be incarcerated at the time?' Simon asked, not totally surprised that the system of imposed punitive imprisonment implemented by Superintendent Musgrave should have its faults.

Fisher's face took on the countenance of an irritated gargoyle. 'I can answer both the coincidence and significance angles. It would seem that I have to be a little bit more explicit to get through to you Chief Inspector. And while I'm not in the habit of berating a senior officer in front of a subordinate, the berating applies to both of you equally. Now the angles, and to put it succinctly, gentlemen, the coincidence and significance of this particular murder are that the murdered body belongs to none other than Andrew Glover. Now do you see what I'm talking about?'

Aghast, Simon looked at Noel who just stared at the carpeted floor; the ramifications of Fisher's announcement abundantly clear to both detectives. 'And the body has been positively identified?' Simon asked in the hope it hadn't.

'Of course it's bloody well been positively identified. Would I tell you the name of the victim if the body hadn't been identified? Detective Inspector Harris from Kings Cross attended the scene, and Superintendent Musgrave was called in seeing the body belonged to him,' Fisher replied in a tone conveying his impatience with such a dull-witted question.

'And it's definitely murder?' Noel ventured to ask. 'Mr Glover might have fallen into the harbour accidently, or it might be a case of suicide.'

Simon winced. Superintendent Fisher stared blankly at Noel before he leant forward, placed an elbow on the desk and rested his face on his hand, his eyes now closed. After a few moments he responded to Noel's in depth and probing questions. 'Detective Sergeant Elliott, to begin with, DI Harris is a very experienced investigator and, if he says it's murder, I would be inclined to believe him. As for the suicide angle, I don't think I've ever heard of someone pointing a gun to the back of their head, blowing their brains out then leaping off into the harbour. Although Graham Gallymore hasn't had a good look at the body, his first impression was that it was more like an execution than a random killing.'

'Sorry, sir, I was just trying to cover all bases,' Noel replied.

In an effort to put the meeting back on equal ground, Simon intervened. 'I take it we can get access to both Gally's and Harris's reports on the killing, sir?'

'Now, what a wonderful and refreshing idea,' Fisher responded sarcastically. 'All of a sudden we're smitten with the idea there might be something going on involving Glover Property Development. We're down to only two surviving members of the family; Paul Glover, who Musgrave says was "In" last night, and Ralph Glover who currently heads Glover Property Development. Seems to me a new ball game just opened up, DCI Webster, so you and your sidekick had better get going, and show a little more competence than you have currently displayed.'

Simon and Noel sat at their usual seat in the coffee shop on the corner of Bathurst and George streets. Felicity, or better known as Flitch to her regular customers, had taken the order of one cappuccino for Simon, and two flat blacks, one for Noel and the other for the absent but expected Ron. 'Cripes, Fisher's a bit upset at the moment. How were we to know Andrew Glover was dead unless someone happened to tell us?' Noel commented. 'It's not as though we need to know the names of every homicide victim throughout the city, only those we're interested in. And how is every LAC s'posed to know the ones we might be interested in?'

'Yeah well, seeing Fisher told us, and as someone had to have told him, it would seem we're at the end of the line of communication. And I'll agree, something is really stuck in his craw at the moment, but I suppose it's only to be expected. It certainly looks like these two incidents are related to Glover Development and Glover Development was, somehow, tied into the Robert Porter murder. That tends to suggest the possibility of a political involvement. If we can work that out, you can bet your booties the chief superintendent already has,' Simon said as he sat back from the table to allow Flitch to place the coffees. 'Thanks Flitch, you can have the rest of the day off now.'

'I wish,' Flitch responded with a smile. 'I start at six and knock off at noon so I have a couple of hours to go. Would you like me to hold Ron's until he gets here?'

'No,' Simon replied. 'He's due any moment, in fact he just came in, but thanks.' Noel shifted over on the bench seat dragging his coffee across the table to make room for Ron. 'Ron, pull up a pew and tell us all about our wondrous lockup,' Simon invited. 'I somehow get the idea I won't like what you have for us.'

'Morning gentlemen, and you're right on that score, Simon,' Ron said as he sat and took a sip of his coffee before responding. 'It seems our Mr Musgrave must have his head in the sand if he doesn't know what's going on. Quite apart from whether he knows or not, this bloke hasn't a clue when it comes to understanding the criminal mind. Hell, I've stayed at holiday resorts run with far more rules and regulations than the way this turkey runs his jail. Give an inmate an inch and he'll take a mile, or more if he can get it.'

'Gee, Ron, thanks for the rundown on the head honcho, but let's have the nitty-gritty,' Simon asked in anticipation of some diabolical disclosure.

'Okay. We all know, well most of us, of the walk-in walk-out system Musgrave has implemented, along with the bundy clock for clocking in and out of the jail. However, Musgrave is delusional. He has this innate theory that those members of society who have been incarcerated are basically honest, law abiding individuals. He believes it's regrettable, but it's only through their own foolishness, and a set of unfortunate circumstances, that the inmates find themselves in the position they are now in. As far as Musgrave is concerned, the question of trust doesn't enter into it as the word of the inmate is sacrosanct. If Musgrave could have his way, and the inmates gave their word they'd stay in their cells, or in the jail grounds, all the bars on the windows and locks on the cell doors would be removed. We wouldn't need warders at all.'

Noel shook his head. 'Come on Ron, we figured Musgrave must be a couple of sandwiches short of a picnic. But can you tell us how the system is being rorted and, more to the point, how was it rorted on the particular nights of Henry's scrap and Andrew's elimination?'

Ron put his coffee down, sat back and folded his arms. 'Now, that is something I can provide you with an answer to; I haven't a clue. You see, Musgrave's bundy approach might work if the bundy card was in the form of a lockable bracelet or anklet that couldn't be removed. The system, as it is, calls for a card that is no more secure than that used by the factory down the road.

'The warders do a head count every so often and, provided the jail has the correct number of heads, everything is seen to be hunky-dory. The problem is that as they never confirm the identity of the head they've just counted, the system is ludicrous and an open invitation for abuse. I'm told some wealthy inmates pay to have someone do their time for them. With so many people coming and going, and a prison bus to help them get there, no-one really knows, or couldn't care less, as to the real identity of who's in or who's out. Inmates can always determine whether they need to be recorded in, or out, to facilitate an alibi. They can be physically out, or in, by having someone else use their bundy card. Now, in the case of Henry and Andrew, if you suspected an inmate with the name of Joe Bloggs to be the perpetrator of a crime, just for argument sake, jail records will more than likely show that Joe Bloggs was in whereas, in reality, he may very well have been out.'

'Holy hell,' Noel remarked. 'Sounds like a cricket match, the batsman goes in until he gets out then someone else goes in until his side is all out and the other side goes in until they all get out.'

'Oh, for cryin' out loud, Noel,' Simon groaned, 'someone said men of few words are the best, so just belt up and think what this means to our investigation. Get in touch with Musgrave and find out if Paul Glover was in on, what day did Andrew get killed?'

'Twenty second, a week after Henry's set-to,' Noel replied.

'Okay Noel, find out if Paul was in on that day, not that it will prove anything conclusively. And Ron, can you find out from your mates in jail if anyone has been doing Paul Glover any favours lately? In the meantime, I'm going to organise a meeting with Gavin Buckmaster up in Macquarie Street and see how the political landscape is holding up at the moment.'

'Sure thing, boss,' Ron replied without any great confidence as to the success of his mission.

# CHAPTER 10

'So, you wish to see the Premier?' the pert young receptionist at the counter asked. The girl was probably attractive although her bright red lipstick didn't quite match the pink coloured hair brushed in the upright mohawk style. The orange, blousy off-the-shoulder, dress enhanced an apparent burning desire to create the unmistakable psychedelic appearance, currently trending among the younger generation.

Anyone who deigned to pass her a second glance might notice, as Simon did, the intricate tattoo displayed on her right shoulder blade, another growing tendency amongst those of the Gen Y elements of society. Being unable to recognise the nature of the tattoo, he decided it must have some esoteric meaning known only to those whacko people obsessed with having their bodies permanently disfigured while playing Russian roulette with a hep C infected needle. The silver stud protruding from the left side of her nostril seemed to provide a perfectly natural enhancement to the overall aura, charm and elegance of the fashion-conscious receptionist.

Having decided a snowball in hell had a better chance of success than achieving the aim of his visit, Simon pressed on regardless. 'No, I wish to see Mr Gavin Buckmaster, you know, the backbench bloke who did some work for Robert Porter before he was murdered. I mean the Robert Porter who was murdered, not the Gavin Buckmaster who hasn't been murdered, well, not yet anyway. It was probably before your time but if you ask someone, I'm sure they'll know who I mean.'

The pert young receptionist employed by the State Public Service to facilitate initial enquiries, and to represent the state legislature as the initial contact point for the general public, appeared to Simon as being no more than eighteen years old. This must be her first job, straight out of school and I bet it wasn't Harvard, Simon thought. Instead of hurrying off to find someone more historically in tune with Simon's request, the pert young receptionist looked at Simon with nothing less than what could be described as a look of patently obvious curiosity; I don't care who this bloke is, it's what he is I'm worried about. And he's just like the others, all wanting to see the boss.

'Look, mister whoever you are,' the young receptionist scalded, 'I find your attitude similar to ninety five percent of the mentally deranged and totally ignorant people who present themselves, along with their egos, at this counter. You would think the majority of people would have some sort of interest in politics, but here we are with no-one having a clue as to who they want to see, and have never heard of the person they need to see. As for you, you halfwit, Mr Buckmaster has been the Premier of this state since the previous Premier died after a short illness. And we even have a new deputy Premier, the previous one quit to chase after his girlfriend who, as it turns out, just happens to be the wife of the new deputy Premier. Apparently she left town and flew off to Paris after some sort of scandal.'

'So, you're sure Walter Ackerman did go to Paris to meet his girlfriend, or whoever she might be?' Simon, somewhat amused by the revelation, asked.

The young receptionist suddenly became serious. 'Hey, hang

about. Who the hell are you and what interest is it of yours anyway?'

'I'm Detective Chief Inspector Simon Webster, if that should make any difference.'

'Crikey, I'm sorry, but I s'pose it does. Why didn't you tell me from the start? You've no idea the pea-brains we get in here and you have to meet them at their own level, which is pretty low. The tattoo washes off and the stud comes off the nose, so I'm really quite normal, apart from when I work here and have to play the part of a normal member of the public. And I can now understand your interest in the previous management of this place, though nothing has changed, just the faces. Anyway, you still wish to speak to Mr Buckmaster?'

'Yes, if he's available.'

The pert young receptionist pressed a button on an intercom, said a few words and turned to Simon. 'Yes Mr Webster, the Premier would be glad to renew your acquaintance. Thirty ninth floor, turn right. You can't miss it.'

'Aah, Detective Chief Inspector Webster. Good to see you again. Come in, come in. Lorraine, grab us some coffee and muffins please, sweetie,' Premier Buckmaster ordered the strikingly handsome, shoulder-length red-haired, receptionist who stood holding the door open for Simon's entrance to the inner sanctum. Whatever images of the Premier's office Simon may have harboured, he was impressed, almost as equally impressed as he was with the Premier's secretary who, probably consciously, solicited Simon's abashed chauvinistic thoughts. Cripes, the place is so big he probably gets a travel allowance to get to the door. No, on second thoughts it's probably just big enough to accommodate a politician and his ego, Simon mused. We vote these halfwits in to run the state, not to live in the lap of luxury.

Trying not to be overawed by the grandeur of the office, Simon nonchalantly sat back in a comfortable leather chair placed beside a glass topped coffee table and crossed his legs. 'Well, it looks as though you're doing alright for yourself; from backbencher to Premier in one easy lesson,' Simon said as he clasped his hands on his stomach.

'Oh, yes, Chief Inspector Webster. And just what, in your opinion, was the one easy lesson?' Buckmaster returned, a smile on his face.

'Someone once said "some rise by sin and virtue fall" and in your case that's probably fifty percent correct, so far. It's generally accepted that one rarely reaches the pinnacle of their chosen profession without getting a little dirt on their hands. But that is neither here nor there as whatever is considered good, or bad, is purely subjective. However, I must confess that, as you are now the man in the chair, I'm curious as to just how you reached such an exalted position so quickly.'

'It's all quite simple really. The previous Premier, Alex Martin, came back from his fact-finding mission to California, found out what was going on here, had a heart attack and snuffed it. Oh, come in, Lorraine. Just put the tray on the table, would you?' Buckmaster said. Simon didn't miss the wink Buckmaster gave the awfully pretty receptionist as she placed the tray of coffee pots and muffins on the elaborate coffee table.

Simon closed his eyes and scratched behind his ear. Yep, the receptionist downstairs was absolutely right; nothing has changed. 'Now, why doesn't that surprise me? The goings on here, I mean. What, with the death of Porter, scams being perpetrated by every man and his dog, plus the indiscriminate screwing around by half the politicians in the place, it's no wonder Martin had a heart attack. And what happened to Wally Ackerman, the deputy Premier?'

Buckmaster rose from behind his desk and took a seat opposite Simon at the coffee table. 'I'll be mother?' he asked and

poured the coffee irrespective of Simon's response. 'Help yourself, the muffins are great.' Simon did as he was a bit peckish,
and the muffins did look good. 'Yes, Ackerman. Now there's a
strange case. After he returned from South America and had to
face all the innuendoes about tossing his wife into the Amazon
River, we saw very little of him. Sure, he had aspirations for the
top job but that went by the boards very early in the piece. With
his wife, Monica, being suspected of murdering Robert Porter,
and his alleged shenanigans in Brazil, the chances of him
becoming premier were zilch.'

As Simon took a sip of coffee, he couldn't help but notice the
cup had been embellished with a picture of the state's bird
emblem, the kookaburra. How absolutely fascinating, Simon
thought. 'I'm led to believe he's left country, chasing after some
floozy to Paris?' he continued seeking confirmation.

Buckmaster crossed his legs at the knees and folded his arms.
'Yes, that's right, but the "floozy" to whom you refer is someone
you know.' Simon didn't respond verbally, the slight inclination
of his head and questioning look enough to convey his curiosity.
'You remember Cheryl Mason, the wife of Peter Mason, the ex-
Minister for Sport?'

'Not the girl who caught the social problem from Robert
Porter before he was murdered?'

'Yep, that's the girl alright.'

'Holy hell,' Simon responded, the news provided by the pink
haired receptionist now confirmed. 'Well, I suppose it was
damned sure she wasn't going to catch anything off Porter after
he was murdered. When you come to think of it, it's not so
surprising she ran off with someone, what with her playing
around with Porter and her hubby admitting to the occasional
fling. But what's Mason doing with himself now?'

'He's my deputy,' replied Buckmaster indignantly. Obviously, the Premier's novel, but ill-founded, presumption that
everyone on the planet knew who the Premier and deputy

Premier of the state were, probably warranted a reappraisal of the current inflated perceptions of public political awareness which, in reality, amounted to sod all. 'Now we've cleared the air as to who's who, what can I do for you?'

'Unfortunately, we've had one recent murder and the possibility of another, both involving people associated with Glover Property Development. Henry Haynes, who worked for the bloke who now heads the company, Ralph Glover, was the first victim. He got his head bashed in near his home at Bondi Beach. Fortunately, they were able to get him to hospital where he remains in a critical condition. This event was followed a week later by Andrew Glover who was fished out of the harbour with a bullet in the back of his head.'

Buckmaster looked perplexed. 'So, what's all that got to do with me? I didn't bash Haynes, and I certainly didn't shoot the other bloke. I'm fully aware of what went on, with Ackerman and his wife lining their pockets with oodles of cash from benevolent developers, but I'm certainly not into the game of receiving kickbacks, either.'

Simon, a little taken aback by Buckmaster's conspicuous lack of emotion to the news of the two vicious attacks, immediately felt the hackles on the back of his neck respond in irritation. 'Well, in view of what we uncovered in the Porter investigation, together with the exposure of politician's indiscriminate rorting of the system, we just thought we would touch base and see if developer's scams and inducements were still on the agenda.'

'Chief inspector, I have absolutely no idea as to what other people are up to. My election to leadership of the government following Alex's death was predicated on extensive lobbying based on cleaning up the corruption you happened to uncover. A new broom sweeps clean and I, along with Peter Mason's support, swept clean. As far as I am aware there is no such thing as a "kickback" being paid to anyone, just as there is no rorting the system, nor overseas junkets. No, I put a stop to all that nonsense.'

'Well, I'm very glad to hear that, Mr Premier. If that is the case, you have obviously achieved the unachievable and I'm sure the electorate will be gratified to see we finally have an incorruptible government running the state, for a change. So, I can take it that with your declaration of integrity and incorruptibility, no amount of money could possibly tempt you to intervene in some decision-making concern that may prove financially rewarding to you, personally?'

Buckmaster pursed his lips and raised his eyebrows as he considered the question. 'DCI Webster, that is an unfair question as every man has his price. Really, it comes down to whether I am prepared to prostitute myself for financial reward at the expense of my principles and integrity. Obviously, as there may be some politicians willing to sell their soul, I'll leave that for your own judgement.'

A soft tap on the door preceded Lorraine's entry into the office, a folder in her hand. 'Sorry to interrupt, Gavin, but we need these travel documents signed as a matter of urgency,' Lorraine crooned in a deep and dusky voice that left Simon a little disconcerted. Cripes, the voice matches the look, he thought. Lorraine laid the open folder on the coffee table where Gavin signed in the required places and handed it back. As she was about to leave, she turned, 'Just one more thing, Gavin, was that The Dodgers or The Yankees game we're going to see?'

'The Yankees. And don't forget the tickets to that Broadway show I spoke about.'

While Simon made his way down to the ground floor, he couldn't suppress the feeling that The Honourable Gavin Buckmaster, MP, was a bit sensitive on the issue of property development. But then again, he probably had other things on his mind.

# CHAPTER 11

*C*hief Superintendent Paxton's office was miniscule in comparison to the office Simon had just left following his discussion with the Premier. But Paxton's office was not pretentious, it was functional, and its smallness provided a certain amount of intimacy the Premier's office lacked. However, the current mood in the chief's office was one of uncertainty; the four "guests", Simon, Noel, Ron and Nigel Fisher, unsure as to what they were there for. Paxton sat back, clasped his hands on his stomach, elbows on the arm rests of his chair and peered over his reading glasses.

'Okay, Nigel, what have you got for us?' his question directed to Detective Superintendent Nigel Fisher.

'Sorry, sir, I didn't know we were supposed to bring anything,' Fisher, somewhat embarrassed by his patently obvious neglect, replied. Undoubtedly, this was not the response Paxton had anticipated as he closed his eyes and slowly shook his bowed head.

'Holy hell, just who are we missing here? I can account for four of the seven and, as I'm obviously Grumpy, that makes two missing. Just what have you got for me on the murder and the

73

apparent related bashing, you idiots, or were they just figments of my imagination? I even have this vague recollection DI Francis over at Waverly passed one of them off onto us.'

'Aah, yes, the two murders,' Fisher said, relieved that the subject of the meeting had finally been resolved. 'Yes, sir, he did, and nothing.'

Paxton baulked before he straightened up and started to chew the end of his glasses. 'Come again?' he asked having missed the essence of Fisher's reply.

'Sir, the "yes" answer refers to the fact that Ian Francis did palm the Henry Haynes murder off onto us because he, Haynes I mean, not Francis, worked for Glover Property Development. As far as the count of two murders go, it is only one, so far. It certainly looked like Haynes wasn't going to make it but the latest bulletin is refreshing. And the same goes for Andrew Glover's murder, which is a very real murder, as that, too, was handed over to us by DI Harris from up at The Cross. The "nothing" refers to what we have for you in regards to our investigations,' came Fisher's confident response; he was well aware the investigation had, so far, produced an abundance of nothing but felt obliged to let his boss know, irrespective of the impending apocalyptic bollocking likely to be forthcoming.

'So?' Paxton enquired with a look of abject bewilderment.

'If I may butt in, sir,' Simon ventured, 'we have commenced our investigation into both incidents and believe they are linked because of their association with Glover Property Development. We already have a couple of suspects, Paul Glover, currently an inmate of the town jail but wasn't the night of Henry's attack but was on the night of Andrew's murder. The other suspect, Andrew Glover, was an inmate of the same place as well. But he was absent on both the night Henry was bashed and the night he got himself killed, although executed may be a better word for it as his killing has all the earmarks of an underworld job. I s'pose if he hadn't chosen to be absent, he wouldn't have ended up dead.'

'What do you mean, Glover was absent'? Paxton enquired with a confused shake of the head.

'Which one?' Simon asked as the question was a tad ambiguous.

Before Paxton could decide exactly which Glover to whom he was referring, Noel intervened. 'Neither was present on the night Henry was done but Paul was when Andrew was executed a week later. I think that is what DCI Webster means.'

'Present where?' Paxton was becoming a bit more than a little confused.

In an attempt to clarify the situation, and as it was his turn, Ron chipped in. 'Yes, that's right, sir, both Andrew and Paul were absent from the jail the night Henry was bashed. They clocked off around two in the afternoon the day of Henry's attack and both returned at different times later that evening. According to the jail's Superintendent Musgrave, Andrew clocked out on the twenty second and hasn't clocked back in, and chances are he won't because he's now dead. The superintendent out there is chuffed because, now Andrew isn't returning any time in the foreseeable future, he has an extra bed space available.'

Undoubtedly, there are some members of the police force who are aware, and some who aren't, of the burgeoning number of convicted criminals and the Musgrave Solution to facilitate the consequences of such burgeoning. Somehow it had never crossed anyone's mind that, with a growing city population, there would most likely be a corresponding growth in the number of criminals sentenced to a period of penal servitude. Naturally, a cell with a bed, along with all the other infrastructure necessities needed to run an establishment the size of a small town, was required to facilitate this growing number of miscreants. Unfortunately, at least for the inmates, the basic requirements of the city's prison had been either totally ignored intentionally, or by the sheer cerebral atrophy of those bureaucrats upon whom the implementation of an adequate infrastructure depended.

The jail, or otherwise known as the town lock-up, had been constructed to provide suitable facilities, or unsuitable depending on which side of the law you were on, for the growing number of evildoers way back in the good old days. Having laid claim to the continent in the latter part of the eighteenth century, the British decided the location was far enough away from Old Blighty to be well suited as a place to unload their surplus felons, or convicts, of whom there were not an insignificant number. The French had Cayenne, or Devil's Island; the British would have Sydney Town.

However, by the time the first sod of the city jail had been turned in the early twentieth century, the population of the penal settlement which, obviously, had to have is own jail to incarcerate those found guilty of wrongdoing in their new homeland, had grown somewhat. With more and more convicts, and increasing numbers of free settlers arriving in the quickly growing city, there was the inevitable increase in the number of miscreants requiring incarceration. As no-one appeared to appreciate the problem, or if they did there was very little they were going to do about it, something had to give. Now, well into the twenty first century, it turned to the quintessential pragmatist, Thomas Musgrave, to provide the solution, not a very good one but at least a solution that was, arguably, better than none. And Musgrave had the courage to implement his unconventional remedy.

Following Ron's disclosure as to the reason for the current state of euphoria of the jail's superintendent, it was abundantly clear Paxton was one of those members of the police force who had no idea of the existence of the Musgrave Solution. 'Ooh, you guys. I'll accept it's still early days and I'm quite interested in the fact we have two related incidents, one a murder, with both victims having come to notice in our last couple of investigations,' Paxton said with a grin. To think "these guys" would try to put one over me with something as outrageous as inmates clocking on and off as they walk in and out of jail. What a joke, he thought. 'Okay, get on with it, and just let me know when you do have something for me. And next time, try pulling the other one.'

∽

'Crikey, he can be a real surly individual at times,' Noel muttered as the three men filed into Simon's office, Simon and Noel taking their seats behind their respective desks, Ron taking the new express racing chair that had been offered to Simon as a replacement for his old battered chair but politely declined for no other than sentimental reasons.

'Can't say I blame him,' returned Ron. 'In fact, I think I feel a tad sorry for him 'cause when he finds out we're not joking…' Ron failed to find the appropriate words and finished with a roll of the eyes and a shrug of the shoulders.

Simon frowned, sat back and lolled an arm over the back of his chair. 'Look, let's get on with it and see what we can come up with. Noel, you work the whiteboard and write down the names as we go. First off, we have the two victims, Henry Haynes and Andrew Glover, but we know Andrew should have been cooling his heels in jail instead of wandering off to get exterminated. Now, link Henry to Ralph Glover and link both Ralph and Henry to Glover Property Development.'

'Gee, this is exciting,' Noel remarked as he used his initiative and drew a line linking Andrew to Ralph. 'Before we start conjuring up other names, boss, how about we look at a motive for the attacks on both men? Like, it's easy to speculate why Henry was thrashed as he was virtually second in command of GPD. With Andrew and Paul due for official release from prison, they might have had it in mind to take back the company, as

Cheryl Whatsaname said. With the way things are, that in itself may have been sufficient motive to try and do away with Henry. But then Andrew gets himself done in and that sort of puts paid to the first motive, unless he bashed Henry before he was blown into oblivion.'

Simon pondered for a moment, his lips pressed firmly together, his arms now folded. 'At a guess I'd say we have two victims and two totally separate incidents involving two guilty perpetrators. Henry was clubbed in a manner not so different from the way Paul Glover belted brother Bruce to death. Graham Gallymore suggests Andrew Glover was the victim of a gang-land execution, a pistol shot taken at close range to the back of the head. And to drop the body into Elizabeth Bay must surely be more than coincidental. Anyway, Gally said he'll have further details after he conducts a more thorough examination of the body.'

Ron looked at Simon, his eyebrows raised questioningly. 'We could just hang around and see if there's another murder. That may give us a better idea of who's aspiring to become a serial murderous miscreant, if there is only one murderer, although I'm inclined to agree with you on the two-killer idea.'

'Oh, that's just great, Ron,' Simon rebuffed scornfully. 'I'll just run upstairs and tell Paxton we believe we may get some idea of who the killer is if we just sit around and wait for the common denominator, or motive, to fit the next poor mortal who ends up dead.'

Noel, having returned to his desk, did a rotation on his chair, came to a stop and shook his head. 'Stuffed if I know, but it sounds like you're saying we have two incidents which may or may not have been committed by the same person. We currently have two people still alive, discounting Henry, who have a direct link to Glover Property Development and were known to both of our victims. Now, if either Paul or Ralph manages to get terminated, we could reasonably expect the other, the living one, to be involved, right?'

Simon shrugged. 'I'll agree to that, but at the moment we have two victims and two potential suspects who might be guilty, either individually or in concert, of the attacks on either one, or both, of the victims. And let's not forget, Andy Crawford has expressed his interest in The Grovel. As he's a racketeer, and a shyster, I wouldn't put it passed him to blow away any competitors on a permanent basis.'

'Ahh, so Ralph could have belted Henry and then killed Andrew. Somehow, that doesn't ring true to me as I doubt his homicidal inclinations,' came Noel's response. 'At the same time, Paul could be guilty of both events. Or Andrew may have bashed Henry before he got himself murdered, possibly by Paul or, more likely, Crawford seeing he's a baddie to begin with. But, being only supposition, we might be completely wrong and it might have been Jack the Ripper who cashed in their chips for both of them.'

Simon rested his elbow on his desk, covered his eyes and slowly shook his head. 'No, no, no. Paul is right up there as the prime suspect for the brutal attack on Henry, probably with the intent to kill him. We know what Paul is capable of, and the attack was conducted in a similar manner to that carried out by Paul on his brother, Bruce. But the Glover family, despite the activities of Paul and Andrew, isn't known for running around assassinating people, at least not with a gun; that's not their modus operandi. But then again, it would certainly fit Crawford's way of doing things.'

Ron, with raised eyebrows, looked to Simon. 'Getting right off the subject of homicidal maniacs, Simon, is there anything to suggest the pollies are involved in any way? You mentioned that both Buckmaster and Mason have claimed to have cleaned up the kickbacks being paid to politicians by developers, especially those who want to build swanky casinos. Don't forget, the whole debacle involving the murder of Robert Porter, MP, was predicated on the development of a new casino and hotel complex. Hell, a tiger can't change its spots overnight, so you can bet there's a shonky going on somewhere.'

'Well, it's for sure a tiger can't change its spots overnight 'cause he ain't got no spots to change. Try a leopard,' Noel interjected.

Simon sat back and pondered Ron's opinion regarding the integrity of politicians, including that of both the Premier and his deputy. Simon, who never held any great admiration for politicians in general, was comforted in the knowledge that he was not the only pebble on the beach; there were others similarly afflicted with the same devastating and incurable disease. 'So, you think Buckmaster and his mate are carrying on in their own inimitable way and still making stacks of black money?' Simon responded, fully aware that Buckmaster's stripes hadn't changed.

Ron shrugged. 'Just because Buckmaster says he's put a stop to things might mean he's put a stop to only those things we uncovered. Hell, there might have been a bundle of other devious things going on that we didn't uncover, and those things may be still going on today. Conversely, it's pretty difficult to find out what's going on if there's nothing going on in the first place. It's only when we become aware there's something untoward going on that we can investigate what that something is, maybe. And don't forget about the wife of the previous deputy Premier who ran that company Eastern Development and Construction. We don't know anything about the company, or who's running it now. Who knows? Maybe Monica Sainsbury Ackerman wasn't murdered and she's back flaunting her fortune and picking up government contracts from under the table.'

'Slim chance of that if she did murder Porter. She'd probably have gone to ground in some Central American country that has no extradition treaty, that's if her hubby didn't send her floating off down the Amazon,' Simon responded. 'And I'll concede you one victory at least; Buckmaster still has his snout in the trough and is rorting the system for all it's worth.'

'Well, I can't say I'm surprised, although I thought Crawford was the gangster, not the Premier,' Noel ventured. 'We know both our victims were involved in property development and that ED and C were running rampant over the smaller developers. Come to think of it, ED and C sounds more like a vitamin pill than a construction company so they probably have the strength to run rampant.

'Anyway, I don't know what Paul Glover's plans are now as he and Andrew had all their marbles in the one bag, that being the Elizabeth Bay mansion. Irrespective of Ralph believing he holds all the aces, I'd say Paul will try and carry on with his plans, despite what Boswell says, and the demise of Andrew. If Crawford is responsible for Andrew's death, another victim is quite on the cards. And if some politician is involved, irrespective of whether he be premier or backbencher, it won't mean anything to Crawford's ruthless methods.'

Simon ran his fingers through his hair before clenching his hands together behind his head. 'Now there's an idea. It seems Andrew had a discussion with Boswell over at the council on September twenty one, and there's no surprise as to the topic. I'd like to get a readout of telephone calls made by Boswell for September as I think the little pipsqueak might be up to some skulduggery. In addition, I think Ron is right but at the moment we know very little as to what's going on in the city. It might be an opportune time for us to see what Paul Stack knows. Seeing the Lees are out of town, he's probably the next best person to talk to. And, who knows, we might even run into our old mate, Jacko.'

# CHAPTER 12

*N*oel headed the unmarked police car east along William Street before making a right-hand turn into Palmer Street. Unable to locate a parking space, not an unusual event at any time of the day, Noel used his resourcefulness and parked in a signposted "Loading Zone", a short walk from The Spinning Wheel. The detectives had been to the illegal gambling casino on previous occasions for discussions with Paul Stack on matters relating to the murder and disposal of Bruce Glover's body into Sydney Harbour. Those discussions were mainly conducted in the early evening prior to the casino's normal operating hours as it was the one time Paul Stack was most likely available.

Irrespective of the number of times visited, both Noel and Simon couldn't suppress the thought that The Spinning Wheel was a squalid den of iniquity, probably frequented by only those who maintained some sort of connection with the underworld. The detective's unflattering night-time impression of the drab premises, with the garish coloured neon spinning wheel that never did, was now reinforced despite the addition of a dose of bright afternoon sunshine.

'Hope he's in as it is a bit early in the day to set up for the night's operation,' Noel said as he pressed a button on the side of the front door to the establishment. 'Maybe we should have phoned first.'

Simon stood with his hands in his pockets, waiting. 'No, if we'd announced our visit you could bet Stack would make sure he wasn't here. I don't think "Sticky" is too amenable to having coppers drop in; something about being bad for business.'

The two detectives finally came to the conclusion it was too early in the afternoon and were about to set off back to their car when the door slowly opened, just a little. 'Yeah, wadda ya want?' came a gruff voice from behind the door.

'Now, if I'm not completely mistaken, that voice sounds like it belongs to Jacko,' commented Simon, a smile breaking out across his face. Simon and Jacko were good acquaintances, not actually friends as the two chose to live in very different circles of society. Still, Jacko was known to all Simon's friends, including Georgie, and all had a soft spot for the gentle giant who now worked for Paul Stack in the capacity of doorkeeper cum bouncer.

'Holy hell, you two! Get inside quick before anyone sees you. If the boss knew you were hangin' around, he'd go bananas,' Jacko said as he hastily ushered the two men through the door.

Paul Stack had imbued into Jacko the fixation that the presence of police at The Spinning Wheel was not conducive to good business practices, a complication Mr Stack did not need. By the same token, Simon and Noel were regarded by Jacko as friends and Jacko wished the relationship to remain that way, irrespective of whether they were policemen or agents of the First Estate out trying to sell indulgences.

'Don't get me wrong, I don't care who else sees me talkin' to the fuzz, especially you two blokes. Geeze , it's good to see you again; been a long time.'

'Yeah, thanks Jacko,' replied Simon. 'We should catch up more often. But right at the moment we would like to have a chat with Mr Stack, if he's available that is.'

'No, he's not and won't be in for at least another hour. I'm the only one here at the moment,' Jacko informed the detectives. 'If there's anythin' I can help you with, we can sit and have a chat without interruptions.' Simon looked at Noel who returned the look with a shrug and a "why not" expression.

Jacko led the visitors into a large dimly lit room with a bar running along most of the wall opposite the door through which they had just entered. Three large, and very cheap, chandeliers hung from the ceiling casting little enough light to prevent the patrons from viewing the cheapness of the place. While the sombre lighting may have prevented patrons from making a reasonable appraisal of the casino's decor, the high class blend of wool, nylon and beverage infused carpet provided visitors the unique sensation of wading through a smelly, sticky glob of glue, a more precise and probably clearer indication as to the true glamour and elegance of The Spinning Wheel.

The remainder of the room was filled with green carpeted tables where the absent-minded clientele, determined to part with their hard-earned cash, tried in a vain effort to prove their infallible betting system could break the bank. Jacko took a seat at a table and nodded his invitation for the detectives to join him. Undoubtedly, the majority of patrons would fail to notice the significance of the tables having been placed strategically close to the bar. Obviously, it was Paul Stack's aim to fleece what little money patrons may have left in their pockets by selling drinks at obnoxiously exorbitant prices while they took a respite from the unwinnable gaming tables.

Having dispensed with the initial polite trivia, Jacko opened the serious side of proceedings. 'Okay, Simon, I don't know what's goin' on, but I guess it might have somethin' to do with a couple of recent kafuffles. I mightn't know much, but I've learnt to keep my mouth shut and ears open, or is that s'posed to be eyes open?' Jacko wondered.

'And a very good lesson to be learnt, Jacko, although I think it's eyes open, but ears will do,' Noel replied with encouragement.

'Right, Jacko, you just admitted that you don't know much, but that infers you know something, so let's have it. How much do you know about the two, er, kafuffles?' Simon asked.

'It's like this,' Jacko started. 'I know Henry Haynes worked for the Glovers, just as Andrew did before he and Paul Glover went nuts. Now, it just so happens that Andy Crawford, you know, the bloke who runs The Red Ruby, he's been to see Mr Stack a few times recently. With the door to Mr Stack's office just over there at the end of the bar,' Jacko said indicating with a nod, 'I found I might be able to hear what was goin' on without lookin' like I was listenin', if you know what I mean. Seems Andy has approached some politician with a plan to develop a site for a new casino, or a sorta club thing, and yes I know, that was the bug-bear in that last politician's murder.'

'Did you hear who the politician was?' Noel asked.

'Naw, but what they were talkin' about had somethin' to do with harbourside land development,' Jacko replied. 'Like I said, I wasn't listenin' altogether, just catchin' snippets.'

Simon placed one hand on his hip and scratched the back of his head with the other. 'And what makes you think this is all tied in with the kafuffles?'

'I don't,' came Jacko's simple reply. 'All I know is somethin's goin' on and I don't know what the somethin' is. I just think it's a bit strange someone starts killin' off people involved in a real estate development just when Andy starts callin' on Mr Stack and starts talkin' about developin' some property. Mr Stack has been good to me, what with givin' me some time off when I needed it, if you know what I mean. But with me bein' responsible for havin' your house shot up, and your next-door neighbour's house burnt down, I feel I should pay you somethin'. As I'm strapped for cash, the only thing I can do is keep my job here and my ears open. Any info I might pick up I'll pass on to you.'

Simon leant across the table and patted Jacko on the shoulder. 'Thanks, Jacko, that means a lot. We know the past has had its hiccups, but that's all water under the bridge. Anyway, what's with this Stack business?'

'I don't know, maybe nothin'. Mr Stack is a good bloke, sometimes, but he ain't all that kosher either. Hell knows, he might be up to somethin' involvin' Andy Crawford and whoever the politician is. Knowin' a little of what politicians can get up to, I've been tryin' to decide whether you'd be interested in what I had heard,' Jacko replied with some pride in the prospect of becoming a police grass.

'Well, thanks Jacko. That's all very interesting,' Simon said as he stood to leave the casino. 'We'll keep in touch, but the main thing is for you not to get yourself into trouble. Just keep your ear to the ground. If you foresee any trouble at all, just give Noel or myself a ring straight away; don't waste your time thinking about it, just ring.' With that Simon took a business card from his coat pocket and handed it to Jacko, as did Noel.

The two detectives left the casino and headed back down Palmer Street. 'Cripes, that sort of sets the cat among the pigeons,' Noel said absently, his mind more concerned with just how far down Palmer Street he had parked the car.

'Yes, it's a bit odd, especially as Buckmaster claims to have rid politicians of their bad habits, which I know is a load of garbage. If Jacko is right, and I've no reason to doubt that he's not, I'd say the status quo has been maintained and Buckmaster, or one of his cronies, is on the fiddle. By the way, just where did you park the car?'

'Ahh, come on, boss, I'm not so stupid that I would lose a police car. It's just a little further down the road,' Noel, with the sudden onset of a horrible feeling, lied. Hell, he thought, I was sure I parked it in that loading zone back there.

'And when you parked it, you did place the identification placard on the dash advising it was a police car on official business?' Simon asked knowing full well the answer.

Noel stopped walking, turned and looked around, hands on hips while he surveyed the scene. 'Yes, that's definitely where I parked it, and yes, I'm sure I put the placard on the dash, or at least I must have as it's the routine thing to do. You do it automatically.'

'Well, buddy boy, I suggest you get your mobile out and track it down as the council has probably towed it away, or it's been stolen, you idiot. In the meantime, we'll catch a cab back to Day Street and you can explain it all to the duty sergeant.'

# CHAPTER 13

'Well, I daresay some people had a good giggle about that, and I think the desk sergeant might have been one of them,' Simon said without a trace of sympathy for his sergeant.

'Okay, so I blundered. We all make a mistake once in our life, and I just made mine. At least I can now look forward to a mistake free future. Anyway, I for one would prefer to leave the subject alone and get on with a murder or two,' Noel said trying to get the matter back onto a more topical subject.

'Sounds like a good idea to me, so pax. Now, which way do we go? We can either chase up what Jacko said in the hope there is a connection between what he told us and the murder, or we could chase up both the murder and the bashing,' Simon said as he stretched back on his chair and started a slow rock, back and forward. 'What do you think, Noel?'

Noel folded his arms while in deep in concentration. To expunge himself from the abysmal depths of stupidity from which he had so easily fallen, and to salvage his shaky reputation, the thought he was about to convey to Simon had to be brilliant, logical, and nothing short of an extraordinary understanding of crime fighting procedures. 'Do both,' he said with all the boldness and confidence he could muster.

'Sounds great, but there are only three of us, and that's counting Ron. We haven't the resources of the FBI or Scotland Yard to play with,' Simon replied, although not totally rejecting Noel's suggestion, 'and we'll have to let Fisher know what we propose to do.'

'Well, seeing you're the diplomatic one, and senior officer, I would suggest you follow up Jacko's comments about the politicians while Ron and I look into the murder. Maybe in the process we'll come up with something on Henry's situation. I think it would an interesting exercise to see whether we meet in the middle.'

Simon pursed his lips and considered Noel's suggestion. After some deliberation he came to the conclusion that the idea did have some merit, quite apart from the exhilarating thought of digging up some diabolical conspiracy, or plot, that might unite the two investigations. Now, that was something that did pique his interest. 'Okay,' he said, 'let's get the ball rolling. Get on to Ron and fill him in on what we've decided and I'll let Fisher know before I start to have a hunt around the hallowed halls of Macquarie Street.'

The room Noel and Ron entered was devoid of furniture, save for one rectangular metal table bolted to the centre of the stone floor, and four collapsible metal chairs placed at the table. The lighting consisted of one fluorescent strip lamp set into the ceiling and covered with a metal mesh grill, the switch located on the doorframe of the solid core door. The one small window, fitted with iron bars, gave a panoramic view of the rolling shoreline but, being located in the stone wall about seven feet above the stone floor, any view provided was inconsequential unless the viewer was extremely tall. Notwithstanding, as the room was within the city prison, neither Noel nor Ron held any great expectations as to the creature comforts provided for the incarcerated reprobates

As the two men sat and waited, Noel said, 'Ron, I don't intend to interrogate Paul about Andrew Glover; maybe just a few questions. Paul isn't known for shooting people and we haven't yet received the pathologist report on what actually killed Andrew. We'll stick with the Haynes case and find out what he knows about that.'

'No, that seems a good idea as I doubt Paul could use a gun to assassinate anyone, even if he wanted to. He's more into clubbing his victims to death,' Ron replied.

After a few minutes of patient thumb twiddling, footsteps could be heard approaching down the corridor. Within moments, Paul Glover, dressed as he would in normal every-day attire and not the expected prison garb of an orange jump-suit, entered the room followed by an escorting warder whose physical attributes amounted to a surprising conflict with the general accepted physicality of a prison warder. Anyone betting on a punch-up involving the vertically impaired warder, with a slight, fragile frame to match, would rate him the underdog in any physical encounter with one of the seven dwarfs. Ron looked at Noel, a whimsical look etched across his face. Still, a man's gotta to do what a man's gotta do, he thought.

'I'll lock the door on my way out,' said the warder in a gruff voice that seemed totally incongruous with the body from which it emanated. 'There's a button just under the table, so when you're ready just give us a bell and I'll be back.' The door slammed shut with a thud as the warder left the room leaving the three men alone.

Noel pulled a chair out from the table and sat, gesturing to the others to do likewise. 'So, Paul, it's been some time now, but I see you're still alive and kicking.'

'Which is more than I can say for Uncle Andrew, poor bloke,' Paul said with something in his voice to suggest he did lament the loss of poor Uncle Andrew, to some extent, at least.

'Yes, so very tragic,' sympathized Noel, 'but at the moment we're more concerned with Henry Haynes following the beating he received on September fifteen.'

'Yes, pity about that. Despite being a cranky bugger, he's alright. I harbour no grudge against Henry.'

Noel quickly picked up on the innuendo. 'So, just who exactly is the target of your animosity?'

'Cripes, Sarge, I'm in the property development game, or was. That's one place where you end up with a lot more enemies than friends, if you have any friends at all, that is. You can't make money by being soft hearted and being pally with people. It's a case of dog eat dog, or do unto others before they do unto you, kind of world. I suppose there's a lot of people I know who aren't on my Christmas mailing list, just as I wouldn't expect to be on theirs.'

'Okay, but getting back to Henry. We were hoping you might be able to shed some light on who might have tried to kill him. I seem to recall both you and Andrew were absent from the prison on the night he was assaulted.'

'Yeah, I think that was the day Andrew and I went into town. But look, I've explained all this to that other detective bloke, Francis, I think.'

Noel nodded his head in acceptance of Paul's comment. 'Yes, we appreciate all this must be an inconvenience, but DI Francis was investigating an assault case resulting in grievous bodily harm. Mr Lange and I are here to continue with that investigation, and to investigate Andrew's murder, so we would like a bit of cooperation.'

Paul leant forward, clasped his hands together on the table and remained silent as if in deep reflection. Finally, with a shake of the head and a deep breath, he continued. 'We left around two in the afternoon. I had a meeting planned so left Andrew sometime around three.'

'And where did you part company?' Ron asked, a pen and notebook at the ready.

'Bondi Junction,' Paul replied. As I said, I had a meeting to attend.'

'With Ralph Glover at Glover Property Development?' Noel quickly responded.

'No, it wasn't with Ralph Glover at Glover Property Development. I've had nothing to do with Glover Property Development since I got put away, apart from a visit from Henry Haynes who wanted to know what I had planned for my Elizabeth Bay property.'

'So, what do you plan to do with it once you're released from jail, officially released I mean?' Ron asked as he finished jotting some notes in his pad.

'Well, I still own the property, along with the house that's on it. Uncle Andrew and I were planning to carry on with the plans we made before brother Bruce had to go and wreck the scheme, and poor Andrew got himself done in. Now I suppose I'll just have to do it all myself,' Paul replied.

'And you can't see any impediment to the development plans brought about by your incarceration?' Noel enquired, his interest stirred by Paul's apparent lack of reality.

'No, why should I? The council had approved all there is to be approved before I was sentenced so, as far as I know, there's nothing to stop me.'

Noel cast a quick glance at Ron who returned with a smug "well, we know something you don't know" look. Both Ron and Noel were aware of the current position as to the Elizabeth Bay mansion, and the fact that the future of The Grovel depended on the outcome of some whimsical deliberation made by one self-indulgent public service bureaucrat, Mr Stuart Boswell.

Noel heaved a sigh and rested his cheek on the palm of his

hand. 'Getting back to Andrew, you say you left him at Bondi Junction around three. Did you see him again on that particular day?'

'No. I came back to the prison around nine-thirty in the evening. You can check my bundy card.'

Knowing the bundy records were easily falsified, Noel ignored Paul's remark and pressed on with the useless question he felt obliged to ask. 'So, you claim you had no involvement in the bashing of Henry Haynes, or the death of your uncle, Andrew?

'Of course I didn't bloody well try to bash Henry to death, and I didn't kill Uncle Andrew either,' Paul replied indignantly. 'Henry and I mightn't have been the best of mates, but I was looking forward to re-establishing the business and working with him. Okay, so I was put away for a minor incident arising from a family dispute. But that's water under the bridge now and it doesn't make me a homicidal maniac. I'm certainly not going to screw up again by killing off any more of my rellies, or work colleagues. And while you're at it, I certainly did not kill Andrew.'

'So, at this stage you're guilty of the non-killing of brother Ralph?' Ron quipped.

'Bloody hell, of course I'm guilty of the non-killing off of Ralph; he's still alive, isn't he? So, what if he is running GPD at the moment? Andrew and I ran the business before we were convicted so I see no reason why I shouldn't run the business once I'm out. I'm sure Ralph and I can come to an agreement on that issue. As I said, just because someone blew Uncle Andrew's brains out doesn't mean to say I have to spend the rest of my life grieving over his death. No, I have plans for The Grovel and, as I'm the sole owner of the place, I can redevelop it any way I damned well want.'

'And you're sure Andrew supported you in your redevelopment scheme? He didn't harbour any thoughts of doing something else with the property?' Ron queried.

'Of course Andrew was with me,' Paul replied indignantly. 'In fact, the day I left Andrew at Bondi Junction I believe he was off to the council to see how everything was placed for us to commence work. As he never did get to tell me the outcome of that meeting it seems like I'll have to go and find out for myself.'

Noel sat back and looked doubtfully at Glover. Methinks a good dose of sodium pentothal mightn't go astray for this bloke. Here we have a murder and an attempted murder, with probably more to come, and I don't know whether to believe this pillock or not. Noel slowly shook his head and reached for the button under the table. Things aren't a complete shambles, not yet anyway.

# CHAPTER 14

$\mathcal{S}$ imon gave the girl with the purple hair working on the information counter a friendly wave as he headed for the elevator. Bugger, he thought as the express lift, bypassing all other floors, sped him to the thirty ninth floor. Here I am off to have a chat with the Premier of the state with nothing more to go on than what Jacko has told me. Totally absorbed with his predicament, he failed to give Lorraine, the Premier's very personal assistant, a second glance as he was ushered into the Premier's office.

'Ahh, Simon, your return so soon has not been anticipated so you'll have to be brief; I have a luncheon engagement.' Having set the scene by letting Simon know the luxury of prolonged verbal intercourse was definitely not on the agenda, the Premier motioned Simon to take a seat while he remained casually ensconced behind his massive mahogany table. 'Now, what's the problem, Chief Inspector?'

'Well, Mr Premier, I'm not sure there is one. However, you will recall the murder of Robert Porter was motivated by plans to develop a gambling casino in the Eastern Suburbs, together with the involvement of Monica Sainsbury-Ackerman.'

'Yes, I doubt anyone involved in that investigation will forget it, especially as you maintain Mr Ackerman pushed her overboard from some boat half way up the bloody Amazon,' Buckmaster said with a wry smile.

Simon shrugged and passed off the comment with a trifling gesture of his hand. 'That's neither here nor there and is still something we can neither prove nor disprove, unless she turns up somewhere else on the planet. But getting back to the point, you claim you have cleaned up the antics of politicians, including the kowtowing to developers and unsavoury entrepreneurs, notwithstanding the size of any kickback that may be offered as an inducement?'

Buckmaster ceased his casual posturing, sat up straight and adopted an aggressive attitude. 'Detective Chief Inspector Webster, I have already told you, I will not compromise the position to which I have been democratically elected, nor my credibility, honesty and integrity, so I'll just ignore your question. Whatever people did in the past happened in the past and that's where it will remain. While members of the other side of the House may pursue issues of a nefarious nature, I do not propose to conduct a witch-hunt for those who may be involved in such activities that may, or may not, exist. Bearing that in mind, I would think you would be the first to agree, DCI Webster, everyone has their price.'

Simon felt the hot sensation of a blush cross his face. Yes, the Premier had just given him a dressing-down, regardless of the fact it had been Simon who had uncovered a blatant misuse by parliamentarians of taxpayer's money during the Robert Porter investigation two years previously. 'Yes, of course. It's just that we have come across some unconfirmed information relating to alleged discussions between an entrepreneur, of questionable repute might I add, and a politician. As we are unable to identify the politician if he, or she, should exist at all, I thought a chat might shed some light on the subject.'

'Know nothing about it and don't want to, even if it is for real, which it probably is. Entrepreneurs are always trying to develop some whacky idea that requires some political support, and politicians can always be counted on to support some whacky idea. Quite apart from that, I have neither the time nor inclination to spend making sure everything is tickity-boo as far as the integrity of everyone is concerned. As I have a state to run, I'd suggest you go and have a talk to Mason, he may know something I don't.'

Simon didn't like Peter Mason, but that was not surprising. In fact, it would be rather extraordinary if it were otherwise; Mason was a politician. Still, que sera, Simon thought as he looked around the coffee shop located in the imposing sandstone building of the State Library. As the deputy Premier was nowhere to be seen, Simon picked up a newspaper from the counter before ordering a cappuccino and taking a seat at a nearby table. He had only read the sports section on the back page of the paper and taken a sip of his coffee before being confronted by a big man with short, black curly hair and a bent nose, obviously broken sometime or other in the past.

'Aah, Mr Webster, long time no see,' the man said before taking a seat opposite Simon.

'Yes, it has,' replied Simon who remained seated in a churlish display of irreverence. 'I see you've come up in the world since I last saw you. What, you were the Minister for Sport and Recreation?'

'That's right, but obviously there had to be changes when Premier Martin died of a heart attack and his deputy resigned. Unfortunately, I can't feel sorry for my predecessor, Wally Ackerman. It was his own stupidity that forced him into such an intolerable situation that he had no choice but resign. Gavin, I mean Premier Buckmaster, lobbied for the top job and asked me to be his deputy. Naturally, I accepted. Who wouldn't?'

Simon harrumphed. 'Crikey, with all the fringe benefits available and shonkies going on with the last premier, you'd have to be nuts not to take it. In fact, that's what I'm here for. I've already spoken to Premier Buckmaster and he suggested I have a chat with you in regards to the scams still being perpetrated by the honourable members of parliament.'

Mason paused as a waitress placed a cup of black coffee on the table. After taking a sip, he regarded Simon with a serious look. 'Well, I don't know what the Premier has told you, but I'm unaware of anything untoward going on. Of course, that's not to say there isn't, it's just that if there is, I don't know about it.'

'Of course, and I presume you will be the caretaker Premier while Mr Buckmaster and his secretary are occupying their time watching baseball and Broadway shows in New York?'

'Oh, so you know about that?'

'Are we supposed not to?'

'Well, it's preferable the opposition remains ignorant of the fact. As far as they're concerned, the Premier is taking a trade delegation to the US to promote the wine industry.'

Whatever Simon was thinking was quickly drowned by a veil of scepticism. 'Oh, yes, and just how many members are there in this trade delegation?'

'Just two.'

'The Premier, and…?'

'Yep, got it in one. It's perfectly natural to have his secretary along to do all the paper work, you know, travel and meal allowance acquittals, reports to write. It saves a lot of time if everything is attended to before you arrive back home,' Mason replied with direct frankness. 'After all, if everything's perfectly normal and it ain't broke, you don't go and change it.'

Simon was fully aware that the final report of the Premier's upcoming US visit had probably already been written. However, not wishing to pursue another trail of scams perpetrated by politicians, Simon continued, 'Moving on to more pressing matters, you don't know anything about an alleged conversation between a politician and the owner of an illegal gambling casino?'

'Yes, you're right; I know nothing, but that doesn't say it didn't happen. The Premier has endeavoured to cut away all the...um, unethical behaviour that might have gone on in the past.'

Holy hell, Sergeant Schultz alive and well. And I bet they've introduced a whole new plethora of scams, Simon thought. 'So, you don't regard the previous deputy Premier chasing all over the world trying to catch your wife as unethical behaviour?'

That question appeared to have some affect on Mr Mason whose bright countenance took on a look of sullen indifference. 'After the results of your investigation into the death of Porter were released, deputy Premier Ackerman resigned. Whatever unethical behaviour he's up to now doesn't count for a brass razoo. Who knows? Who cares? He's not a politician, not now anyway. As far as Cheryl goes, she can do whatever she likes. She owns the place I'm living in at the moment down at Kogarah Bay, and by the time she gets back, if she ever does return to Australia, I'll be gone.'

'So, you've decided to give Cheryl the permanent flick and move on?'

'Look, DCI Webster, I'm currently the deputy Premier of the state and deserve to live in a bit more prestigious domain than the suburban bungalow in which I currently reside. While not wishing to cast aspersions on those who live in Kogarah, I think I should be seen to reside in a bit more up-market location.'

'Don't tell me; Elizabeth Bay?'

'Well, somewhere over in that area,' Mason replied, avoiding a definitive answer with all the dexterity and mental agility of a seasoned politician. 'And while I have no intention of discussing my domestic plans, I take it you are referring to Paul Glover's place, The Ghetto, or some such idiotic name?'

'Well, now that you've mentioned it, yes. There is some doubt as to the future ownership of The Grovel,' Simon replied. 'Depending on a council decision, the place may be sold off way under market value. I take it you would be interested in purchasing the place should the opportunity arise?'

Mason took a sip of coffee then took a deep breath. 'Maybe,' he said, nodding his head, 'I've heard the names of a few interested people bandied around, including Andy Crawford's, and if he's interested, I'm not.'

'And if he isn't interested?'

'Well, that might open up a whole new ball game, but I somehow think he's serious about the place. Crawford's a thug and wants The Grovel as a high price casino cum bordello; a high price prestigious bordello maybe, but a brothel by any other name.'

Simon paused to consider Mason's bit of gossip. 'And can you tell me the source of your information?'

'No names, no pack drill, DCI Webster. And it's hearsay so it's not admissible. Look, DCI Webster, I'll level with you. I feel somewhat uncomfortable as Mr Buckmaster appears to have an ongoing problem. My gut feeling is that whatever the problem, it just might involve the development of a particular Elizabeth Bay property. While I have nothing to even suggest I'm right, I have this funny feeling Mr Buckmaster might be predisposed to a bit of unethical behaviour if the price, or reward, is right. Simply put, I think our Premier is in cahoots with someone, and that someone will be some unscrupulous person not averse to something, if not illegal, at least immoral, or maybe unethical is a better word.'

Cripes, talk about loyalty. I wonder if all politicians are ready to plant the dirk between the shoulder blades, Simon thought. 'Well, at least I can say you're not backward in coming forward,

Mr Mason. Okay, as we're talking about redevelopment scams, what do you know about Ackerman's wife, Monica and her construction company located here in Sydney?' Simon asked in a "shake the tree and see what falls out" exercise.

Mason shifted uncomfortably on his chair. 'Hell, according to you, Ackerman killed her off somewhere in the Amazon jungle. I haven't seen or heard anything to the contrary, or anything to confirm whether she is or isn't, dead, I mean. Mind you, there are rumours circulating that might tend to suggest Monica is alive. I've even heard she's currently in Panama City working for some construction mob involved in widening the canal.'

Simon folded his arms and screwed his eyes tightly shut. After a deep breath he was able to get back on track having mulled over Mason's latest revelation. 'And you think Buckmaster's current preoccupation may be related to a redevelopment scam?'

Mason shrugged and gave a non-committed nod. 'Well, I would think the shonkies you revealed during the Porter murder are still being perpetrated, despite what Buckmaster may have told you. He certainly doesn't need Monica Ackerman to show him what to do. And you can bet whatever his current distraction is, it will be illicit, one way or the other.'

'So, apart from the gut feeling, there's nothing to indicate what's going on?'

'There has been some gossip concerning the property over at Elizabeth Bay, but I think that's all it is at the moment; gossip. No-one has come out with anything definite and to believe the claptrap you hear, you do so at your own peril. Mind you, having a private secretary as good looking as Lorraine might prove to be Buckmaster's distraction. If she were my secretary, I'd say I would be somewhat distracted. But seriously, it could be that someone is out to try and muster some political muscle. If you add that to my gut feeling, I'd say Buckmaster is being tempted with an offer involving The Grovel. And should that be the case, it would mean there's some sort of collusion going on between Buckmaster and, most likely, Andy Crawford. But look, I really must be going. If I hear anything on the grape-vine, I'll give you a buzz.'

With that The Honourable Peter Mason, MP, pushed his empty cup and saucer to the centre of the table, rose from his chair and strode from the room.

# CHAPTER 15

$\mathcal{N}$oel looked dejected. But then again, Simon wasn't over brimming with jubilation either. Things weren't going well for the two detectives and Superintendent Nigel Fisher was well aware of the fact. Simon accepted that Jacko may be short on the personal attributes of sophistication and culture. However, there are those pretentious, self-indulgent "would be if they could be" members of society only too willing to exercise such self-proclaimed attributes, much to the amusement of others, totally unaware that they are no more a sophisticate or enlightened guru than Jacko. But Jacko was honest and a good bloke without any such pretentions. And what's more, as Simon believed what Jacko had to say, there was every possibility that something, if not corrupt at least dishonest, was being perpetrated.

'Okay, Noel, I'll trade you. You find out what's going on up in Macquarie Street and I'll find the culprits of these dastardly deeds.'

'No way. We agreed you'd do the political side of things and I'll get on and find the guilty weasel, or weasels. But something tells me you've had as much success as I've had, and fussy

Fisher wants some answers,' Noel replied as he absently flipped through the pages of his notebook. 'And what's up with Fisher anyway?'

'Well, you can't blame him for being a tad touchy,' Simon replied. 'After all, we did have some input into the collapse of the last premier and his deputy. And following my talk with Buckmaster, I'd say the pollies are still playing games despite his protestations that everything is squeaky-clean. Although, I must say Mason came up with a bit of news which tends to confirm what Jacko told us about Crawford and an exclusive club. Mason's words were almost the same as Jacko's with Andy Crawford's plan to convert some old mansion on the harbour foreshore into some type of exclusive casino cum bordello.'

'Oh, and ain't that just ducky. And how did Mason come by that snippet of info?' Noel asked with a sceptical tone. 'I can understand how Jacko might have, but Mason?'

'He wasn't at liberty to say, or wouldn't, although it seems pretty common knowledge. Mason knows, Jacko knows, Paul Stack knows, and obviously Crawford knows. At a guess I'd say our Mr Crawford has spoken to a politician and I've no doubt it was either Mason or Buckmaster.'

Noel's countenance brightened as the veil of ignorance was slowly lifted. 'So, you think Crawford may have hijacked a politician to help him get his hands on The Grovel and turn it into a den of iniquity?'

'Most likely, but if it's true I think it might come as some surprise to Paul Glover. He believes he's the owner of the place and anyone who thinks otherwise can get knotted. Problem for us is that it would extend our investigation beyond Glover Property Development and into the realms of The Grovel. Should Paul get the idea he may lose it, for one reason or another, he may resort to violence against anyone who poses a threat.'

'So, you don't think he would be interested in going along with Crawford's scheme?'

'Doubt it,' Simon replied. He believes he holds all the approvals to go ahead with his townhouse complex, which he doesn't because they're in the name of GPD. Problem for him is he can't do anything now because, as a convicted murderer, he's without a license to trade. I'd bet Crawford is already aware that Paul's chances of developing the place amount to zero, so maybe he's manoeuvring to buy the property out from under him, if Boswell decides Paul has defaulted on statutory payments, which he probably has. In their quest for the outstanding debt owed by Paul, Boswell may well decide to invoke legitimate provisions under the Local Government Act and claim the property for the council. Once council has title, they'll no doubt sell it to a specific client chosen by Boswell at a fraction of the market price. And whoever does obtain the title to the place, you can bet it won't be for much more than the amount of Paul's outstanding debt, especially with Boswell and, or, a heavyweight politician pulling the strings.

'No, I think Crawford has recruited a politician to help him get the place and then to oversee the paperwork for his exclusive club. Obviously, the politician would expect some recompense for his effort and that would be a cut of the casino profits. And I've no doubt that, with a politician on your side, the casino would be seen to run at a loss as far as the tax office is concerned.'

'But what if Crawford did join with Paul and not a politician? Paul has all the experience in dealing with council and could get a new set of plans approved in Crawford's name. At the moment he still owns the place which would make things a lot easier for Crawford. So why does Crawford need to cajole a polly into the scheme?' came Noel's next in-depth searching question.

'Neither Paul nor Crawford has any credibility. One's a convicted murderer and the other is a well-known gangster running an illegal casino. To get all the approvals, in either

Paul's or Crawford's name, together with a property rezoning, plus a complete new set of plans to develop The Grovel into a casino, they would need someone with a squeaky-clean record working for them, and that might include Boswell. And don't forget the tax angle. Okay, so let's say Buckmaster is the polly. He knows enough about rorting the system when it comes to tax minimization and I've no doubt he knows how to organise money laundering.'

Noel pursed his lips, relaxed back on his chair and folded his arms. 'But Mason could fit that role just as well as Buckmaster, rorting the system I mean.' Now having some difficulty in visu-alising the scene, Noel moved to the white board and examined the names. 'Okay, Mr Ackerman is chasing after Cheryl Mason who's in Paris and Peter Mason couldn't care less if his misses never returns home. Meanwhile, Mrs Ackerman is probably dead and floating off down the Amazon, or overseas somewhere sipping a pina colada.

'We believe Andy Crawford, with a little help from an unknown politician, wants to develop some harbourside place which we think is The Grovel. Both Paul and Ralph Glover want The Grovel for one reason or another, while Boswell is deciding who currently owns the property, which might turn out to be the council, ergo, Boswell. We think Buckmaster, who claims he's squeaky-clean, is in league with Crawford, while Mason wants to upgrade his living standards by moving to the Eastern Suburbs, possibly Elizabeth Bay. Sorry, boss, but I smell a rat.'

Simon looked discouraged. How can a simple murder and the brutal assault of an innocent victim which, on face value, appear to involve bureaucrats become so complicated? Easily, when those bureaucrats are politicians, he thought. 'Come to think of it, that's an oxymoron, or at least a contradiction in terms; a squeaky-clean politician? I don't think I've ever seen one of them, but I think you're pretty close to the mark. The only other piece of info Mason provided was that he doesn't know for sure that any politician is talking to Crawford, not that I would put much trust in anything Mason had to say on that score. The best he could do was infer that, if a politician is involved, it would probably be Buckmaster.'

'We could always go and ask Crawford what's going on,' Noel suggested.

'We could,' Simon replied, 'but has all this beat-up about The Grovel anything to do with Andrew reposing in the morgue, or Henry recovering in hospital? Sure, we've uncovered some info on what might be going on, or supposedly going on, and it appears to be linked with The Grovel. Unfortunately, it's not helping us find the miscreant, or miscreants responsible for our two victims.'

'So, you think Buckmaster and Crawford are conspiring to manipulate ownership of the property'?

Simon pursed his lips and gave a shrug. 'Who knows, and only time will tell what's going on, but the killing of Andrew Glover has all the earmarks of an underworld job which means Crawford or Stack had to be involved. And on top of that, I'd say Mason is absolutely right on the casino issue. If there is something going on involving Buckmaster, I'd say he'd be a very silent partner and have whatever kickbacks he receives deposited in some Swiss bank account. I somehow think he may be stupid enough to have forgotten the scandal that erupted when the last premier and his deputy got involved in rorting the system.'

'So, in effect, every individual we've talked about has a motive for doing away with anyone who has shown an interest in The Grovel,' Simon said as he scratched his ear lobe. 'Even Andrew could have tried to murder Henry as he might have viewed Henry as an impediment to retaking the management of GPD. Obviously if he did do it, he would have had to have done it before someone murdered him. I think the only person we can delete from the suspect list is Henry, and only because he was the first victim.'

Noel rolled a sheet on paper into a ball and had a three-point shot at Simon's waste paper basket – and missed. After a shrug and a frown, he said, 'Irrespective of who bashed Henry, I'd say Ralph's interest in both The Grovel and GPD might be fatal. Paul, and I guess everyone else implicated in the place, is probably well aware of Ralph's interest. If Boswell decides Paul is the legal owner, Paul will go ballistic when he finds he can't do anything with the place. Now, if Ralph can hang on to GPD and not get himself killed, maybe he and Paul can work something out.'

'Yep, and at the moment it's like you said, Crawford wants the place, Paul wants the place, Andrew wanted the place, Ralph wants the place and I have an idea Boswell might want the place for no other reason than to make a financial killing. And I'm sure even Mason wouldn't say no to it. On top of all that, Crawford and the Premier, or his deputy, are working hand in glove, well, we think they are, with a scheme to convert The Grovel into a swanky whore house; okay, gambling den.

'No, something is wrong somewhere. It all gets back to who owns the place and it seems we won't know that until Boswell makes a decision. And, if what we've got scribbled up there on the board is anything to go by, it could make Boswell vulnerable to pecuniary offers, which is probably the object of his little exercise anyway.' Simon thumped the table with his fist. 'Right, that does it. Although I prefer not to ask questions I don't already know the answer to, it's time we try and have that little chat with Paul Stack.'

'Okay, so was there anything else Mason had to say?' Noel asked as he fidgeted with the whiteboard marker.

Simon folded his arms, surveyed the ceiling and swivelled his chair from side to side before responding. 'Nothing, apart from the fact that he has doubts whether Monica Ackerman is alive or dead, which is par for a politician's decision-making ability. I'm certain she's either one or the other, unless she's stranded in the ether somewhere.'

Notwithstanding the limited knowledge provided by Jacko, the idea of speaking directly to Paul Stack was, to Simon's thinking, a good one. Jacko had provided Simon with enough credible information to warrant a closer look into the current activities of the very wealthy and flamboyant gangster, Andy Crawford. Simon couldn't suppress the notion that however lawful his activities might appear on the surface, they were bound to be shonky, if not downright illegal. No-one could amass such a fortune as Crawford had by being squeaky-clean, and Crawford was a Stack associate.

The two detectives alighted from the police car after Simon had dismissed the station constable who had driven the detectives from Day Street to Palmer Street and the The Spinning Wheel casino. Although Simon had authority to draw a police car from the station's vehicle pool, he preferred not to drive on this occasion, quite content to sit back and let someone else run the gauntlet of city traffic. It was another thing for Noel, his previous vehicle debacle denting the confidence of the pool management to the extent that his access to a police vehicle had been revoked until further notice.

'It's still daylight, but I s'pose someone has to be here by now,' Noel commented as he reached for the door buzzer.

Simon frowned. 'It's not just someone we want to see. It's Paul Stack, and if he's not in I'll get the idea he's trying to avoid us. Hang on, someone's coming.'

A lock was turned and the door opened a smidgen. An eye peered out for a moment before the door was opened to the visitors. 'Blimey, it's you two again. Quick, inside before anybody sees you,' Jacko directed.' Jacko's initial response to the presence of the two detectives was no different from any previous response; a welcome with all the geniality of an enraged wasp. Although the detectives were in mufti, there was no doubting they were readily identifiable as members of the constabulary, and Jacko was well aware of his boss's distaste for coppers.

'I s'pose you want to see Mr Stack?' he asked as he led the two men into the same room they had been on the previous occasion.

'Yes, but before we see him, Jacko, have you heard anything of interest lately?' Simon asked.

Jacko stopped his leading and turned to Simon. 'Funny you should ask, but all of a sudden it seems Andy Crawford is layin' low. No-one's seen him for a while, but maybe Mr Stack knows more on that score. I did hear him boastin' to Mr Stack that he had paid the polly a great heap of dough, but I don't know the details.' Simon looked at Noel, his eyes conveying the "now that's interesting" comment.

'And anything on our two victims?' Noel asked.

Jacko looked trouble. 'Gee, fellas, I don't know. Last time Crawford was here there seemed to be an argument goin' on, and honestly, I didn't want to hear, not that I could help it. I got the idea Mr Stack didn't want to hear either as he eventually called me in to escort Crawford from the premises. Mr Stack was a mess, all hot and sweaty and he kept on sayin' "I don't want to know" over and over. I don't know if it had anythin' to do with the murder, but it all seems too coincidental to me.'

'Okay, Jacko. You're doing well, so just keep your ear to the ground. Now, Mr Stack?'

Jacko knocked before opening the door to Stack's office. 'Sorry, Mr Stack, but you have a couple of visitors, Detective Chief Inspector Webster and Detective Sergeant Elliott.'

'Jiminy Cricket, Jacko, when will you learn? These people aren't visitors, they're interlopers, and I didn't invite them here.' The invisible voice emanated from behind a large mahogany table, the voice's owner slowly materialising from obscurity as Stack rose from his chair to inspect the interlopers. Simon couldn't help thinking that there had been little change in Mr Stack's physical appearance since their last encounter nearly two years ago. He was still the small, rotund man, maybe with a little less hair than his balding pate had displayed on Simon's previous visits to The Spinning Wheel. It seemed Paul Stack's penchant for a garish wardrobe had not changed, the gangster now attired in a pair of red slacks and a bright green shirt giving Simon the heady thought that he was confronting a traffic light. But to each their own, and who would be stupid enough to criticize?

Stack had the knack of being able to completely disappear from those sitting in front of his table, either because the table was far too big, or his chair perched him way too close to the floor. Either way, on regaining his seat Stack had to lean forward and strain his neck to view the seated visitors, as the detectives now were, a most unsettling situation, at least for the visitors.

'Okay, gentlemen, what is it you want? You collecting donations for the policemens' ball?'

'No, not quite,' Simon replied. 'I just thought we'd pay you a cordial visit and ask how things are going.'

'Codswallop, you blokes know nothin' about cordiality,' came Stack's response. 'Let's cut to the chase and stop wastin' time.'

Simon nodded and gave Noel a slight but meaningful shrug. 'Okay, Mr Stack, what are you and Andy Crawford up to? We know Crawford paid a donation to a certain politician and the amount of that payment would suggest there's a shonky going on, and we want to know what the shonky is.'

Paul Stack seemed unperturbed by Simon's question. In fact, he casually sat back in his oversized leather chair and disappeared from the view of the two detectives. After the sound of a drawer being opened and a match being struck, the desk was enveloped in a cloud of blue cigar smoke. While now beyond the view of the two detectives, Stack said, 'Mr Webster, I'm fully aware you don't expect me to answer that question. As to if there's something going on between Crawford and myself, which I steadfastly refuse to either confirm or deny, that something, if it existed, would be a matter strictly between Mr Crawford and myself.'

Untroubled by Stack's failure to clarify whatever might, or might not, be going on, Simon looked across to Noel and gave an imperceptible nod of the head. 'Okay, Mr Stack,' Noel countered, 'we believe Mr Crawford may be involved in one recent murder, and a near-fatal assault, both victims known to you personally. While we acknowledge you are under no obligation to assist in our inquiries at this point of time, we would stress that any future information or revelation implicating you in any way, irrespective of how trivial you may consider it to be, would almost certainly result in legal action being taken against you. Now, how about some answers?'

Upon re-emergence of the head, this time with a smouldering cigar protruding from the corner of his mouth, it was fairly obvious Stack had been somewhat irritated by the inference of Noel's statement. 'Now, look here. I'm in the gambling business and run an honest illegal casino. Some time ago you made accusations relating to a body fished out of the harbour, which I had nothing to do with. Now you have the temerity to come here on the presumption I know all about the attack on two blokes just because they had an interest in real estate. Sure, I was acquainted with the victims, and so what if one of them was a convicted murderer?'

Both Simon and Noel remained silent although Simon's raised eyebrows conveyed the question; 'So.' Stack's cigar was now held between thumb and forefinger, his elbow resting on the desk. His initial outburst of anger had now tempered, his face etched with a look of troubled concern. 'Look, Crawford made it quite plain to me that other contenders for the property, including

GPD, would soon realise it would be in their best interest to forgo any involvement in a certain property. He may have been a little more explicit in what he said regarding who the other interested parties might be, and the consequences of staying in the race for The Grovel. I can't recall the exact words he used and if I do, I'll try very hard to forget them,' Stack said as he brutally ground the butt of his cigar in a glass ashtray.

'And it was this conversation that had you call for Jacko to throw Crawford out of the place? Taking such extreme action suggests whatever prompted you to remove your friend from the building would be quite significant and something you would be unlikely to forget in a hurry,' Noel commented, more as a question.

'Okay, so Crawford got me angry. Look, maybe I should start at the beginning,' Stack suggested as he removed another cigar from the ornate cigar box on his desk, bit off the end and unceremoniously dispatched it with a spit to the floor. Now, with the unlit cigar in the corner of his mouth, Stack continue. 'Crawford's interested is in the Elizabeth Bay mansion currently owned by Paul Glover. He wants to convert it into a swanky elite sort of club for high rollers with lots of money, you know, lots of champaign and women. He wanted me to come in on the plan with both my money and experience within the industry. You know, the bigger the investment, the bigger the return. However, I figured that with all the paper work he'd have to go through to get the idea accepted by planning authorities, and the time that would take, it wouldn't be worth the trouble, quite apart from the fact Crawford has no legal claim whatsoever on the property.'

Before continuing, and after conducting a careful inspection of the unlit cigar, Stack apparently resolved his dilemma and made the significant decision; the cigar remained unlit. 'Crawford believes there may be some contentious issues regarding ownership of the property and he's started to butter up some heavyweight politician to gain support for his plan. He claims the casino would be a good investment for both the local council and the state as it would bring in considerable revenue in the form of the gambling tax. Now, as far as I know, other possible contenders for the property are, or were, Paul and Ralph Glover, Henry Haynes from GPD and Andrew Glover. I suppose there may be others I'm unaware of.

'Anyway, when Crawford came to see me, he told me all other contenders would be dealt with in the appropriate manner. When I asked him what he meant by the "appropriate manner", he left me under no illusion as to what he meant. That's when I told him to get out of the place as I didn't want anything to do with him, or his money-making schemes. And now we have two of the contenders dead, or at least one dead and one nearly. Honestly, I had nothing to do with their unfortunate incidents, but I wouldn't mind betting Crawford does. He might not have pulled the trigger in the shooting case, but probably had someone do it for him, if he was involved, that is.'

A silence prevailed as the two detectives pondered Stack's disclosure. 'How much buttering up, and which heavyweight politician are we talking about?' Noel asked with all the cynicism the inevitable question demanded.

'A lot and don't know, but I'd guess it has to be someone able to move mountains,' Stack replied. 'With the amount of money that had to have changed hands you would expect a decent return. You know, the quid pro quo, so he wasn't paying off the tea lady. You'll have to ask Crawford, that's if you can find him.'

'What do you mean, if we can find him?' Noel asked.

'Haven't seen him for a few days now,' Stack replied as he was engulfed in a pall of blue cigar smoke, the decision not to light up having been rescinded. 'But, if on the off-chance you can find him, I'd ask you not to let him know I've been speaking to you. He's a bit strung out at the moment and everything is very confidential, or so he says. In fact, I think he'd be quite angry with me if he knew what I've told you.'

Simon wiped a smoke effected eye and sat back on his chair. 'And just how angry is Mr Crawford likely to be?'

'Very. As I said, he's admitted any opposition would be neutralised, and with one opponent already eliminated, who knows who else may end up the same way. And if it's not Crawford poppin' people, there just might be an unknown serial killer on the loose.'

'So, he's not around at The Red Ruby?' Noel asked.

'Doesn't appear to be, and it's sure as hell I'm not going around there to find out if he's in or not. He's probably hanging around just cooling his heels until the time is right to make his move.'

'I suppose we can take it that whatever friendship you had with Crawford no longer exists?' Simon enquired.

'Look, I really don't care if I never see Andy Crawford again. He's way too big for his boots now. Once you start trying to push people around and eliminating opposition, someone's bound to get hurt. I somehow think Henry and Andrew Glover found that out, not that Henry deserved what he got, poor bloke. The closer you get to Crawford, the chances are someone will think you're in cahoots with him and, to tell the truth, he's the last person on the planet I would want to be in cahoots with.'

As the two detectives left The Spinning Wheel, Simon turned to Noel and shook his head. 'Well, that's some sort of a revelation. Trouble is, Noel, I can't help feeling our Mr Stack is not averse to telling the odd porky pie when it suits him, even if he swears on a stack of bibles that he's telling the truth, and no pun intended.'

*S*imon pushed his chair back from the desk with his foot and surveyed the mess of scribble Noel had painstakingly scrawled across the whiteboard. 'Well, what do you think, boss?' Noel asked as he proudly stepped back from his simple diagrammatic solution to the ongoing problem at hand; the horrendous attack on Henry Haynes and the demise of Andrew Glover. 'It's quite simple really. Both attacks are centred round The Grovel and involve two of the rivals competing for the place. Obviously, the attacker of Henry has to be Paul Glover who wants to run Glover Property Development by himself and carry on with his townhouse redevelopment, irrespective of the fact that he's lost his license to trade.

'Both Ralph and Henry might have been able to complete Paul's redevelopment scheme in accordance with Paul's approved plans. Maybe Ralph still can. However, it might have crossed Paul's mind that, in view of the cancellation of his license, both Ralph and Henry may be scheming to usurp all of his, or at least GPD's, council approved paperwork. As a consequence, Paul would have assumed that both Ralph and Henry pose a threat to the millions he expects to pocket. I'd put my money on Ralph Glover being the next victim as he's the last person standing in Paul's way. We already know Paul's predilection to committing a simple case of fratricide and I don't think any time spent in a prison would have changed his homicidal tendencies.'

'Yeah, well that's all very clear and maybe you're right, but from fratricide to parricide in Andrew's case, wouldn't have been just one small step but a giant leap for Paul. His modus operandi is bashing people to death, not shooting 'em,' Simon growled. 'But hell's bells, Noel, I don't know, it just seems too easy. And don't forget, the last person to have seen the victim is usually the perpetrator of the crime. Paul claims he never saw Henry the night Henry was bashed and, according to the jail's records, Paul was safely tucked up in jail the night Andrew was executed.'

Noel harrumphed. 'Yeah, sometimes. I know that's one of the police's teachings and it's probably right in most cases. Obviously, the last person to see Henry fit and well would have been his assailant, and I doubt anyone would have seen Andrew Glover alive after his assassin had done his work. I'll go along with the principle when someone actually kills the person outright, but we haven't a clue as to what happened in Henry's case.'

'Okay, okay, point taken. So, you think Ralph is next in line to cop a belting over the head?' Simon asked.

'Without doubt, and I bet Ralph has worked that out for himself.'

'So, you think we'd better get out to the jail and arrest Paul before he runs rampant again? Problem is we don't have any real evidence to charge him with either murder or GBH. We can probably screw him for both attacks on the motive side, but the opportunity question is debatable. The means is simplified by the fact that whatever was used to attack Henry was a blunt instrument, and that could have been anything from a baseball bat to a fence paling. As for Andrew, his death is way out of Paul's league; Paul wouldn't know one end of a gun from the other. But even with Henry's assault, the only evidence we have is circumstantial with nothing concrete enough to get past a preliminary hearing. Okay, so Henry's on the mend, but doctors say he's incapable of remembering anything of the incident, except having a beer at the pub. They also say that he's still not well enough to be interviewed, and it might be some time before he is. Anyway, this has nothing to do with me. You're the one working on the murder side of things,' Simon said with feigned indifference.

'Well, what do you suggest I do now?' Noel asked, conscious of the fact his case, so far, was based solely on supposition. 'Okay, so we suspect Paul's guilty of being Henry's assailant, but we have grave doubts that he would have been the shooter of his uncle. Irrespective of whether he's one or the other, we would still have to establish that the Musgrave solution provided him with the opportunity to commit either, or both, of the crimes. That, in itself, might prove difficult as we know how easily the system can be exploited. And if we charge Paul with both events, we would have to charge him with being a fibber as he claims he wasn't involved in either case.'

'Then maybe you should go and speak to him, not that he's likely to reveal anything you don't know already. Best you let Fisher know your thoughts on the matter before heading off; he'll want to know something, even if it's nothing,' Simon said as he pulled his chair closer to his desk and started writing notes on a pad. 'In the meantime, I have to work out my next step as I'm sure there is something going on involving politicians. I want to know what that something is because, whatever it is, it's going to be some unscrupulous scam. Oh yes, and have you received the list of telephone calls made by Boswell?'

'Yes, and I think you'll find a very interesting number

called,' Noel replied as he headed for the door. 'The list is in my "In" tray.'

The ringing of Simon's phone caused Noel to defer his venture to Superintendent Nigel Fisher's office and await whatever earth-shattering news Simon would no doubt convey on completion of his exchange with whoever the ringer might be. After a very brief conversation, Simon replaced the receiver, looked at Noel and gave a shrug with an "I haven't a clue" pout. 'Hang on, I'll come with you,' Simon said as he picked up his coat, 'it seems Fisher wants to see us as much as you want to see him.'

'Now gentlemen, I believe you wanted to see me, Sergeant?' Fisher asked as he settled himself back in his chair.

'Yes, sir,' Noel replied, 'although I believe you want to see both of us, now?

'Yes, that's right. These murder cases; anything new?'

'That's what I was on my way to see you for, sir. I believe the killing is Grovel related. If I am right, it could put either Paul or Ralph Glover, maybe both, in a pretty precarious situation. Being the only remaining Glovers, at least one of them might be a candidate to join both Andrew pushing up daisies and Henry, who someone expected to be in the same condition as Andrew.'

Fisher nodded his approval of Noel's logic. 'Yes, that seems perfectly reasonable. And Simon, you agree with your sergeant?'

'Yes sir, but only up to a point. We know there's a queue of people lined up wanting The Grovel for one reason or another. In order to pursue the murder case, while keeping tabs on The Grovel, we decided to split the investigation in two, Noel doing the murder while I look to see if there's a tie-up with the real estate and the involvement of some political pundit. Knowing that Andy Crawford, with the possible collaboration of an unknown politician, is eyeing off the place suggests there might be some conflict with other aspiring owners. I just haven't worked out who's involved and the extent of their involvement.

'Despite the fact that Ralph sent Henry, prior to him being hospitalised, out to the jail to see Paul about The Grovel, I very much doubt if Ralph would do anything untoward to get the place. I think Noel should continue with his investigation into GPD and the murder while I continue with my side of the investigation. Maybe it would be a good idea if we just sit back and wait to see if there's going to be another murder as that might shed some light as to what's going on.'

'Aah, yes, another Websterism. They probably used the same system on The Ripper murders; wait long enough and the culprit is bound to make a mistake, eventually, which he didn't. No, I think you had better continue the investigation in the hope we can forestall someone else being nudged off the planet. Okay Sergeant, now you've whittled it down to two suspected victims, just who exactly is going to be the next casualty and, more importantly, who's going to be the villain?'

'My money's on Ralph being the victim and Paul the perpetrator, although Paul may opt for the dual role of villain and victim. We already know Paul's capable of murder and I think Cheryl Drake wouldn't be too happy knowing she dated a murderer one moment, and a victim the next. And if someone wants The Grovel bad enough, there's every chance he will be the next victim,' Noel replied.

Fisher nodded. 'And what about the death of Andrew Glover?'

'Ahh, yes,' Noel replied, nodding. 'It looks quite simple really although we haven't established clear motive or means. However, the opportunity thing is a different matter. As Andrew Glover chose to take a day off from jail, it provided someone an opportune moment to blow his brains out. The motive, we think The Grovel. The means we have to confirm with Graham Gallymore as he's yet to identify exactly what was used, apart from the fact we know it was a gun. Although only speculation, we think Andy Crawford could be the guilty culprit but, then again, pure speculation and he may not be.'

'You know, Simon,' Fisher said, 'you seem to have a pretty smart sergeant working for you and I like the way he hedges his bets; at least he'll never be totally wrong. From the information he has, I'd say his assessment of the situation is quite plausible. So far, and only conjecture, both the murder of Glover and the assault on Haynes seem to have nothing to do with anything else but The Grovel.'

Simon was a little surprised by Fisher's acceptance of Noel's assessment, bearing in mind that everything was either hearsay, which is non-admissible, or circumstantial. 'Yes sir, Noel and I get on very well and I think we're a pretty good team. But, so far we have nothing to establish a firm direction for the investigation to follow so we're sort of waiting to see what happens next.'

'Well, let me give you some trivia for you to work on. I called you up here to provide you with some information you might consider relevant to your investigation. Sergeant Elliott seems to have an idea as to who the principle players are; he just doesn't know who the baddie is, or conversely, who the goodie is.' Fisher, inwardly enjoying the anticipated reaction the two detectives would most likely display on hearing his bit of trivia, was playing the game; I know something you don't, so let them wait.

After a prolonged pregnant pause, Simon couldn't contain himself. 'Ahh, for cryin' out loud, get on with it, sir. What's this piece of trivia that's so damn important you have to carry on like a pork chop?' Noel, while he might have agreed with his boss's frustration, nearly fell off his chair at Simon's display of gross insubordination and lack of respect, and to a superintendent, even.

The response from Fisher was, to Noel's way of thinking,

quite composed and relatively free from the expected outpouring of wrath and rage. 'Now, now, Simon, just calm down and take your Valium,' which Simon didn't take anyway. 'Okay, I appreciate I may have prolonged the news, but I found Noel's explanation of events quite enlightening. However, it now transpires that Ralph Glover and his girlfriend, what's her name, Drake, Cheryl Drake, have both been admitted to hospital with serious but not life-threatening injuries. Seems they were over at Elizabeth Bay wandering around some deserted mansion when they were set upon by some maniac wielding a garden spade, and in the middle of the afternoon. Fortunate no-one was killed but whoever it was did some damage.

'Anyway, as a result of this latest event I'd say Noel here could be correct in his assessment of the situation with one of the latest victims being another member of GPD, at least he is at the moment. On top of that, the attack took place at a deserted mansion with the name of The Grovel. How coincidental.'

'Bingo,' Noel exclaimed. 'See, told ya. I knew it had to be Paul.'

Simon shook his head and pressed a comforting hand against his forehead; he had a migraine. 'Okay, so we know Ralph has an undisclosed interest in The Grovel which could mean the bashings might be Grovel related. But, by the same token, the basher might have been Andy Crawford ridding himself of another Grovel opponent, or Paul trying to rid himself of any impediment to his taking back GPD once he's out of jail, officially that is. However, as far as I'm concerned, these bashings don't alter the case one iota. We know something's going on between some unknown political figure and Andy Crawford. We also know it involves converting a council zoned residential dwelling into some seedy club for high rollers, along with all the other attractions and amenities such a place would provide.

'I've done some homework and found that to run a nightclub, the property would have to be rezoned as a commercial site, not residential. So, if Crawford is the casino man, whoever the politician is would be the right person to lean on the council to get all the rezoning and paperwork approved.'

Fisher nodded. 'That seems appropriate. And you don't think the murders and the bashings could possibly be just a matter of sheer coincidence?'

'Coincidence, my eye. There's no such thing as coincidence,' Simon growled. 'One murder and now three bashings, where everyone knows everyone else and everyone linked to both The Grovel and Glover Property Development. No, someone's running rampant and I bet there's more thuggery to come. And I still reckon The Grovel will continue to be the common denominator.'

Fisher dropped his head a little and regarded Simon with raised eyebrows and a very doubtful look. 'Well, I'm sorry Simon, but at the moment we don't even know which politician it is who's conspiring with Crawford, if Crawford is conspiring with anyone. Sure, everything is a bit nebulous at the moment, but until the council decides who actually owns The Grovel, we can speculate all we like.'

Simon heaved a sigh and rubbed his eyes with his hands. 'Yeah, okay, but delete council and insert that little weed Stuart Boswell. Anyway, what do we know about the injuries to Ralph and Miss Drake?'

'Now that's the funny thing,' replied Fisher, 'As Elizabeth Bay is in the Kings Cross LAC, Dave Harris attended. He knows of our interest in the Glover family and gave me a ring soon after the attack. It would seem the assailant was interrupted in the job of assailing by a couple of council workers doing a check of power lines and tree branches. One of these workers immediately called for an ambulance and then the police.

'Harris didn't need to be told by the ambo officer that it was a very vicious attack, which could easily have been fatal; Harris could see that for himself. In fact, he believes if the attack hadn't been interrupted, we'd probably have another two totally murdered victims. I know it's a very long string to the bow, but anyone who shoots someone in the back of the head has to have murderous intent. From what I hear, the Haynes bashing was so savage the perpetrator probably had the same result in mind. Poses the question; did the council workers interrupt a proposed fatal attack on Ralph and Cheryl, or did the thug intend to just rough 'em up a bit?'

'And neither Ralph nor Cheryl could identify their attacker?' Noel asked the obvious question.

'Well, despite the fact that neither saw the attacker's face as he was wearing a sort of knitted balaclava thing, both Ralph and Cheryl say it was definitely Paul. However, it's doubtful their evidence would stand up in court,' Fisher explained.

Noel shook his head dejectedly. At least Paul had stuck to his modus operandi; bash 'em over the head; a gun was another matter.

# CHAPTER 17

'Well, there you go, boss, I told you Paul had to be the killer, or at least one of the killers. I'll get right on to Musgrave and start to build a case against our illustrious Mister Glover. And just for my own edification, can you explain what Fisher meant when he said the victims could have been "totally murdered"? If you're murdered, you're dead. There's no question of being totally dead or even just a little bit dead. It's like being pregnant; you either are, or you aren't. I never knew there were degrees of dead.'

Simon looked at Noel with the look one gives when trying to assess whether the person is just having a bad day or should be committed. 'Noel, I haven't a clue in the world and as I've never been pregnant, or even a bit pregnant, I'm unable to comment. Maybe Fisher is just trying to be smart and get one back on me. You know I have this thing about it being an exercise in tautology by referring to a dead body. All bodies are dead or they would still be a person, not a body. It therefore follows that when referring to a body, I understand it to mean a person has ceased living and has become a body. Everyone on the planet makes that transition eventually. But that's beside the point. You go and do your thing while I take an aspirin and stick pins into those dummy politicians. Even though you have one dead and three in hospital, I still maintain some politician will be involved in The Grovel.'

Noel raised his arms in a gesture of acceptance of the assertion. 'Yeah well, I have solid proof of three attacks against people who work, or was working, for GPD, whereas all you've got is a bit of flimsy hearsay evidence on some nebulous conspiracy theory. Anyway, I'll grab Ron and we'll go and have a chat with Musgrave and Paul Glover, that is if he's in.'

Simon rested his elbow on his desk, held his chin in the palm of his hand and tapped his cheek with his fingers. 'You know, Fisher might have something there. If the murderer of Andrew and Henry's assailant turns out to be one and the same person, it means that person is in possession of a gun. Why use a shovel to beat the tripe out of his victims, and be interrupted in the process, when a gun would have dispatched the trio straight away? Hell, he may as well go for a sheep as for a lamb.'

'Which reminds me, have you ever asked the butcher for long loin chops?' Noel enquired.

'No, never heard of long loin chops; short loin, yes.'

'So why do we call them short loin if there is no such thing as a long loin chop?'

'How the bloody hell would I know? Maybe there's a medium loin chop. Go ask a butcher,' Simon countered, slightly exasperated by the question.

'Okay, keep your shirt on. It's just that Sue asked me to get a short leg of lamb the other day. She said to make sure to ask the butcher for a sheep's upper leg, the leg on the upper side of the hill. According to her, when sheep graze, they always graze in one direction. This makes their legs on the lower side of the hill a bit longer than those on the higher side, which are obviously a bit shorter. The butcher looked at me as though I was nuts before he cracked up. When I told Sue, she just smiled and patted me on the head.'

Simon rested both elbows on his desk, covered his face with his hands and slowly shook his head. After gaining control he said, 'Noel, just forget I ever said anything about a sheep and a lamb. Fisher, poor deranged copper that he is, obviously thinks you have some potential as a detective. As for being domesticated, you're a bloody disaster. Just shut up about whatever you put on the barbie and get out to the jail and arrest someone, anyone.'

Superintendent Musgrave was a computer troglodyte, his ability limited to one function; view the records of the coming and goings of jail inmates. To perform the most basic functions was way above his level of expertise, the computer having to be logged on each morning by Jessie prior to making Superintendent Musgrave his heart-starting mug of coffee. 'Yes, here we are,' he said and turned the screen to give Noel and Ron a clearer view. 'Seems our Mr Glover has been out more than in lately, but that's only to be expected with his imminent release. And yes, he was out on the day in question and came back at, now let's see...'

Before Musgrave could impart the complete record of Paul's sojourn into the community, Noel looked at Ron, raised his eyebrows and said, 'Now we have motive, means and opportunity. I'd say it might be just about time we had a chat with Mr Glover.'

Musgrave returned the screen for his own closer inspection. After a moment of intense scrutiny, a frown crossed his face. 'Jessie, got a minute?' he said after pressing a button on his intercom system.'

'Right with you, Tom,' came Jessie's melodious response.

Within seconds Jessie entered the office and proceeded to take a position beside Musgrave where she could view the computer screen. Needless to say, the position adopted was one of close intimacy, her well-endowed chest firmly snuggled into Tom's shoulder. 'Now, what seems to be the problem, Tommy?' she crooned.

'The police here would like to have a word with Paul Glover, but according to the screen he's out.'

Jessie leant further forward and peered at the screen, her long, painted index finger-nail following the entry across the screen. 'Seems he's been out for a few days now, which is contrary to the rules,' Jessie remarked as her finger finished its journey across the screen. 'My, he has been a naughty boy.'

Musgrave shook his head. 'Blast! So, I was reading the information correctly. I suppose, on the brighter side, the longer he's out the more time we'll have to accommodate someone waiting on the outside for a cell to become available on the inside. Er, thanks Jessie. That will be all, for the moment.' The pause was significant, its implication not lost on the two visitors.

Following Jessie's departure, Noel, somewhat mystified by Musgrave's demeanour, sought clarification. 'You mean the redoubtable Paul Glover is not within the precincts of the establishment?'

'Unless there's a glitch with our computer records, which I doubt, I'd say Mr Glover has been playing truant for a few days now, which is most unlike him. He goes out regularly but he usually comes back regularly,' Musgrave said in vain defence of his courageous incarceration policy.

Noel glanced at Ron who was engrossed in an in-depth study of the ceiling. 'Ron, have you got anything to add?'

Ron clasped his hands on his stomach and arched his index fingers. 'Well, the way I see it, we're of the belief Paul may have committed one murder and put three others in hospital while supposedly being confine to jail. We know the system is open to a bit of skullduggery, so whether Paul is in or out is probably a matter of conjecture. I guess the only thing we can do now is go on a manhunt, find the stupid git and see what he has to say for himself.'

Noel nodded before addressing Musgrave. 'It seems we have a bit of a problem here, Superintendent. If you should come across Paul Glover somewhere here in jail, or he sees fit to return, if he's out that is, we would really appreciate it if you could whack him into solitary confinement and give us a ring. We really do need to speak to him before he gets carried away and tries to pop someone else off, which he seems to have a propensity to do. In the meantime, we'll go and see how his brother is getting along in hospital.'

Musgrave just nodded. Somehow Noel got the idea the superintendent was not a happy man, but no doubt Jessie would attend to whatever the problem was.

'Holy hell, Ralph, I knew you and Cheryl had been attacked, but cripes, it looks like you've been put through a mincing machine,' Noel chided as he pulled up a chair next to the bed.

'Gee, thanks Sarge. I feel like I've been put through a mincing machine,' Ralph managed to say with the best he could do for a grin. 'Obviously Paul doesn't play cards or he would have led with a club, not a spade.'

'So, you're sure it was Paul who attacked you?' Ron asked as he commandeered a chair from the next bed in the ward.

'Well, it was Cheryl who first realised what was going on. I copped a thump to the back of my head and went down like a sack of potatoes. Apparently, the attacker used a shovel to clout us. I heard Cheryl scream out for Paul to stop, but all she got for her protest was a belting as well. He wade in on me a few more times once I was on the ground, although he did pause to apologise before he belted me again. That's all I remember.'

'But you didn't see his face?'

'No, he was wearing a mask or something.'

'Then how do you know it was Paul?'

'Cripes, of course it was my brother. Everything about him said it was Paul, even his smell.'

'And Cheryl is convinced it was Paul.'

'I won't answer that as I'm sure you're aware Paul and Cheryl were an item, once.'

'Of course we know,' Noel replied with a scornful role of the eyes. 'However, she obviously had no idea he was a raving looney at the beginning of their relationship.'

'Well, she certainly found out she was dating a mental pygmy with all the charisma of a witless warthog soon enough,' Ralph responded.

'So, have you any idea as to why Paul should attack you? Like, why in the world would he want to bash you both like he did?' Noel asked.

Ralph tried to shrug and achieved a wince of pain for his effort. 'I can give a couple of reasons, the first being the fact that he's lost his licence to trade as Glover Property Development. As I'm currently the boss of the Company, I could knock down The Grovel and build the townhouses, or submit plans for just about anything else I'd like to put there. Paul's out in the cold as far as GPD goes, apart from the fact that, at the moment, he's still the legal owner of The Grovel.

'Look, Paul had every intention of doing away with Cheryl after he murdered our brother, Bruce, because Cheryl twigged as to who the killer was. On top of that, Paul is aware of my interest in The Grovel and that I'm currently the boss of GPD, which probably causes him no small amount of angst.'

'And just what is your interest in the place?' Ron asked as he idly toyed with the catheter supplying a drip to Ralph's arm.

'Please, don't do that,' Ralph protested. 'Madam Lash will be doing her rounds soon and if she finds me dead because you turned the drip off, my injuries will be nothing to what she'll do to you. Now, as far as my interest in The Grovel goes, I've had my eye on it for a while now. Initially, it was purely for financial gain but, after some thought, the option of refurbishment and returning it to the grand old home it used to be seemed quite appealing. Cheryl certainly likes the idea, despite the fact Bruce was murdered in The Grovel's lounge room.'

Noel harrumphed. 'Yeah, but you and everyone else on the planet wants The Grovel for one thing or another and, at the moment, I'd say the council must be favoured to take it. That little flea-brain Boswell will do all he can to ensure the council gains legal title to the place so he can onsell it at way under market value. No doubt, whoever the buyer is will pay Boswell a whopping kickback as you can bet the sale of the property will have been agreed to way in advance. It's also possible our mate Andy Crawford is chatting up a heavy weight politician in the belief that, with a little political wheeler-dealing, he can gain title and turn it into a cosy little den of iniquity. On top of all that, we have your brother who regards the place as the end of the rainbow with oodles of money to be made but can't because he's a convicted murderer.'

'Aha, seems like you're right, Noel. The Grovel is the focus of what's been going on,' Ron exclaimed. 'So, Ralph, have you any idea where we might be able to find brother Paul?'

'Well, brother Paul won't be at any monastery. Maybe the jail would be a good place to start as that's where he's supposed to be but, according to you blokes, he's out and could be running around anywhere.'

Noel frowned. 'That's okay Ralph, we'll find him some-where, but just one point. What happened to your idea of taking over from where Paul left off? With all the council approvals to redevelop the place into a bunch of ritzy townhouses settled, whoever gets the place is halfway home to bucket loads of money, even if they don't proceed with the townhouses. Remember the saying, "location is everything", and Elizabeth Bay is a prime location. And now you want the place for yourself and Cheryl?'

'Okay, so I've changed my mind. This redevelopment thing can get very stressful and it's about time I slowed down a bit. Cheryl and I get on pretty well and I can't think of anyone I'd rather slow down with. If The Grovel should become available, I'd certainly be in the market for it as it would satisfy my future goals perfectly. I'm sure council would have no objections to rezoning the property back to low density housing and provide the approvals needed to refurbish the place back to its former glory. People would give their right arm to own a place in Elizabeth Bay. Unfortunately, it seems the only chance anyone has to acquire The Grovel would be if, or when, council shafts Paul, which is on the cards. Of course, I accept your point that some unscrupulous council bureaucrat who occupies a position of influence may decide to take a bribe from someone to ensure the corrupt sale of the property.

'Mind you, just on the off-chance I ever did get the property, the first thing I'd do is change the name of the place to something more appropriate, like Murder Mansion, Killer Cottage or Homicide House, as it certainly won't keep the same stupid family anagram.'

*A*lthough Simon had prepared himself mentally for the upcoming discussion with the state's top politician, he was under no illusion it was going to turn out to be a complete waste of time. Expecting a straight answer from a politician, any politician, was like try to suck blood from of a stone. Aah well!…

'So, Mr Buckmaster, the rumour has it Mr Crawford aims to take over ownership of the mansion commonly referred to as The Grovel in the not too distant future, with a little help from you and some council bureaucrat. Once title to this little bit of real estate is in his possession, he hopes to establish some high-class gambling casino open to only those people with heaps of money to throw away,' Simon prodded. While wishing to express his thoughts using a somewhat more vernacular idiom, Simon resisted the temptation; after all, he was talking to the Premier.

Gavin Buckmaster had a smirk on his face, his arms folded and, without saying a word, conveyed his sentiment as clearly as if he had belted Simon over the head with it; so, what are you going to do about it, copper? 'Well, that just proves you shouldn't take any notice of rumours. I would suggest the credibility of your information is as far-fetched as the reduction of taxes and certainly does not reflect the situation at all,' he managed to say with some diplomacy, and a straight face. 'I have absolutely no interest in purchasing the place, that's up to someone else to organise when it comes up for sale. As far as turning it into a casino, that decision is entirely in the hands of someone else.'

'I take it the someone else to whom you refer is Andy Crawford?' Simon asked.

'Maybe, but not necessarily so. You see, council has already approved Paul Glover's plan for the demolition of the house and the construction of a townhouse development. In approving the development, council was required to rezone the property for medium density housing. Unfortunately, it turned out that the developer, Glover Property Development headed by Paul Glover himself, hasn't met the financial obligations set by council. Now, along comes a fine upstanding gentleman with a business proposal. In light of the predicament of the current owner, Paul Glover, council wants to recover unpaid levies, bring the impasse to finality and secure the future of the property. Obviously, a Mr Boswell from council is thinking the outstanding debt can be met by the sale of the property and provide council with a windfall into the bargain.'

'So, I take it if that is the case, the property won't be auctioned off, but sold at a predetermined price set way below market value?'

Buckmaster pursed his lips and nodded. 'That may well be so, although I am unaware of the specifics involved. While not wishing to put a name to the interested entrepreneur, I believe the fine upstanding gentleman, whoever he is, will be happy to pay the asking price that will be set by council, provided it's reasonable and council agrees to his business proposal. As he wants the place for his own purposes, which are confidential at the moment, he feels the need for a bit of political support behind him to gain title to the property. To gain this support, the entrepreneur has considered it only appropriate to offer a lucrative share in a business arrangement. While I do not wish to confirm the nature of the business, I will say it should, in all probability, provide a high annual turnover and a substantial profit margin. Notwithstanding the pecuniary incentive, after careful consideration of all factors, including the advantages and job creation for the district, I was grudgingly forced to accept the offer.'

'So, your involvement will be purely as a silent partner?'

'Indublit... indubit... Ahh hell, of course, very silent. My decision to accept his offer in the venture was made purely for political reasons and for the specific benefit of the state. Unfortunately, there are people out there in the electorate who probably view the involvement of their Premier in any business arrangement, apart governing the state, contrary to their moral and ethical expectations. No, all I have to do is maintain a low profile and ensure the mansion doesn't get bulldozed.'

'I therefore take it you're working on the assumption council will divest Paul Glover of the ownership of The Grovel, despite the fact it's currently zoned as medium density residential in accordance with his redevelopment plans. I s'pose once council has acquired the place, they'll amend it back to low density to facilitate the continued existence of The Grovel, which I believe is what you envisage happening.'

'That's how it might appear,' replied a very confident Premier.

'And of course, your Minister for Local Government will approve the establishment of your commercial enterprise, albeit that the venture would be operating from a privately owned domestic dwelling.'

'Now, what on earth gave you that idea? You brought up the subject of a commercial enterprise. I don't think I've mentioned anything about a commercial enterprise, or a casino and, as someone will be residing in the residence on a permanent basis, I think any residential zoning, be it low or medium density, will satisfy the requirements. And what goes on in a private residence is just that; private. Mind you, while the place may anticipate a profit, we do intend to pay our taxes. Well, some tax. And as far as any of my ministers go, I'm the boss and they'll do as they're told, or they'll be sitting so far back on the backbenches they won't have a clue as to what's going on in the chamber.'

'Yeah well, I can't help thinking the taxes you pay will amount to no more than five cents in the dollar, if you pay any at all,' Simon replied with a hint of scepticism. 'And as for being the boss, Julius Caesar thought he was the boss, and look what happened to him.' Simon frowned. Buckmaster was aware of the current situation regarding The Grovel, but Simon wasn't sure how the Premier's involvement could ensure the safety of the old mansion. 'Okay, Mr Buckmaster, how do you propose to save the house from demolition?'

'Now that's where my knowledge, experience and being the boss, of course, can achieve the seemingly unachievable. I have just directed our Minister for the Environment, at either the cost of returning to the backbenches or a promotion, to do whatever is necessary to ensure The Grovel is heritage listed under the Heritage Act. Obviously, council will have to renege on its decision to rezone the place as medium density, together with the townhouse approvals, but that's their problem. We have a temporary injunction in place prohibiting any redevelopment until we get that all sorted. The heritage authorities will only be concerned with any restoration work to the outside of the building while we would have a free rein to do whatever we like done with the building's interior.'

My, my, you do advance your cunning, Simon thought. 'And

I suppose any work to the outside of the building will receive automatic approval by the heritage officials?' Simon questioned.

'Of course. I'll have to use my influence to make sure everything we need to get done gets done, including possible pecuniary incentives to ensure the required outcome. To that end, it will be up to me to ensure all the necessary approvals required by the council, and any other statutory authority, are guaranteed before we start. Most of the work will go on inside the place so we will need to satisfy all building covenants, you know, health and safety regulations, but I can't see any difficulties that cannot be overcome.'

Simon sat back into the chair, crossed his legs at the knee and folded his arms. 'And all this is taking place while Paul Glover is in total ignorance of what's going on?'

'Yep. Come to think of it, I very much doubt if Paul Glover will continue to be the owner for very much longer, although that will depend on whatever decision the council chooses to make. It seems Mr Glover has been a bit remiss in not keeping up his financial obligations on the property.'

Buckmaster continued his smug attitude which only failed to impress and provided Simon with greater resolve to vilify this supercilious pillar of virtue. 'Yeah, well you don't earn much money being locked away for a couple of years,' Simon replied as he tried to decide on just how to dethrone another premier; maybe a quiet word to an investigative journalist. I'm sure the constituents would love to learn the Premier is abusing his position to facilitate a very select gambling casino, despite what this pelican says. And on a prime piece of harbour foreshore real estate, not that government ministers in the past haven't done exactly the same thing, but not involving a gambling casino.

'And I suppose you're wondering just how ethical my actions are?' the Premier asked with all the sarcasm expected of a squeaky-clean and morally incorruptible politician.

'No, not at all,' Simon replied unexpectedly. 'Whether your

actions are ethical or not are totally subjective and up to the individual to decide. I must admit, I will get a giggle out of the whole thing if it's decided Paul Glover remains the owner. Even if the house is listed under the Heritage Act, it won't make an ounce of difference as Paul would still be the owner; he just won't be able to bring the bulldozers in. He might decide to sell it at market value to anyone interested in the place, and that includes all those people who believe they're experts in early Federation mansion restoration. Although selling the property might not provide the profit expected, it would certainly provide him with an awful lot of loose change.'

Buckmaster's smirk broadened a touch as he shook his head. 'Oh, I don't think we have to worry about any opposition to my gaining control of the property,' he crowed.

'So, you do propose to gain control of the property for yourself?' Simon queried having picked up on the use of the personal possessive pronoun.

'Okay, not necessarily my control, but maybe jointly with a partner, who may or may not be Andy Crawford. Just because you have this fixation of him being my associate doesn't guarantee he is. But be assured, DCI Webster, Mr Boswell will see his way open to ensure the future of the property will meet the wishes of both myself and my associate.'

Now it was Simon's turn to smirk. 'It's of little consequence whether you divulge the identity of your partner in crime or not as I'm sure Mr Boswell will, in time, be happy to furnish us with details of ownership of The Grovel. Irrespective of who the council decides is the owner, once title is transferred the ownership will become public knowledge. And it's irrelevant how "silent" a partner you wish to remain, you will be implicated.'

Buckmaster, his elbow on the desk and his chin held in his hand, slowly shook his head. 'Look, Chief Inspector Webster, you can speculate, postulate or formulate whatever hypothesis you wish to dream up, but don't expect me to confirm or deny any of your hair-brained ideas as I have far more important things to do than play mental gymnastics with you. And shut the door on your way out.'

My, my, Simon thought as he entered the express elevator to take him back to planet Earth. Grovelgate is alive and kicking.

'Here he comes now,' Noel said and nodded to where Jacko was in the process of boarding the Manly ferry. As it was a Monday, and The Spinning Wheel didn't open on a Sunday night, Jacko was able to sleep in and make his way to Circular Quay in his own good time, thus avoiding the morning rush. The fact that The Spinning Wheel didn't open on a Sunday prompted the question; was Mr Paul Stack the consummate morally deficient racketeer?

'Hi, Jacko,' Noel called out as both he and Simon shuffled along the bench seat to make way for the amiable giant.

'Simon, Noel,' Jacko acknowledged with a nod. 'Lovely day for a boat ride,' he said as he settled himself comfortably on the seat. In fact, it was a very pleasant day for the forty-minute ferry trip from the city over to Manly. At Simon's suggestion, it was decided they should occupy the outdoor seating on the starboard side of the ferry, thus being able to take advantage of the warm October morning sunshine.

'Can't say I've ever been on one of these things before, so I s'pose I can cross this off my bucket list. But I'm sure you didn't invite me here to enjoy the scenery,' Jacko remarked as he slipped on a pair of sunnies.

'No, much as I would like it to be a social occasion, Jacko, we're in a bit of a mess with what's going on, or at least what we think might be going on,' Simon replied.

'Yeah,' I must confess I'm gettin' a little confused myself,' Jacko admitted.

'How's that, Jacko? What seems to be the source of your confusion?' Noel asked.

'Well, it's sorta strange. I told you about how Andy Crawford called around to see Mr Stack on several occasions, and I know their discussions involved developin' this place at Elizabeth Bay. Now everythin' has gone quiet, no Andy Crawford callin' round and Mr Stack runnin' around without showin' too much concern for the runnin' of the club. He used to be in every night of tradin' but now he leaves a lot of the decisions to the staff. Everythin' is goin' okay at the moment, but…'

'So, you'd say Mr Stack has other things on his mind?' Simon asked as he gazed at the naval ships moored at Garden Island.

'Definitely, and that's the problem. I know he and Crawford had a run-in, and I know Crawford has been chattin' up some politician. There ain't nothin' Crawford does that's not illegal, or at least pushin' the boundaries, and I can't help thinkin' that whoever the pollie is must be just as corrupt, or even more so, just by talkin' to the bloke. Mr Stack believes Andy has become far too big for his boots and shoots off at the mouth anyway.

'Now, I'm a bit of a sticky beak, and as Stack seems to have other things on his mind at the moment, I want to know what those things are. Once you start gettin' nosy you just become more nosy. Look, I don't know what's worryin' him, but it must involve Crawford. Ever since they had that row in Mr Stack's office, things have changed, and not for the better. But, hell, I could be completely wrong. It might be nothin' more than a lady friend and that would be enough to give him the willies, or at least keep him preoccupied. Who knows?'

Simon's countenance took on one of sheer boredom, his interest far more centred on the rhythmic pulse of the ferry engines, the sunshine and the beautiful harbour. Days like this, you wouldn't be dead for quids, he thought. Paul had to be guilty of Henry's mugging, along with the bashing of Ralph and

Cheryl, and Andy Crawford had to be the most likely candidate to have eliminated Andrew Glover. It was easy to establish a motive for all the attacks, but motive is subjective and will not get a conviction on its own; in fact, it won't even get you to court.

# CHAPTER 19

Superintendent Nigel Fisher was displeased. An unsolved murder, three people recovering in hospital from injuries inflicted by some annoyed thug, and all events probably related; one council bureaucrat trying his best to fleece the probable rightful owner out of a much sought after harbourside mansion; a very affluent racketeer probably paying off both a member of Parliament and a weasely bureaucrat in order to gain the said mansion, and another racketeer who's probably doing something that no-one seems to know what that something might be. To top that off, his chief inspector, Simon Webster, is probably hell bent on bringing down his second premier of the state only months after bringing down his first state premier with allegations that the Premier probably tossed his murdering wife into the Amazon River. Yep, Superintendent Nigel Fisher probably had cause to be irate.

'Look Simon, this is all very messy and getting messier. I strongly suggest we get the investigation into the murder victim bundled up in a nice neat package and some arrests made,' Fisher growled, his "suggestion" issued as a directive, and received as such. 'I agree the murder is involved with The Grovel and, according to you, we already know who the murderer is but, unfortunately, we seem to be just a little bit short of evidence.'

Simon nodded his agreement. 'And there you have hit the nail on the head, sir. Apart from both Paul Glover and Andy Crawford having some sort of a motive, everything is circumstantial. It certainly looks a bit suspicious, especially with Ralph and his girlfriend getting clobbered while at The Grovel, but maybe we're being somewhat presumptuous at this stage. I believe the murder and the bashings are related and whoever gets murdered next should give us some indication as to just who is winning the race to secure the mansion.'

'Hey, hang on a moment. You believe there'll be another person murdered?' Fisher asked, somewhat perturbed by Simon's prediction.

'To put it bluntly, sir, the answer is yes. I'm sorry, but we currently have one body, three hospitalized, one missing racketeer cum casino operator, and one missing incarcerated, or supposedly incarcerated, murderer. On the other side, we have a politician out to make more money by any means available, one bureaucrat who likes to push his weight around to achieve whatever he wants, and a casino owner who has something on his mind and we haven't a clue what that something is. Now, it's a bit odd that both our missing imbeciles happen to be our prime suspects responsible for the death of Andrew Glover, currently in repose at the morgue. By the same token, as the missing duo both have their own interest in The Grovel, one, or both, might already be dead. Yes, I think it safe to say the worst is over with only the bad to come.'

Fortunately for Simon, Fisher's aggravation was distracted by his 'phone which he answered rather impolitely. 'Fisher. Yes, yes, we are. And there's no doubt. Damn. Forensics been advised? I take it a crime scene has been established? Okay, I'll get Webster out there straight away. And thanks, Superintendent.'

Fisher replaced the receiver, sat back and massaged his eyes with the ball of his hands. After a sigh of resignation, he scratched an ear and raised his eyebrows. Instinctively, Simon had a premonition that whatever the superintendent was about to divulge was not going to be good news.

'Good news, boss?' Simon enquired flippantly.

'What is it with you, Simon, you some bloody oracle or something? That was Musgrave.'

Simon's blood ran cold, he squeezed his eyes shut then asked the question. 'Okay, who is it, or was it this time?'

'Paul Glover.'

'You're kidding?'

'Not according to Musgrave. He was found dead in his cell. Apparently he told a warder, on his voluntary returned to the jail, that he was not feeling too good and was going to have a lie down in his cell. Gallymore has been called in, so best you get yourself over there and see what's going on.'

'On my way, boss.'

'Hi, Gally, Superintendent,' Simon said with a nod as he entered the cell having first donned a set of protective coveralls. Already at the scene were Graham Gallymore, together with his forensic assistant, Superintendent Musgrave and a warder strategically placed to prevent probing eyes from inquisitive inmates.

'Okay, where is it?' Simon asked before he realised it was a pretty stupid question. In a ten by ten cell there weren't too many places the body of an inmate could be.

'Oh, you mean Mr Glover? He's the dead body on the bottom bunk,' Graham replied, indicating with a sweep of the hand. 'In fact, I think you'll find he's the only body in the cell. Whatever killed the poor bloke, it must have been a little painful as his face certainly doesn't reflect any enjoyment in the process.'

'Cripes, what happened?' Simon asked on seeing the grotesque figure, the face contorted in a mix of rictus, intense agony and overwhelming fear.

Gally shrugged. 'Can't say until I open him up. There are no external injuries to suggest anything untoward, so I can say with some confidence he hasn't been shot, stabbed, strangled or clubbed to death. But again, I'd be remiss to make a suggestion until I take a closer look.'

'How long has he been dead?'

'Oh, not long, probably a few hours.'

'First impression?'

'Poison, but don't quote me. From the state of the bed I would say he may have suffered some form of seizure. Apparently he had a dose of the trots before he expired, hence the unpleasant smell. By the way, just how many more Glovers have you got stashed away?'

Simon, arms akimbo, looked at the floor and slowly shook his head. 'Gally, I only know of one remaining Glover, and that's Ralph. He's recovering in hospital with his girlfriend after brother Paul here objected to them looking over a piece of real estate. Apparently, he took a shovel to them, beat them senseless.

'Paul's been absent from jail for some time and, from the look of him, I'd say once he realised he'd developed symptoms a bit more serious than a cold, he scarpered back here. Although based on the very iffy identification provided by Ralph and Cheryl, they're both adamant it was Paul who attacked them, before he pegged out that is, not that he could have laid into 'em after he pegged out, I s'pose. Considering our primary suspect is now dead, I don't think anyone will object to the three assault cases being declared closed. The only bloke who'll get any comfort out of this is probably you, Superintendent; another bed becomes available.'

Superintendent Thomas Musgrave remained quietly solemn.

He was more concerned that another nail had been firmly driven into the Musgrave Solution.

Simon looked dubious as Gallymore's assistant scoured the place for clues as to what might have brought about the agonizing death of Paul Glover. 'Well, if that's not a case of what goes around comes around, I don't know what is. And I don't think Claudius can be blamed for this one,' he remarked to anyone who cared to listen. 'I take it this wasn't suicide, Gally?'

'Well if it was, our Mr Glover was undergoing a major conflict of interest being both a sadist and a masochist,' Gally replied as he removed his pair of rubber gloves. 'No, I think it's safe to say he's been put away by someone else. I'll have a better idea when I trace what did kill him, and that should give us a time-line.'

'Seems we might be able to explain away Andrew Glover's body, but this one's a bit unexpected. But then again, nothing comes as a complete surprise, and bad news comes in threes. Fisher will be on my back and Paxton will be on Fisher's back. No, that's okay, Gally, he's all yours,' Simon added in response to a questioning look from the pathologist.

Simon doodled on a pad – in fact he was drawing little stick men, all with a question mark over their head. Noel, at the other end of the office, folded a piece of paper into the resemblance of an aged American fighter aircraft which, on completion of meticulous construction, was jettisoned into the air. Not surprisingly, it fell to the office floor with as much success as the original aircraft which had been dubbed, inauspiciously by those in the aviation industry, The Flying Coffin.

The atmosphere in the office was one of total apathy and lack of interest. Without any debate on the subject, both detectives had arrived at a similar conclusion; who cares anyway? Of the two murders so far committed, both victims were convicted homicidal maniacs about to be let loose on the poor unsuspecting community. Simon and Noel did agree on one point; the attempted murder of Henry was a pity. If his sometimes-cantankerous attitude could be overlooked, Henry had been a decent chap with no seemingly obvious connection with the murders, save that he worked for a Glover. The hospitalization of Ralph Glover and Cheryl Drake was unfortunate, but they would recover and, no doubt, continue to be contenders in the battle of Grovelgate.

'So, what now, boss?' Noel asked as he folded his arms and pushed his chair out from his desk with his foot. 'If we sit here for another five minutes, we'll probably have either another murder on our hands or I'll be struck down with a terminal case of apathy. But then I s'pose the more murders we have, the fewer suspects.'

Simon frowned and threw his pen onto the desk. 'Yeah, okay, but you don't have to be so glib about it. Now Paul and Andrew have both been shuffled off this mortal coil, my brain is telling me there's Andy Crawford, Paul Stack, Brainless Boswell and Gavin Buckpasser left in my book of suspects.

'What my gut is telling me is that if we do nothing, that lot will do a self-extermination job and go about eliminating everyone out of the contest. After they've finished killing people, there should be only one person left standing, and that person will probably be guilty of murdering the last victim. Hang on a tick,' he said as he answered the phone and, after a brief discussion, replaced the receiver. 'Grab your coat, Fisher wants us up in Paxton's office, and while I'm no prophet, I bet I know what it's about.'

Superintendent Fisher was already seated in Paxton's office when the two detectives arrived, two vacant chairs already placed conveniently next to Fisher's in front of Paxton's table. The chief superintendent looked grim as he vigorously polished his reading glasses with his handkerchief. 'Well, Fisher, if things weren't so serious, I'd say Tweedle Dee and Tweedle Dum had just arrived. Take a seat gentleman as we need to have a little chat,' he said as he carefully placed his spectacles on the table in front of him.

'Thanks, sir,' Simon acknowledged the invitation to sit, not necessarily the facetious introduction.

'I take it you gentlemen know what I wish to have a chat about,' Paxton's question obviously rhetorical, there being no other subject other than Grovelgate. My, my, the boss is a tad upset, Simon mused, his glance to Noel with raised eyebrows and inclined head conveying his tacit warning; careful, he's cranky.

'Superintendent Fisher has briefed me on the violence that appears to be linked to a property in Elizabeth Bay currently owned by Paul Glover who, as we all know, was supposedly in prison for murder. Unfortunately, he is now dead having been murdered and, to my mind, that investigation falls squarely within the realm of the investigation division of the police department to which you two gentlemen have been assigned. Strange as it may seem, I'm not overly concerned with your progress with that investigation, apart from the fact there are now two people dead and you've found absolutely no-one to charge with their murder, yet. However, Simon, I'm a trifle troubled your investigation has led you to make a couple of visits to Macquarie Street to speak to our Premier, Gavin Buckmaster. Is that correct?'

'Yes, sir, I can confirm information to hand suggests the Premier is involved in an attempt to procure premises located at Elizabeth Bay. The aim of this involvement, in collaboration with an underworld figure, is to set up a casino for trendies, socialites and those who wish they were.'

'Were what, Chief Inspector?' Fisher interjected.

'Trendies and socialites, sir.'

'And you don't approve?' Fisher returned.

Simon shrugged. 'Well, as I fail to fall into either of those categories, it's not a matter of whether I approve or not. Our Premier is associating with those known to be involved in illegal casinos and, being a politician, it's hard to imagine he's not involved in some sort of duplicitous venture which is, if not corrupt, at least questionable.'

'And you're out to nail him?' Paxton accused.

'No, not at all, sir,' returned Simon, 'but if the cap fits you have to wear it. After all, we are talking about a premier of the state and only God knows the number of corrupt premiers, prime ministers and presidents of countries currently stacking away oodles of dubiously obtained money in Swiss bank accounts. And we all know that, in the majority of cases, it's big business that runs a country with the bosses of conglomerates and multi-nationals pulling the political strings to the financial benefit of their respective corporations, and the politicians. Come to think of it, Boswell would do very well in politics as he's probably the most venal character I've ever met, and he's only a public servant.'

Paxton picked up his reading glasses, held them to the light for inspection and, satisfied they were still clean, replaced them on his desk. 'Okay, Simon, while I may not necessarily agree with you, just who are these criminals you're referring to?'

'Well, we're not quite sure, but we think we're certain it could be either Paul Stack or Andy Crawford, or maybe both of them. We've discounted Graham Lee as he's the most law-abiding criminal you'll find, and he's out of town. Hearsay evidence would suggest it's Crawford, but then it could be Stack. There is one other person currently stirring the pot and that's the council bloke, Stuart Boswell. He's either after the property for his own use, or he's fishing for the best deal he can drag out of the contenders. I've no doubt that with so many people after the place, Boswell would be only too happy to sell his decision to the highest bidder. Obviously, that raises some questions as to what action the Premier might be predisposed to take to ensure success of his venture, whether it be with Crawford, Stack or anybody else.

'Boswell, while not be directly involved with the Premier, would have to be a very brave public servant not to be compliant with the Premier's wishes which, in reality, would be the wishes of the Crawford or Stack league. Irrespective of who's talking to the Premier, it still comes down to Boswell's decision on owner- ship. I have grave doubts that he's given any thought to the possible repercussions from those who will ultimately miss out on obtaining title to The Grovel.'

'So, at the moment you have no confirmed evidence the Premier is consorting with any known criminal?' Paxton snapped, the question in demand of a negative response.

'Sir, at the moment we have no firm evidence of anything against anyone. Even the evidence provided by Ralph Glover and Cheryl Drake concerning their hospitalization wouldn't stand up in court as they didn't see Paul's face when he attacked them. Apparently, their identification is based purely on their recognition of Paul's body odour. I don't suppose that really matters now as the chances of bringing Paul to court are pretty remote seeing he's dead.

'While we think it may have been Andy Crawford who shot Andrew Glover, we have no evidence to even suggest he did. And let's face it, Andrew Glover was shot with a twenty- two calibre pea shooter pistol, whereas Crawford, in keeping with his image, would've used something like a Beretta forty-five and completely blown Glover's head off.'

Paxton's countenance took on one of tired frustration. After a slow hand massage of his face, he sat back in his chair and folded his arms. 'Look, we're running three and two now and strangely, things can only get worse. If you think Crawford is guilty of murder, go and invent some evidence; stitch him up, do whatever it takes.'

Fisher looked confused. 'Three and two, sir?'

'Okay, so I was beaten on the weekend three and two but I mean three in hospital, and two dead, not the golf score.'

Simon shook his head. 'Sorry sir, but your idea won't work, and even if it did, so what. With the Musgrave Solution, he'd be out walking the streets as soon as he's signed in, that's if you can find a judge who'll send him down. After all, the judiciary here appears to lack any appreciation of the value and sanctity of human life. It's not at all like in the old US of A where, if you take a life, they'll permanently remove you from society, one way or the other.'

'Yes, and that's all very well and good, but that's not your problem, Chief Inspector. Your job is to get a conviction, so go get one,' Paxton demanded. 'And lay off the Premier, that's an order.'

# CHAPTER 20

'Come on, Noel, grab your coat,' Simon commanded. 'The only bloke with any genuine credibility around the place is Jacko. I think Sticky Stack is as reliable as a politician's promise or the weather bureau's latest forecast. Hell, we gave Jacko our business cards and told him to get in contact with us if he had any news. It seems like we should've taken Jacko's card.'

'So, Paxton got up your nose just a little?' Noel enquired guardedly. Simon was irritated and Noel was anxious not to exacerbate the situation with some frivolous remark.

'Well, what do you think?' Simon growled. 'We've been ordered not to talk to Buckmaster who's involved in a diabolical conspiracy aimed to defraud the rightful owner of his property. Just because Paul hasn't lived in it for a while, nor paid his rates, shouldn't mean he gets the place whipped out from underneath him, even if he is dead. On top of that, Andy Crawford, who is undoubtedly pally with Buckmaster, is also as guilty as hell for the killing of Andrew Glover, or at least we think he is. Come to think of it, now Paul Glover's dead I haven't a clue as to who owns The Grovel. Maybe it's now part of a deceased estate. To top that off, Mr Crawford has now disappeared off the face of the planet. It's time to find out exactly what Jacko knows, and then go find Mr Crawford.'

'With you, boss,' Noel acknowledged. 'But where does Stack and Boswell fit into this mess, or conspiracy as you call it?'

Simon, his enthusiasm to ferret out the magnitude of the fiddle probably being perpetrated and the participants involved, now aroused by Chief Superintendent Paxton's caustic comments, stood hands on hips, a disturbed look on his face. 'Look, if Crawford is colluding with Buckmaster, then Stack is colluding with Boswell, or it could be the other way round. All four of them are aspiring to make money out of The Grovel and I think Stack's idea is similar to Crawford's. Don't forget, Stack was openly trying to prise The Taipan Club away from Graham Lee to further his casino interests. Crawford's line of attack is to use a political heavyweight to secure the place while I suspect Stack will have made Boswell quite a substantial offer for a favourable decision. I can't help thinking that Boswell will find it a lot easier to hijack The Grovel for a particular client, seeing it's probably now a deceased estate. And there's always Mason to consider as he's publicly declared he wants the place for himself. Trouble for both Boswell and Buckmaster is that if they don't deliver, they may end up dead. But that's their problem. Anyway, let's get going as I'd like to see Jacko alone when we get to The Spinning Wheel.'

'Yeah, but what about the murders? We've got two of 'em stacked up now, both done by different methods; shot and poisoned, and that's not counting Henry's attempted murder by bashing. It might not be the O.K. Corral but we've got nearly as many bodies as they ended up with, and I wouldn't mind betting there's more to come. As there isn't any consistent modus operandi, I have this funny feeling we have three killers running lose. So, do we go chasing after brutal murderers? Ooh no, we're off trying to dig up some scandal involving some property development. Fisher and Paxton will have apoplexy,' Noel, not sure if Simon hadn't screwed up his priorities, said face-tiously.

'Okay, so you've got two dead bodies which should have been three. If you count up all the people, both alive and dead who have, or had, an interest in The Grovel, another won't make that much difference to the averages,' Simon remonstrated.

The drive from Day Street to Palmer Street was made in silence, Simon contemplating the problem Paxton had placed firmly on his shoulders, while Noel fortified his determination not to lose the police car he was now driving. After finding a legitimate parking space, for a change, the two men set off along Palmer Street heading for The Spinning Wheel to confront Jacko with some discrete questions concerning his boss, Paul Stack. In their previous interviews with Stack, there hadn't been any hint, or suggestion, that he held any specific interest in The Grovel. On the other hand, Simon believed that, as Crawford had discussed his proposed intentions for the property with him, Stack would be like a rat up a drain pipe wanting to participate in such an apparent lucrative scheme, albeit not necessarily Craw-ford's scheme but maybe one hatched by Stack himself.

Notwithstanding Crawford's rejected invitation to invest in his business proposition, Stack had his own substantial financial assets to go it alone without Crawford, if he could get his hands on The Grovel. And good luck to "Sticky" if he does, Simon thought, Crawford probably deserves to be stabbed in the back, metaphorically speaking, that is.

Jacko was caught in his usual perplexing situation; not thrilled to have two police detectives knock on the door, yet pleased to see Simon and Noel. 'G'day boys, come on in. There's no-one home at the moment and the boss won't get here for a couple of hours.'

'Thanks, Jacko,' Simon replied as the three men entered the dingy casino and sat on the very worn and stained red uphol-stered chairs they had sat on their previous visit. 'Okay, Jacko, there's a few things we need to get straight, the first being the whereabouts of Andy Crawford.'

Jacko grimaced and shook his head. 'Gee, do you mind if I take the one on sport instead? That one's too difficult for me as I haven't a clue where he is. The Red Ruby appears to have shut up shop and no-one's turnin' up for work, and that's very strange for Crawford. I hear the place will open up again as everythin' is still there, like, they haven't moved out on a permanent basis. I s'pose you've checked his home?'

'Yep, and there's no car and no-one home. Do you think Mr Stack knows where he might be?' Noel asked, pen poised to take appropriate notes.

'Short answer; maybe. I really don't know what the boss knows and if I did, I probably wouldn't be workin' here.'

'And why's that, Jacko?' Simon asked.

'I think I might be pushin' up daisies,' came Jacko's simple reply. 'Somethin's goin' on and I think Andrew Glover's death may have somethin' to do with it. Stack and Crawford are at each other's throat, or were last time I saw 'em together, and either one could end up dead. It's all somethin' to do with this property thing at Elizabeth Bay.'

'Hey Jacko, how about we go and have a look at The Red Ruby and see if we can turn up anything that may help us?' Simon suggested. 'You say you have a bit of time on your hands, and you've already admitted you're inquisitive.'

'Yeah, love to, but only if it's kosher. I'd hate to get in trouble with the coppers,' Jacko replied with a broad grin.

'Well, we haven't a warrant or anything official like that but, as you say there's no-one home, no-one will know, will they?' Noel teased.

Although the front door was safely secured, it didn't take Simon long to have the door open, a skill Noel had been unable to master since observing Simon's ability to gain access to a certain politician's securely locked stately manor in one of Sydney's up-market suburbs. 'Holy hell, and we thought botulism was thriving at The Spinning Wheel. Now I know why you don't mind working for Sticky, Jacko,' Noel said after finding a light switch.

Neither detective had been in The Red Ruby before, a non-event for which they were now grateful. Crikey, at least you could say "Sticky" tries, Noel thought. The Red Ruby was defi-nitely a walk-in incubator for the production of yet undiscovered lethal microbes and assorted noxious germs. By comparison, Graham Lee's Taipan Club, another illegal casino located in the same area, could be considered a palatial and thoroughly hygienic establishment, compliant with all the health and safety rules. But The Red Ruby was something else. Crawford had money, lots of it, but it was for sure he hadn't spent a nickel on creature comforts for his patrons.

The main gaming room looked more like a garage having a bare concrete floor that failed to hide the irremovable, and no doubt toxic, stains accumulated over the years. Some feeble and unsuccessful attempt had recently been made to remove a large stain from just in front of the bar area where the concrete was still damp, probably the result of some poor inebriated sod spilling his beer, Noel thought. The few table and chairs that were available were of the metal collapsible variety that made standing preferable to sitting. And the place had its own over-powering smell. The fetid air, which Simon attributed to stale beer and cigarette smoke, didn't appear to emanate from any one particular location, although the nauseatingly dirty bar area prob-ably contributed significantly to the stench of the place.

'Noel, you and Jacko have a look around and see if there's anything to suggest what's going on. I'll take a look in Craw-ford's office, once I find it,' Simon ordered. 'We're after anything that might tell us something, even why the place has closed down.'

The three men, all unsure of what they were looking for, went in search for anything that might reveal something about whatever they were supposed to be looking for. It was obvious the casino hadn't been purpose designed, but more likely adapted from something that may have been long, long ago before the advent of TV, a dance hall catering for those nimble geriatrics capable of a foxtrot or barn dance. As a consequence, with few rooms or furniture available to secrete anything of police interest, the search presented little difficulty.

Rectangular in shape, the wall opposite the entrance to the casino had a door at each end with a drinks bar positioned in front of the wall between the two doors. A further door was located immediately behind the bar. Although the dish washer, also behind the bar, was stacked with empty but unwashed glasses, there remained two drink glasses on the bar, one unfinished beer and the other empty; not such an earth shattering find. Now, what would Sherlock deduce from that Noel thought as he contemplated the significance of the two glasses. Probably nothing, so get on with it.

Continuing his rummage behind the bar without any hint as to what he was searching for, Noel's fantasy, prompted by some vague recollection, strayed to the kingdom of King Arthur. Yeah, well, at least you blokes knew what you were looking for which would make it a lot easier for us if we did. No wonder you found what you were looking for, eventually. Noel's valiant but unproductive search for the vital piece of evidence, which might suggest what it was he was looking for in the first place, was interrupted by Jacko's plea for assistance.

'Hey, Noel, have a locked door here. Do I break it down or do you want to take a look?'

'No, leave it, Jacko, Simon knows how to fiddle locks. He's in Crawford's office at the moment so I'll let him know.'

Jacko had entered the room located behind the bar. This room appeared to be some sort of a store-room with a few tables and chairs piled against the rear wall. There were doors at each end of the room, one of them unlocked and provided access to a further smaller room occupied as what appeared to be the bar manager's office. It was the door at the other end of the store room that was now the object of Jacko's interest.

Having brought Simons attention to the door, both Noel and Jacko watched expectantly as Simon worked on the lock, the task taking a little longer than anticipated. However, Noel had been correct; Simon knew how to fiddle locks, the door being finally opened to reveal…a door. But this door was different. It was a door to a small cool-room, which was not so surprising as the illegal casino, notwithstanding the failure to secure a liquor licence, did have a bar with alcoholic beverages available for its patrons. And after all, those who frequented such places generally found it much easier to part with their cash with a skin full of liquor.

'Go on, Jacko, you wanted the door open, so you can have the pleasure,' Simon urged.

'No problems, Simon. I wonder if there's any grog inside.'

'You won't know until you look,' Noel added as he flicked a switch located on the frame of the door after reasoning it had to be the switch for the cool-room's internal light.

Jacko did and wished he hadn't. On entry to the cool-room he made an immediate and unsteady retreat, a vacant look across his face. 'Err, sorry fellas, but I think we've found Mr Crawford, and he don't look too good at the moment.' The cool-room was still operating as both Simon and Noel viewed Andy Crawford who, apart from a sprinkling of ice crystals across his face, looked peaceful and serene while slumped against a stack of cardboard boxes full of beer cans.

'Damn and blast, another one,' Simon swore under his breath. Well, Sticky Stack was right about one thing, Simon thought; old Andy has certainly been cooling his heels. 'Noel, get Gally over here, but only if he hasn't anything better to do. This makes it three and he's probably working overtime already. And best you give Fisher a ring and let him know what's going on. Oh yes, and get Dave Harris down from The Cross seeing we're in his bailiwick, and ask him for some back-up. We need to secure the place as a crime scene.'

'Right away, boss. I suppose this puts paid to us having to find evidence on the Andrew Glover murder?'

'Noel, I haven't a clue what it puts paid to, apart from getting me really cheesed off at having bodies turn up while we're in the middle of an investigation. It does make it quite difficult as no-one seems to stay alive long enough for us to arrest them for any particular murder.'

# CHAPTER 21

*D*etective Superintendent Nigel Fisher's office was crowded. Apart from Simon, Noel and Ron, even Graham Gallymore had managed to tear himself away from the gruesome task of examining the seemingly endless supply of cadavers Simon was providing. Everyone was seated with the exception of Chief Superintendent Paxton who stood nonchalantly at the back of the room, the silver braid of his uniform a silent, but effective, symbolic display of intimidation.

'Right, let's get this show on the road,' Fisher's succinct declaration drawing the gathered group's attention to the matter at hand. 'So far we have two bodies in the morgue, both having a common interest, that being the desire to own Paul Glover's mansion known as The Grovel.'

'Sorry sir, it's three,' Noel corrected.

'Three what?'

'Bodies, sir.'

Fisher grimaced. 'Oh yeah, that's right. I keep forgetting about the first bloke, the one pulled out of the harbour. He started a trend and now you only have to turn your back for a moment and we're saddled with another body. Yes, well, getting back to our three bodies. Doc Gallymore, now you've had a chance to have a squiz at our victims, what can you tell us?'

Gally, full of confidence, slouched back in his chair, stretched his legs out and clasped his hands behind his head. 'Well, as you know, despite the intent, Henry is still in hospital as a result of an aneurism. Whether his condition can be directly attributed to blunt-force trauma or, more succinctly, being bashed over the head with a blunt wooden instrument, is debatable. From his injuries I would say something like a pick handle was used. Irrespective of the cause of Henry's injuries, whoever bushwhacked him certainly had murder in mind as it was a very vicious attack.

'Andrew Glover is a completely different kettle of fish, no pun intended seeing he was shot in the head and thrown into of the harbour. His passing was similar to a gangland assassination, not inferring that Andrew was a member of any gang. I tend to think anyone with a bullet in the back of the head from close range tends to have a very fishy-like smell about it. Interestingly, Andrew was shot with a small calibre pistol which we have narrowed down to a Walther P22, a dainty little thing that you can pick up in a very nice shade of pink.'

'You're kidding? A gangland hit using a pretty little pink shooter?' Fisher asked somewhat bemusedly.

'Just because you're a gangster doesn't mean you have to go running around with a 357 Magnum; a victim can be either dead with a .22 round or very dead with a 357 round. The victim sure ain't going to debate the issue,' came Gallymore's dispassionate and enlightened response.

'Live and learn. Okay, how about the next one who was…' Fisher paused in deep concentration.

'That would have been Paul Glover, the owner, we think, of The Grovel,' Ron interrupted.

'Ah yes,' Fisher nodded, 'the murdering scoundrel who bashed his brother to death. Now, how did the Grim Reaper reap Mr Glover?'

'Poisoned,' Gallymore responded. 'Had a bit of difficulty with this one, but we eventually concluded he'd received a dose of ricin, not that you need much of it to kill a horse, and not a pleasant way to die either, if I might add. The effects are a bit nauseating and there are a lot more pleasant ways to doff yourself if you're considering the suicide angle.'

'But he was in jail at the time and we take it he didn't commit suicide. Does that mean he was murdered by an inmate?' Fisher inquired, his knowledge of ricin minimal to non-existent.

Gallymore ceased his slouching, sat up straight and folded his arms while he considered the question. 'Not necessarily in jail and probably not. You see, it depends on how Glover came by the poison; it can be inhaled, injected or ingested. It seems on this occasion it was ingested so the symptoms may have taken hours, or even days, to become manifest. Obviously, someone fed him such a miniscule amount, but still enough to kill him, that he never noticed. And whether he and Andrew Glover were both in jail, where they were supposed to have been and not out making targets of themselves, is another matter.'

'Tasteless?' Noel enquired, 'the poison, I mean.'

'Never tried it as I would be dead, although I am told on good authority that it has a bitter taste. It would need to be disguised in a meal or a strong drink,' Gally replied.

'Like strong coffee, I mean really strong undrinkable coffee, sort of thing?'

'Sounds good to me, and if you're into strong coffee, you'd drink it and be none the wiser until you become horribly sick, or die,' said Gally with a shrug.

Fisher, a tad exasperated by the lack of success of having no-one identified as the perpetrator of any of the dastardly deeds, was anxious to move on. 'Okay, Graham, and what about our thoughtless thug, Mr Crawford. He's the last person I expected to peg out.'

'Well, it seems our illustrious, but very dead, Andy Crawford was terminated with the same gun that pushed Andrew Glover off the planet. I know you boys are the detectives but I'd say whoever did the job was known to Mr Crawford.'

Fisher's head twitched sideways in curiosity. 'And why is that, Gally?'

'No sign of violence.'

'And where was he shot?' came Fisher's next ambiguous question.

'Sorry, sir,' Gallymore apologised, 'I thought Simon gave you an initial report of the incident. Mr Crawford was shot in his casino.'

Noel grimaced. 'Ouch, nothing hurts like being shot in your casino; tends to make your eyes water.'

A stunned shroud of silence descended over the room as all eyes turned to Noel. Fisher, too occupied with processing Gally's response to appreciate Noel's dismal attempt at some humour, plunged on regardless.

'Ahh, for Christ sake, I know where he was shot. I mean, what part of his body got shot?' Fisher explained in exasperation.

'Oh yes, I understand. Andy Crawford was shot in the femoral artery; bloke bled to death. Maybe the person taking the shot missed the planned target, which might have been ...'

'Yes, we get the drift. If that was the case, the shooter had a definite dislike for the shootee,' Fisher interrupted.

Gally nodded in agreement. 'I think it's fair to say that in most cases the murderer harbours some hostility towards the person they set out to murder. Mind you, in this case the victim took a small calibre bullet so maybe the shooter didn't dislike the victim with any great intensity. If he did, he would probably have used something a tad more lethal, like a shotgun. The chance to causing lethal damage with the little popgun used is minimal, but obviously Crawford was unlucky. Once the femoral artery was stuffed, he probably had only a minute or two to live, poor sod. The only assistance provided by the shooter was to drag the body into the cool room.'

Simon's slowly shook his head, his eyes peering at nothing in particular. 'So, he was killed while at the bar?'

Graham Gallymore raised both his hands in a gesture of affirmation. 'Yep, blood all over the floor, although someone had tried to clean up the mess. There were two drink glasses found on the bar which we took for analysis; Andy's fingerprints were all over one of the glasses.'

'And the other?' Fisher enquired, his spirits rising in anticipation.

'Clean as a whistle, I'm sorry, sir. Whoever Crawford's drinking mate was had accounted for the obvious. As no-one would think it unreasonable for the owner of the place to have a drink at his own bar, it's not surprising to find a glass with his fingerprints on it. At the same time, his drinking partner wouldn't have been dumb enough to leave his fingerprints all over the glass he had been using, if the drinking partner was the shooter.'

Having now covered the attacks on four people, all having an interest in the future of The Grovel, Chief Superintendent Paxton entered the fray and moved to the front of the office and sat on a corner of Fisher's desk. 'Gentlemen, although I am strictly an observer to this meeting, there are a couple of points I would like to clear up. Simon, initially you were of the belief the Premier was somehow involved in this case. In view of the current circumstances, and the escalating body count, may we have your thoughts as to his alleged involvement?'

'Well, sir, following your directive, I have not approached the Premier, which would be quite difficult at the moment anyway as he's leading a trade delegation to New York at the moment.'

'Yeah, some delegation,' Noel blurted, 'a delegation of two, the Premier and his secretary.'

'I'm sure Chief Superintendent Paxton is not a bit concerned as to the morality of the Premier's overseas trade delegation, Noel, so just let me finish,' Simon chided. 'We were aware he was in consultation with the owner of an illegal casino, Andy Crawford, or at least we think it was Andy Crawford. The purpose of these discussions related to the redevelopment of The Grovel over at Elizabeth Bay into a high-class casino cum club for big spenders. The Premier had already intervened by having the building listed by the National Trust, this action taken to permanently negate any plans Paul Glover may have had regarding his townhouse development scheme. Obviously, Crawford's plan had its difficulties as the property is still currently owned by Paul Glover who, we now find, died intestate.

'Notwithstanding, the future of The Grovel is currently in the hands of the local council and some little trumped up bureaucrat named Boswell. He currently has to decide if they, the council, can legally recover outstanding statutory monies owed by taking possession of The Grovel and having it offered for sale at some ridiculous bargain price. Obviously, should that happen, the future of The Grovel, and its subsequent owner, would be prede-termined by Boswell after being suitably remunerated for his decision. Of course, we haven't heard anything tangible of the Crawford Buckmaster plan, and I have my doubts we will in the future, seeing Crawford's now dead.'

'Just stop there, Simon,' Paxton ordered. 'Three dead bodies and a stack of motives all linked back to one harbourside mansion. Standing where I do on this investigation, I get the idea that as soon as you come up with a suspect, that suspect gets themselves shunted off to that big casino in the sky. Of all the people you know who have, or had, an interest in The Grovel, just which ones are still left alive, for the moment, that is?'

Simon shrugged and pressed his lips together as he quickly reviewed the contenders. 'Well, there's Boswell who hopes to make money on the property by either buying it himself at a ridiculously cheap price or by taking a bribe from someone else who wants the place, which is probably closer to the mark. Deputy Premier Mason, urged on by his ego, has declared his interest in the place in the belief his position demands a more substantial residence than a suburban bungalow. Then there's Paul Stack who hasn't openly declared his interest, although I have an idea Crawford's idea appeals to him. Crawford apparently asked him to join the venture but, according to Stack, he declined the offer; said it was too difficult. In reality, I think he has designs on the place himself in order to implement Crawford's little scheme. I've discounted Haynes as he's been in hospital while all this has been going on. Of course, there's always Ralph Glover who's interested but he's been eliminated from the suspects list for the same reasons we've discounted Henry Haynes.'

'So that leaves you with three potential suspects; Mason, Stack and Boswell,' Paxton confirmed.

'Yeah, potential suspects or potential victims,' Simon muttered

Paxton nodded. 'Yes, I appreciate the position two of these three may be in as it appears one of them is a murderer. And what about Buckmaster?'

'Well, sir, I don't think the murderer is any one of the three,' Simon said with a twinge of discomfort. 'At a rough guess, I would say at least two are murderers, and the one who isn't has ticked all the boxes ready to graduate into the realms of the wicked. Now, as far as Buckmaster is concerned, with his partnership with Crawford dissolved, he might see what Stack has in mind, after all, I believe both the Crawford and Stack ideas were much the same. I know that's being a bit presumptuous as we haven't any evidence to suggest what either had in mind. I don't know, but with so many murders being committed, Buckmaster may get the idea things are getting out of hand and decide not to push his luck. Somehow I get the idea politicians are quite keen on seeing how much they can get away with, and Buckmaster is certainly a master of pushing his luck.'

# CHAPTER 22

*T*he back lawn of Simon's Collaroy bungalow, a sunny spring Saturday afternoon, the birds singing, convivial company, plentiful refreshments and the sweet smell of a freshly mown lawn; what could be better? The four guests, consisting of Ron Lange and his partner, Judy, along with Noel and Sue, were seated on director's chairs around a small circular metal table upon which a variety of nibblies had been provided by the hosts, Simon and Georgie.

Despite the utopian conditions, Simon wasn't sure if he should be delighted or undelighted. It was only a matter of time before the inevitable gauche discussion relating to the outbreak of a severe case of highly contagious homicide would be addressed and, until then, the topic would remain hanging in the air like the sword of Damocles waiting to stuff up a pleasant afternoon's get-together.

In an effort to delay the inevitable, Simon had brought forth discussion relating to the Manly rugby league team's successes, or failures, the likely winner of the forthcoming Melbourne Cup and even touched on the forbidden topic of politics. To defer the pending matter still further, Simon turned to Judy. 'And I believe you have a new tenant and we have new neighbours?'

'Yes, apparently so, not that I've met them. The property manager told me a sweet old couple has taken a long-term lease over the place, which suits us down to the ground. It's not far from the shops and they wanted a place where she could do some gardening.'

'Come on, Simon, I told you days ago they had moved in,' Georgie scolded. 'Obviously they keep very much to themselves as I've seen her only a couple of times, and nothing of him. I don't expect we'll have the drama of hydroponic cultivation of drugs, or murder, going on this time, thank heavens.'

Noel harrumphed. 'Yeah, well Dorothy gave the impression she was a harmless little old lady but you considered her bad enough to do her in.'

Judy, well aware of Ron's involvement in matters relating to the city jail and the occasional murder, couldn't contain her curiosity any longer. 'Simon, Ron told me about that poor man, Henry Haynes, who's in hospital. Do we know if he's going to live as I believe the beating he took brought on an aneurism?'

Simon lobbed his empty beer can into the garbage can strategically placed for such lobbing before responding. 'Yep, that was really a shame as we all thought Henry was going pretty well. Unfortunately, the doctors can't categorically state whether the assault brought about the aneurism. The only thing they can confirm is that the battering he received failed dismally to provide Henry with any positive therapeutic benefit.'

'So, if he hadn't been knocked senseless, he wouldn't be in the predicament he's now in?' Judy asked in an effort to obtain a conclusive answer.

'Mightn't is as close as they will say. And yes, while you're at it, Noel, I'll have anotheree,' Simon responded as Noel took another can of beer from the Esky located next to his chair.

'And have you worked out who it was who hit him, and

why?' Sue asked as she contemplated whether her glass of wine was sufficiently empty to require a refill.

'We have no witnesses, no weapon, and no real motive, no matter how much we might like to speculate. Irrespective of what we haven't got, we at least know the modus operandi was consistent with that used successfully by Paul Glover on his brother, Bruce. Quite apart from being a rampant homicidal maniac, the assault on Ralph Glover and Cheryl Drake is claimed to have been carried out by Paul before he succumbed to a lethal dose of poison. Come to think of it, it would probably have been difficult for Paul to commit an assault after taking a lethal dose of poison. Even if he hadn't snuffed it, it would have been difficult to get a conviction for the attack on Ralph and Cheryl based on body odour, which is pretty flimsy evidence.

'Anyway, the whole thing is now hypothetical as our major suspect in both bashing incidents is dead. And before we're consumed with lethal chitchat and speculation as to who's done what to whom, what do we know about the LOL and her hubby?' Simon, although not particularly interested, asked.

Georgie topped up her glass with a Chardonnay and handed the bottle to Sue. 'Her name's Moira and the husband's Ted, so that makes him Eric, I suppose. She's stuck her head in a couple of times to say hello, seems a bit dithery but quite a pleasant lady. As I said, I've seen neither hide nor hair of him, but if he's older than she is, I suppose he doesn't get around much nowadays. Despite their age, I get the idea they haven't been married for too long, which seems a bit odd.'

'Why odd?' Ron asked somewhat surprised by Georgie's apparent discrimination of the older generation. 'It's kinda nice to see the elderly tucked up comfortably and not living their lives as lonely outcasts waiting for their use by date to come up.'

Georgie rolled her eyes to the sky. 'Yeah, and next you'll be telling me Dorothy was a sweet little old lady too. They say you can't judge a book by its cover, and she was a great example of that cliché.'

'Aha,' Noel exclaimed, 'but you did away with dear old Dorothy anyway. I suppose if Moira doesn't measure up, she'll kick off unexpectedly as a result of some diabolical plot you'll have dreamt up.'

Georgie gave Noel the evil eye and slowly shook her head. 'Noel, I'm not even going to go there, so just belt up. Dorothy died of natural causes, and I wasn't held responsible.'

'Yeah, but maybe she died with just a little help from your eight legged friends,' Ron quipped.

The mood of the group was becoming more relaxed and was directly proportional to the amount of wine and beer partaken. Fortunately for those who had to drive, it was getting late and a bit chilly with the nor-east sea breeze now cool and gusty; time to call it a day. Before clearing away the chairs and other paraphernalia, a high-pitched voice was heard.

'Yoo-hoo.'

It was Georgie who identified the perpetrator of the "Yoo-hoo" as the sweet little old lady from next-door, her small rounded face topped with light blue, tightly permed hair, peering over the fence. 'Oh, Moira, come on over and meet my husband. I do apologise, I should have given you an invite.'

'No, not at all, my dear. Teddy and I aren't into socializing very much these days, you know, getting a bit slow on the old feet. I only wanted to ask if one of your charming young gentlemen would be so kind as to give me a hand to move some flower pots. I'd do it myself but they're a little too heavy for me to manage. The flowers will grow much bigger if I plant them in the ground,' the little old lady explained.

'No problems, Noel and Simon would be delighted to help, Moira. And don't ever be afraid to come over if you have any need of help with anything,' Georgie replied.

With that, Simon and Noel headed out to save the little old

lady the inconvenience of relocating numerous potted botanical specimens from the driveway to the back lawn where, it was clearly obvious, Moira had yet to prepare suitable plots to accommodate the potted plants. 'Cripes, she's right; they are a bit heavy,' Noel grumbled as both men struggled to relocate the half dozen terracotta pots in which the unidentified plants currently resided.

'Well, that was a bit of an effort,' Simon said as they walked back to finish cleaning up Simon's back yard. 'And no, I haven't a clue what sort of horticultural specimens she's growing. To me, all plants are weeds if they're in the wrong spot.'

'Yeah, okay. I know more about brain surgery than I do about gardening,' Noel conceded, 'but sure as hell, the chances of a little old lady who likes gardening turning out to be another raging psychopathic killer seem pretty remote.'

'Okay, what now, boss?' Noel asked as he rocked back and forth, his facial expression one of depressed optimism. 'Every time we come up with a suspect, that suspect ends up dead, and right at this moment Paul Stack's life insurance premiums must have hit the roof.'

Simon sat dejectedly, his elbows on the table, his face resting in his hands. 'Look, just because the type of gun used on Andrew Glover and Andy Crawford is available in a pretty pink colour doesn't mean Stack's the guilty party. And the fact that he wears lairy clothes doesn't necessarily mean he uses a lairy shooter. Mind you, I will concede he certainly had motive, and he did express his vehement dislike for Mr Crawford.'

'Yeah, well how about we get a bit of protection organised for Ralph?' Noel suggested as he rolled a piece of paper into a ball and had a three-point shot into the waste bin beside Simon's desk. Neither detective cared to view the result which had been a foregone conclusion. 'You know, with him now being the sole remaining Glover, and probably holding a legitimate claim on The Grovel, someone might decide to eliminate him from the competition, permanently.'

'It's not a bad idea, but any attempt on his life might provide us with more clues as to what's going on. We still have Stack, Buckmaster and Mason all eager for the place and, of course, there's always Boswell to consider,' Simon said as he stooped to drop the shot into the bin. 'I'd like to have another chat with the Premier but I guess he's still away.'

'Yep, and we know the mission he's on has very little to do with the wine trade,' Noel remarked sarcastically. 'And if there's another attempt on anyone's life, I just hope it's not Ralph. The other four you mentioned are far more suitable to get their heads blown off. Anyway, how about we go have a chat with Boswell? That should brighten up our day.'

'Not a bad idea. At least it'll boost the blood pressure.'

'Ah, my old mate, TBones,' Noel said with a tone of surprise; the information desk was attended.

'Bloody hell, two coppers and it ain't lunchtime yet. I s'pose you're here to see Mr Boswell. He's pretty busy as he's had people coming and going all morning. Anyway, you know where he is, down the corridor and on the left. I'll let him know you're on your way,' he said and reached for the phone.

A knock on the door elicited a gruff voice. 'Come in, it's open.' On entering the office, the detectives were greeted with the not unexpected sarcastic reception. 'Ah, DCI Holmes and his faithful Sergeant Watson,' declared the weedy little man behind an inordinately large desk as the two detectives entered the office. Noel, recalling Stack's office desk and now seeing Boswell's, couldn't suppress the thought that the size of the desk is directly proportional to the ego that sits behind it.

'Not quite, but if you just keep going the way you are, you pretentious prat, I'll haul you in for obstructing a police investigation,' Simon responded, his blood pressure already on the rise.

'Now, don't be like that, who is it, ah yes, DCI Webster. It's been a bad day already,' Boswell said, trying in vain to be a little more polite. 'I suppose you're here about The Grovel, and a very interesting case that's turning out to be. I believe the legal owner has passed away, along with most of the other members of the Glover family. Yes, a very interesting case with a significant debt still owing to the council, and growing by the day.'

'Yeah, well we're not too concerned with the financial complication, that's your problem. However, I'm now led to believe the government has recently had the place registered under the Heritage Act,' Simon announced rhetorically to see what reaction the comment may elicit from Mr Boswell.

After a shrug and a shake of the head, Boswell sat back and folded his arms. 'Yes, that came as a bit of a surprise in view of all the trouble we've gone through to have the place rezoned for medium density housing. On top of that, there was all the paper work for the approval of Paul Glover's plan to demolish the place and build a townhouse complex. But that was before he reneged on his financial obligations.'

'So, who owns the place now?' Noel asked.

'That's classified information regarded as Commercial in Confidence at the moment and is released on a strict "Need to Know" basis. While we have a number of people interested in the future of The Grovel, the heritage listing has complicated the issue with a need to have the current zoning reverted back to its original classification of low density housing. Obviously, the consequences of such action may influence the number of people interested in the place.

'With my limited knowledge of heritage listed buildings, any renovation work must comply with the regulations applicable to the specific listing. In the case of The Grovel, I would think any external renovations would have to be consistent with the original plans. The place does have some historical value, being of the architectural Gothic design, despite having been constructed in the early Federation period. I would have to see the heritage listing to see if the internal structure is included because, if it is, some prospective owner may decide to opt out of proceedings.'

Simon nodded. 'Ah yes, you decide who presents the most lucrative plan consistent with the heritage listing and then rezone it either as a commercial or residential site depending on whatever activity is planned to go on inside the place.'

'Now, DCI Webster, if that comment was made outside this office, I would sue you for libel,' Boswell declared in feigned annoyance, well aware Simon's appreciation of the situation was spot on.

'Mister Boswell, apart from the fact it would be slander, not libel, I would like to remind you that we have three bodies in the morgue, all murdered and all having expressed an interest in The Grovel before they were brutally done in. Now, I've already warned you about failing to cooperate in a lawful investigation. Should you choose to remain recalcitrant, we would be forced to lay charges against you which would, I have no doubt, prove detrimental to your career aspirations. I would therefore strongly suggest you start to cooperate. Now first off, I take it the names Mason, Stack and Buckmaster are included in the list of interested people?' Simon asked with a hint of irritation.

'Well, it's no skin of my nose, but I think those who have been brutally murdered, as you so graphically put it, won't be expressing interest in anything now. But to answer your question, DCI Webster, yes, Mr Mason is interested in buying The Grovel for his own family use. That would mean rezoning the property back to its original state of low density, which it will be anyway, now it's heritage listed.

'I believe the Premier was supporting a Crawford venture to convert The Grovel into an exclusive club, although any idea to change the occupancy of the place would probably entail rezoning it as a commercial site, which it could be, provided it didn't not contravene the heritage listing. For some reason Mr

Crawford has lost interest and his idea taken up by Mr Stack who, with the Premier's support, wants the property for the same reason Mr Crawford wanted it. And that's it, so there's nothing outrageous going on. But unfortunately, gentlemen, I have an important meeting to attend so I must call a halt to our little discussion, brief as it may have been.'

As the two detectives walked back down the corridor, Noel said, 'Meeting my eye, he just didn't want to answer any more questions. And I take it you smelt it too?'

'Sure did, Doctor Watson. So Sticky Stack has been to see Mister Boswell while in the process of talking to Buckmaster, and it's not about the weather. How very interesting.'

'Yes, but the field is narrowing and Crawford isn't talking to anyone now he's dead. Funny, but Boswell gave me the impression he was unaware of just why Crawford has lost interest in a whole lot of things. The only person we can rule out of this mess is Ralph,' Noel uttered to himself as they left the building and headed back to their car.

After driving from Bondi Junction back to the city and parking the car at the Day Street Police Station, the two detectives took the stairs to their office. 'You know, boss, Buckmaster has gone to a lot of trouble to get the place listed under the Heritage Act and he'll want compensation for his efforts,' Noel said as he removed his coat and hung it on the hat stand.

'Yes, but I'd say Stack would be willing to reward both Buckmaster and Boswell quite substantially for anything they have to do to ensure he ends up with The Grovel. And all this just because Stack usurped Crawford's idea of a swanky casino,' Simon replied as he flopped down on his chair without removing his coat. 'I vote we do absolutely nothing and let these deranged lunatics sort it out for themselves. Every time we think a person has a motive, someone comes up with the same motive and all we end up with is another body. Maybe that's their idea; let's confuse the coppers.'

'Well, I'm all for doing nothing because the whiteboard looks more like a Jackson Pollock masterpiece and we're no closer to knowing what's going on.'

It was mid-afternoon when Simon's phone rang. 'Jacko, good to hear from you, I think. What news have you got? You're kidding, when? Okay, touch nothing and we'll get right onto it. And thanks, thanks heaps.' Simon hung up the phone, closed his eyes and slowly shook his head. 'Now, ain't that just dandy as another one bights the dust. Fisher's going to just love us.'

Noel, distracted by both Simon's conversation and his subsequent response, was aware that the phone call was not the harbinger of favourable news. 'So, I take it that wasn't the lottery office?'

'No, Jacko. He just found Stack's body.'

'Dead?'

'Of course, dead. Would I be referring to his body if he were alive, you moron?'

'At the Spinning Wheel?'

'Yep. Get on to Dave Harris up at The Cross seeing it's in his bailiwick, again, and you better have Gally meet us there.'

'Sure thing, boss.'

Jacko was waiting on the footpath outside The Spinning Wheel. The road had been cordoned off to traffic with several police cars already parked outside the casino, their red and blue lights flashing. 'Hi, Jacko,' Simon said in greeting the somewhat agitated giant. 'Not the nicest way to spend your day?'

'You can say that again. The forensic bloke Gallymore is inside at the moment,' Jacko volunteered.

'Yeah, but before we go in, can you give us some idea of what happened here?'

'Sure. I turned up for work around mid-day, you know, clean

up the place from last night's tradin' and set up for tonight. I found the front door unlocked, which it never is, at this time of the day anyway. I started to have a look around expectin' some thief to be robbin' the bar. Strange, but that's how I first met you, me robbin' a bar and you blokes commin' around to blow the job. Anyway, I looked in Mr. Stack's office and there he was not lookin' too well at all. In fact, he'd snuffed it, poor bloke. And that's when I thought I better give you a call, you havin' given me your card.'

'Well, thanks Jacko. We'll need to get a written statement from you but we'll worry about that later,' Simon said and entered the casino. 'Hi Gally. How, when, where and why?'

'Oh, hi Simon, Noel. You keep this up and I'm going to need more space over at the morgue. At least with the overtime you're providing I'll forget the row boat and buy a yacht, but re your questions. The how I'd say would be poison, although I'll need to take a look inside, inside Stack, I mean. The when, I'd say only about two hours ago. He's still warm, not that I've taken his rectal temp yet. The where, right where he's sitting, and the why; that's your problem. If I can get him back to the lab ASAP, I'll get to work on it straight away as we will have more of a chance of finding out what killed him. It will also save having to put him on ice for a while.'

'Gee, thanks, Gally. I've already let Dave Harris know what's happened so he should be along shortly to help out. I take it you've had your boys do a search of the area?'

'Thanks. And yes, we've had a quick look around, but didn't turn up anything obvious. No doubt Harris's people will do a thorough search when they get here. By the way, you are aware that this is the second cadaver you've provided in this area in the space of days. If you think there's going to be more, please let me know. I'll take the time to set up a temporary morgue here to save me the travelling time.'

'Yeah, well how the bloody hell do you think I feel?'

bemoaned a very disconcerted and ruffled Simon. 'I just wish people would stop killing off suspects. Aah, G'day Dave,' Simon said amiably as David Harris entered the room. 'You know, we're going to have to stop meeting like this, Dave, people will start to talk,' he added as DI Harris pulled a face at the sight of Stack's sickly-looking body. 'I thought you might like to know what's going on because, as sure as hell, I don't. And yes, I know it's connected with our investigation.'

'Crikey,' DI Harris declared, 'and I thought the bobbies had problems dealing with The Ripper. You'll easily reach his target of, how many bodies…'

'Five, so we have only one to go. Come on Noel,' Simon directed, 'let's get the hell out of here and go have a beer somewhere before we go home.'

# CHAPTER 24

*A*s the bus trip from the city to Collaroy was just as fast, or slow, as driving their own private vehicles, both Simon and Noel had given up on the tedious and onerous task of driving to work, except when special circumstances prevailed, which was not often. With the approach of summer and the evening sunset getting later, by the time Simon alighted from the bus at Collaroy shops, it was still light. He looked forward to daylight saving when, with clocks advanced one hour, he would be home in time to whip down to the beach for a swim. Aah, the joys of summer, he thought.

Simon unhurriedly ambled back along Pittwater Road, turned right into West Bank Lane only to have his attention immediately drawn to the white sedan, with a flashing blue light on the roof, parked outside what appeared to be number twenty-four. 'Good grief and bollocks. What is it now, as if I haven't got enough on my plate?' Simon muttered to himself, certain in the belief that whoever the visitor was wasn't making a social call. Whatever the reason for the constabulary's uninvited presence, someone was about to receive a very grumpy and sour detective chief inspector. After all, Simon did not have a good day at the office.

On entering the lounge room, Simon immediately recognized the two plain clothed detectives, both of whom rose from their chairs to greet him. Georgie got up from the lounge where she had been sitting nursing a cup of coffee. 'Oh, hi darling,' she said and gave Simon a peck on the cheek. 'You remember Detective Inspector David Spring-Brown and his sidekick Sergeant Gaskill, from Manly CIB?'

'Yes, can't forget them, not after the last debacle with people getting killed by flashes of lightning, or pushed over a cliff. Good to see you again,' Simon said cordially. 'I hope you're not chasing after some homicidal nutter again as I'm already up to my neck in murder victims. We've got one of those frustrating cases where the suspect becomes the next victim. Anyway, before we get started let me get organised,' he said as he removed his coat and undid his tie. He then flopped down in his favourite chair and, without undoing his shoe laces, worked each shoe off with the other foot.

'Look, I've just made some coffee so would...'

'Yes, I'd love one,' Simon replied pre-empting Georgie's polite offer, the annoyance and exasperation of the day still persisting. 'Okay, I haven't had the best of days, so let's go easy. Now what brings you out to Collaroy?'

Spring-Brown placed his empty coffee mug on the table, sat back, crossed his legs and folded his arms. 'We've got a bit of a problem with your next-door neighbour, or at least we might have. But before we get into the nitty-gritty, I think I should fill you in on a bit of the background. Moira Sampson, and that's her maiden name, moved into a retirement village with an elderly gentleman over at French's Forest a couple of years ago. As his name is of little consequence, apart from the fact he's now dead, we will refer to him as Body One. No autopsy was conducted as he was old, frail and appeared ready to kick off, and there was no overt evidence to suggest foul play.

'Even though Moira was the sole beneficiary of this gentleman's will, there was nothing to suggest Moira encouraged, or coerced, Body One into making her the sole beneficiary, nor was there any obvious evidence of Moira having assisted Body One on his way. While the demise of Body One didn't prompt any alarm bells, the fact that not long after Body One's probate was granted, Moira took in another aged gentleman ...'

'Don't tell me, he became Body Two,' Simon interrupted as if there was no doubt that was what Spring-Brown was about to reveal.

'In spades,' the detective inspector replied. 'Again, there appeared to be no call for an autopsy as Body Two was long past his use-by date, and it was accepted that he had died of nothing but old age. In fact, his death was similar to Body One, as was his cremation which was carried out with all the dispatch the body of a bubonic plague victim might have expected. Again, because of the nature of the death, no suspicion was aroused.'

'Okay, this is all very well and good, but Moira and her husband, Eric, I think, just moved in here recently. If you're suggesting Moira has done away with Eric, neither Georgie nor I have seen anyone's body hanging around, or even a live body for that matter, at least I haven't. Have you Georgie?'

'Good grief,' Georgie exclaimed, 'I think I would have told you if I had seen a stray corpse stashed away. Anyway, what makes you think there's a body to be found, Inspector, apart from Moira having a two from two record, so far?'

It was Sergeant Gaskill who took up the conversation. 'We've already mentioned Moira was the sole beneficiary of Body One's will. Now, as it would happen, Moira was also the sole beneficiary of Body Two's. While she could, no doubt, afford to buy a place of her own, she chooses to rent, as she did in the retirement village. Moira has never tried to hide the fact that the passing of Body One and Body Two were to her financial advantage. After inquiries with her bank we find, and not surprisingly, she has a bank account you wouldn't be able to jump over.'

'So, she's a lucky lady having two old codgers bequeath their fortunes to her, not that she's any spring chicken herself. And now you think old Eric is about to get the old heave-ho, if he hasn't already?' Simon asked in an effort to display some interest.

Detective Inspector Spring-Brown raised his eyebrows and, with an enquiring look, cut to the chase. 'What we'd be interested in is if you know anything about Moira Sampson, or Eric Tindale, like, have you spoken to them, what sort of people do they appear to be, in fact, anything you know about them.'

'I've spoken to Moira a couple of times and she even came in for coffee on one occasion, in fact it was the day they moved in, not that Eric came over,' Georgie explained. 'She seems to be in total control of her faculties, well nearly, considering she's getting on, that is, and appears to be a lovely little old lady.'

'And I've spoken a couple of words to her over the fence, but that's about it,' Simon added. 'Anyway, you haven't mentioned what's prompted your enquiries, apart from the fact she might be a serial killer on the loose?'

'That's just it,' Spring-Brown said with a shrug, 'the governing body of the retirement village from where Moira used to live is just suggesting we might like to keep an eye on the household. There's nothing to suggest anything untoward or unlawful has been committed, but they're a bit concerned any older gentleman who cohabits with Moira might end up as Body Number Three.'

Sergeant Gaskill took it upon himself to explain. 'What we mean is, we would appreciate any information you come across that, in any way, might suggest the old bloke next-door has met foul play. Even if he hasn't, if he suddenly dies, or you notice a dead body in the back yard, we would like to be informed. It has been noted that Moira is a keen gardener, and flowers just might not be the only thing she plants in the ground.'

'I'm sure if we noticed a body in her back yard, it would certainly be dead, as most bodies are,' Simon interjected

'Are what?'

'Dead.'

'Oh, yes, I see,' Gaskill replied, not quite sure what it was he could see.

Simon drained the dregs of his coffee and placed the mug on the coffee table before he sat back and folded his arms in a somewhat confrontational manner. 'So, we have a watch alert out on a little old lady, Moira Sampson, who hasn't the strength to lift a flower pot, in the belief she may be a serial killer. And all you have to go on is the fact that her last two partners, both of whom had at least one foot already in the grave, finally cashed in their chips, as we might all expect to do when we reach a certain age, and both were given a swift, but no doubt dignified, farewell. The concern now is that poor old Eric has the potential to end up Body Number Three?'

'That's about it,' returned Spring-Brown, 'but another body turning up in similar circumstances as the first two might raise enough suspicion to warrant an autopsy, irrespective of whether Eric is past his use-by date or not. If, as we now expect but can't prove because they were cremated, Body One and Body Two were poisoned to death, Moira might try to dispose of Teddy some other way to negate the prospect of an autopsy being conducted. Of course, that's if Teddy needs disposing,' Spring-Brown added, on reflection.

'As Moira couldn't be stupid enough to think three dead spouses wouldn't raise some suspicion, it's reasonable to think she might be a tad uneasy should an autopsy be carried out on Teddy, if, or when she does do away with him,' Sergeant Gaskill continued. 'That's why she would have had the first two cremated as soon as possible after their death, if she is a serial killer, that is.'

Having listened intently to the discussion, Georgie's pragmatism came to the fore. 'Yes, alright, but if Eric does expire suddenly, wouldn't that suggest she's out for the thrill of the kill, not the money she might receive from a benevolent geriatric? And how do you pin a motive on a thrill killer?'

Spring-Brown just raised his eyes, tightened his lips and nodded his head. 'Good point, especially as there didn't seem to be any major medical problems with Body One or Two, except they're now both dead. The difficulty, Mrs Webster, is that most people's health starts to decline in later life, and most deaths usually aren't such a sudden event. There's generally some intrinsic health problem to which they eventually succumb, and their death doesn't come as any great surprise.'

'And as their death doesn't come as any great surprise, no autopsy,' Georgie acknowledged with a nod of the head. 'I know when I'm old, infirmed and ready to peg out, I'd prefer to do it in my time, not have someone nudge me off the planet when they think I'm ready.'

# CHAPTER 25

*N*oel immediately recognized the morose atmosphere as he entered the office a little after Simon's arrival. Following the daily ritual of coat removal and the booting of his computer, He took stock of the whiteboard, the names, the arrows, the question marks; it was a mess Bletchley Park would have had trouble deciphering. 'Anything I can help you with, boss?' he asked, well aware that Simon was not in the best on spirits.

'Noel, if all these killings and Grovelgate were our only concerns, we would be laughing.' After a moments silence, Simon gave a wholesome sigh, pushed his chair back and settled his legs on top of his desk in a relaxed manner before setting off on the Spring-Brown revelations. After completing the long and tedious summary of possible murder and mayhem involving the next-door neighbours, Simon shrugged and waited for Noel's reaction.

'Ah, come on now, Simon, there seems to be a lot of maybes being thrown around. Maybe she's a serial poisoner, maybe she poisoned her previous two partners, and maybe she's going to poison her existing partner. Who knows, who cares?'

Simon had a definite look of grim fatalism etched across his face. 'It's as if we didn't have enough on our plate and along comes that twit, Spring-Brown. If I remember correctly, I got hauled over the coals for starting an investigation into something that might happen and not something that had happened, not that the something that might happen didn't happen. And now I have to keep an eye out for something that might happen, if it hasn't already, but we don't know if it has.'

Noel gave a shrug, pressed his lips together and, in an effort to bolster his boss's flagging spirits, said jovially, 'Okay, boss, we're both in this together, if there's anything to be in, that is. Let's hope Spring-Brown is wrong because I wouldn't like to be living next- door to the little old lady of West Bank Lane, if he's not. And I'd certainly find a reason to decline any invitation for dinner she might like to make.'

Simon's rumination of what might or might not happen regarding little old Moira was rudely interrupted by the annoying ring of Simon's phone. After a rather lengthy discussion, with Noel eagerly listening to a one-sided conversation, Simon hung up and turned to Noel. 'That was Graham Gallymore. Seems both Paul Glover and Paul Stack took a dose of the same poison, ricin.'

'Ricin,' Noel said with surprise. 'I thought that took days to become lethal?'

'Who knows? I'm just the conveyor of the news. What I do know is that ricin comes from the same plant as castor oil, which is supposed to taste horrible. Your mummy probably threatened to give you a dose of it when you were naughty, the oil bit, not the ricin part or you'd be dead,' Simon said without too much concern as to what poison had been used. He was of the opinion that the future prospects for the two Pauls would have been the same, irrespective of the poison used, ricin, strychnine, cyanide; they'd all make you feel terribly ill before you expire.

'And did Gally tell you how they were poisoned?'

'Yep, ingested.'

'Time frame?'

'Both dead within hours, although those hours would have been pretty unpleasant,' Simon replied.

'Well, as far as I'm concerned, that puts the ball fair and squarely in Boswell's court. We know Stack visited Boswell's office a few times, including the day he died. On top of that, Paul's whereabouts prior to his death are a bit hazy to say the least, Paul's death, I mean, not Stack's. I'm betting he went to see Boswell at some time to see whatever was going on regarding The Grovel,' Noel remarked as he proceeded to the white board and put a large red line through the names of those who had come to notice but who had, for various reason, expired.

On completion of his artistic scrawling, Noel stood back and considered the current state of affairs. 'You know, boss, of all the names we started with, the only ones remaining alive are Mason, Buckmaster, Boswell and Ralph Glover. Now, with Ralph still in hospital and Buckmaster currently over in New York screwing his heart out with his secretary, it doesn't leave us with too much to focus on. And don't forget, Boswell's coffee is so strong you could pour a bottle of tabasco into it and no-one would be the wiser. Just drinking it without a poisonous additive would be enough to kill a horse, if horses drank coffee, that is. That, to my mind, makes him a candidate for poisoning people.'

'Good thinking', Noel, but that would only account for two deaths, which is better than none, I s'pose. Maybe we should pay Mr Boswell another visit, and this time he won't have an important meeting to attend.'

'Wouldn't waste the time,' interrupted Detective Inspector David Harris as he stood by the office's open door. 'With so much going on in my bailiwick, I thought I'd come over to find out what's going on in your patch of turf and, more importantly, fill you in on the latest gossip.'

'Oh, hi David,' Simon greeted the neatly dressed, friendly faced colleague. 'And exactly what bit of gossip inspires you to make such a significant and earth-shattering comment?'

'He's dead. My boys are at the scene now. We've left a message for Graham Gallymore but he's been on the phone, not that I think there's any doubt he's dead; he's got a letter opener in the shape of a sword stuck in his chest.'

"Who's dead?' Noel asked in bewilderment.

'Boswell,' came Harris's succinct response.

'Oh, what a shame,' was all the commiseration Simon could offer.

'You're joking?' Noel's protest offered as both a question and a statement.

'Wish I was. Here I am at the twilight of my career and we've never been so busy, and it's all your fault,' Harris replied as he sank down onto the office racing chair. 'If you hadn't pulled that Glover bloke out of the harbour, none of this would've happened.'

'Well, how was I to know there was going to be a body on the end of the bloody anchor?' Simon responded indignantly. 'Anyway, who have you arrested for Boswell's murder?'

Now it was Harris' turn to respond indignantly. 'Cripes, hang on a bit. The body's still warm. You know, if you keep this up, you're going to establish some sort of record for the number of victims one investigation can deliver; you've got Andy Crawford, Andrew Glover, Paul Glover, Paul Stack and now Stuart Boswell. That's five Gally has on the tables over at the morgue, and we're not counting those involved who have been hospitalized. And the press is right onto it now claiming we have a serial killer running rampant.' Simon was reluctant to mention the next-door neighbour, Moira Sampson-Tindale who, while not involved in the current spate of murders currently under investigation, was cause for some concern, at least for Simon.

'Well, it looks like our rampant serial killer has to be our illustrious deputy Premier Peter Mason, unless some unknown witless yobbo comes along and knocks him off before we can get to talk to him,' Noel said as he drew another red line on the whiteboard.

Simon finally took on an expression of aggravated determination. 'Look, this is plain bloody stupid; five people dead and three survivors who should be after being belted-up by one of the already dead, obviously before he snuffed it himself, unless he's a real live zombie. And all this over some piece of real estate where the rates are higher than the national debt. I'm going up to see Fisher and tell him what I think of the whole shemozzle.'

# CHAPTER 26

*A*fter Simon had removed his coat, he sank back in his favourite chair, kicked off his shoes, loosened his tie and gladly accepted the glass of wine Georgie offered. He felt exhausted; not so much physically exhausted, but mentally. The Grovelgate investigation Simon had initially found to be both stimulating and thought provoking, now failed to maintain either curiosity or interest. Grovelgate had shot itself in the foot by producing more homicide victims than could be reasonably expected to materialise in the course of a normal murder investigation. As a consequence, Simon was not the only member of the constabulary now thoroughly overcome with a sense of monotonous repetition, each new victim radically affecting the course of the investigation the police were currently pursuing.

Georgie, curled up on the sofa with a glass of wine, her legs tucked under herself, offered some comforting words of wisdom. 'Come on, sweetheart, there can't be too many potential victims left running around. No matter how bad things are now, they can only get better.'

'Oh, that's just dandy; thus bad begins and worse remains behind. We may as well sit back and wait for anyone with an interest in The Grovel to kill off anybody else with a similar interest. The last man standing must be the killer, at least the killer of the last victim to peg out,' Simon grumbled as he gazed into the depths of his glass. 'I have an idea each of the victims may have been a murdering nut case having done away with some poor sod who was probably a murdering nut case themselves. While I think this is probably the case, I have to have some answers before next Wednesday as that's when I told Fisher all will be revealed. Trouble is, I'll have to spend more time pondering the problem rather than running around trying to catch some degenerate flagrante delicto, like in the process of murdering someone.'

Georgie harrumphed. 'So, all you have to do is dream up reasons why and how each of the, what is it, four, five, unfortunates happened to get themselves knocked off, and all over a piece of real estate. It hardly seems worth it. Anyway, to more important things. Moira, you know, the lady next-door, she had one of those digger things in this morning to dig up the back yard.'

'What, you mean a bobcat?'

'Yes, that's what I said, one of those things.'

'No, you said…Ah, forget it. Okay, she had some gardening to do and she's too old to swing a pick. I can't blame her for getting someone in, and she does have those azaleas to plant. Which reminds me, have you seen anything of Eric yet?'

Georgie shook her head. 'No, not a thing, and I haven't heard a word from next-door, which is a bit odd. People at that age usually start to lose their hearing and tend to turn up the telly a bit louder than others might. Still, I've learnt not to stick my nose into whatever our neighbours get up to. The closest I've come to having a conversation with Moira was today when she asked if I could give her a hand to wheel her wheelie bin up to the roadway for collection. We chattered about the weather and mundane things but she didn't mention Eric.'

'You don't think she might have done away with him and had the bobcat dig his grave, especially in view of what Spring-Brown had to say?'

'Cripes, don't ask me, you're the detective,' Georgie replied somewhat indignantly.

'Okay, just asking. After all, some pretty strange things have gone on in 26 West Bank Lane. I might let Spring-Brown know she's been digging up the back yard; might be nothing but could be something.'

Simon finished his wine, placed the glass on the coffee table, sat back and scratched the back of his head. Why was Georgie so damn logical? And honestly, the neighbours are Spring-Brown's problem; I've Grovelgate to worry about. Who cares who bumped who off as long as we can show that someone had a motive for bumping someone off? And who cares if we don't marry up the correct murderer to the respective body, as long as we have a murderer, dead or alive. The means and opportunity we can stitch up later. Simon was in deep thought, his spirits now almost as low as a backbencher's IQ.

With a scarcity of any real or admissible evidence to present, Simon's forthcoming Wednesday's revelations were presenting the detective with a sizeable amount of trepidation. 'Well, I s'pose I'll have to fudge it again,' he said having come to terms with the dubious position he had placed himself. 'Last time I revealed all was at The Grovel. Everything seemed to go alright, apart from the fact we had only one body to deal with, and that was Bruce Glover's. Problem this time is that with five deaths and no arrests, someone, and the press, will be out for blood which will probably be mine. Anyway, we can talk about it on the weekend.'

Saturday afternoon at 24 West Bank Lane, the weather fine and warm with a gentle northeast sea breeze, as it should be in late October. The usually gregarious congregation sitting on the director's chairs on the back lawn, consuming the occasional wine or amber ale, was in a rare sombre mood. In four days time Simon would have to reveal to the state's top politicians and police management those responsible for the murder of a sufficient number of victims to field a basketball team. Everyone now sitting on the back lawn of Simon's bungalow couldn't help but think such revelation was going to be based on pure guesswork. Simon's main worry was that he thought the same thing.

'I still can't work out why Henry was put away in the first place assuming, of course, it's Grovel related,' Ron muttered with a shake of the head.

'No, it's not as though he had any obvious interest in the place,' Simon said as he snapped open another can of beer, 'maybe the fact he had been to see Paul and Andrew while they were in jail was seen as a declaration of GPD's or, more precisely, Ralph's interest in The Grovel.'

'So, you're working on the presumption that Paul Glover attacked Henry with, or without, the intention of killing him?' Ron asked.

Simon gave a shrug and raised his eyebrows. 'Can't think of anyone else right at the moment, but we still have a couple of days to go so someone else might put their hand up and claim to be the guilty individual.'

The group's attention was distracted from the topic at hand by the sound of the side gate opening and shutting and the appearance of Detective Inspector David Spring-Brown. 'I knocked on the front door but figured you must be out the back here; hope you don't mind my intrusion.'

'That depends' replied Simon amicably. 'Here, pull up a seat and have a coldie, or are you on duty?' Simon asked as he indicated to a collapsible director's chair that required uncollapsing before use.

'Well, yes I will and officially no, but….'

'Oh ooh. Something tells me something rotten has happened in the State of Norway,' Simon predicted as he handed the inspector a can of beer from the Esky.

'Denmark, but a little closer to home this time, I think,' Spring-Brown corrected before he snapped open the can and took a long draught. 'Gee, that's good. No, I'm here to ask if you have seen anything of your neighbour yet, you know, the old bloke, Eric.' The sudden disclosure of the purpose for the visit by the Manly CIB detective had an immediate effect on the group, especially Georgie who was of the firm belief Eric had already been planted under the azaleas in Moira Sampson's newly established garden.

'No, not a sign of 'im, and haven't heard as much as a whisper either. You would have thought we'd have overheard some conversation, or something going on, but nothing, and I'm here all day,' Georgie volunteered.

'You mentioned Mrs Sampson came over for coffee one day, I think the day she moved in. Is that correct Mrs Webster?'

'Yes, that's right. She didn't stay long and we only had a brief chat but, goodness, she did seem to be a nice little old lady, but you can never tell these days, can you?' Georgie replied.

'And she drank coffee, not tea?'

'Yes, she said she didn't like tea, not that she minds making it for other people. Apparently, she really likes the idea of putting a gum leaf in the pot, you know, the swagman's billy thing.'

It was Judy who couldn't control her inquisitive nature any longer. 'Inspector, you obviously have been conducting an investigation into the life and times of Simon and Georgie's new neighbours and there's something obviously amiss here. You have further information that prompts your visit, and the fact she drinks coffee in preference to tea is overwhelmingly significant to the investigation?'

Detective Inspector Spring-Brown acknowledged the significance with his lips pressed together and a nod of the head. 'Sounds pretty stupid at this juncture but yes, it could very well be significant. You see, the body of an aged male has been recovered from the Manly garbage tip. Garbage in the vicinity of the body clearly indicated the body came from Collaroy. While there was no return address attached to the body, we're inclined to think someone was trying to permanently dispose of a cadaver.'

'Well, it can't be Eric because he's buried under the azaleas out in the back yard,' Georgie said, the indignation in her voice not going un-noticed.

Spring-Brown, taken aback somewhat by Georgie's revelation, shook his head as if trying to clear the cobwebs; maybe he hadn't heard correctly. Finally, having come to the conclusion there had been nothing wrong with his hearing, he asked, 'And what makes you think that, Mrs Webster?'

'Because if she is a serial killer, and I think we both agree there's a good chance of that, the fact she just had a bobby dog in to dig a garden plot, just when her boyfriend goes missing, or reportedly missing, is just a little too coincidental.'

'Bobby dog?' Spring-Brown asked, now a little confused not having heard the term before.

Simon rolled his eyes, shook his head and then proceeded to enlighten the inspector on the mechanical contrivance used to dig up the neighbour's back yard. 'She means a bobcat.'

'Of course, how very stupid of me,' the inspector replied before examining his empty can of beer and deciding he'd better have another.

'So, I take it you've had this body sent off to the pathologist?' Noel asked.

'Yes, although we haven't had a positive identification yet. We've asked the boss over at the retirement village at Frenchs Forest to come and have a look, so he may be able to give us something to go on. We didn't want to approach Moira at this stage as the body might not belong to her.'

Ron gave Simon a wry smile. 'You just can't help yourself, can you, Simon? As if the stack of murders you have isn't enough, you have to bring your work home with you.'

Simon slouched forward, stared at the ground and slowly shook his head.

# CHAPTER 27

*J*t was certainly a case of déjà vu for Simon as he
paced the floor in front of the ornate, unlit fireplace. It
was not so long ago that he had paced the same floor while
addressing a similar group of people, which now included
members of the police force, a prospective property developer, a
bureaucrat, politicians and Jacko, not to mention the lovely
Cheryl Drake, the person who had started the steam roller off on
the current demolition mission based on nothing more than the
belief something might happen.

Noel had never felt comfortable visiting The Grovel and
now, with the sun slowly setting over the city and the shadows
growing longer, his uncomfortableness was just as acute as ever.
To Noel, it seemed ironic that such a piece of real estate could be
the cause of so much death, destruction and shonky dealings.
With uninterrupted views across Elizabeth Bay and the harbour,
The Grovel, despite its dilapidated condition, was still a very
imposing two storied Gothic style mansion with all the characteristics demanded by Boris Karloff or Vincent Price. The multi-
tude of unsmoking chimneys protruding from the roof gave hint

to the once opulent interior of the mansion with many rooms provided with an open fire.

While the Premier had ensured the continued existence of the mansion in its original state, the surrounding grounds of the property were another matter. On the detective's previous visits to The Grovel, nearly two years ago, both men couldn't help but notice the state of the overgrown garden with weeds and bushes running rampant. Nothing had changed, albeit the weeds and bushes were running a little more rampant, the old Morton Bay fig tree was a little older and the figs a little riper, while the resident colony of flying foxes had now multiplied to plague proportions. Gee, Moira would go berserk in this place, all this room to plant belladonna, hemlock, strychnine, and the occasional body maybe, Simon had thought on seeing the garden again.

Noel had been to the mansion earlier in the day to try and make the place fit for a meeting to which some high-powered individuals had been invited, including the Premier of the state, recently returned from, ostensibly, an overseas trade mission. The room in which Simon now paced was either the living room or the drawing room; Noel had never been able to figure out the difference. Although having vacuumed, dusted, and committed his limited domestic talents to making the room habitable, it still oozed all the grandeur and oppressive atmosphere of the House of Usher. The long period of unoccupancy had aided the room's deterioration for, despite Noel's efforts, there was nothing he could do to eliminate the damp and musty smell that pervaded the place. The old ineffective chandelier still hung from the unusually high ceiling, its initial illumination, that was poor to start with, having dwindled to a dull glow long before it had reached the occupants of the room.

From Noel's vantage point next to the fire place, he surveyed the occupants with a touch of apprehension as Simon was, hopefully, about to reveal all to the expectant audience. The approval for the evening's little soiree had been given the nod by Detective Superintendent Nigel Fisher following Simon's irate discussion with him and the subsequent referral of the matter to a higher authority. That Simon was about to expose, hopefully, the identity of the guilty culprits to the murder of five victims, and in the process solve the Grovelgate case, was the extent of Noel's knowledge of the night's entertainment, the content of the forthcoming disclosures promising to be a revelation to Noel and everyone else present in the room. With an audience that included Premier Buckmaster, his deputy, Peter Mason and Chief Superintendent Paxton, Noel had definite reason for apprehension. He had seen Simon perform a similar act in the Hercule Poirot style, but not in the presence of such exalted and elite bureaucrats where a minor slip-up could prove somewhat detrimental to any career aspirations Simon might entertain.

Along with those Noel considered as "upper crusties" there were those of the lower plebeian class and included Superintendent Musgrave from the City Jail, Superintendent Fisher, Detective Inspectors Dave Harris and Ian Francis from the Kings Cross and Waverly stations respectively, Ralph Glover and Cheryl Drake, both recently discharged from hospital, no thanks to Paul Glover, the forensic boffin Dave Gallymore, Ron Lange and Jacko. Winding up the little group, and at an undetermined position on the social scale, was the council's inimitable information counter director, TBones, making a total of fourteen people crowded into The Grovel's lounge room. For any unplanned contingency, two uniformed constables had been positioned inside and adjacent to the room's only door.

The expectant audience, now seated on the old floral upholstered lounge, the three matching lounge chairs and the dusty dining chairs Noel had purloined from The Grovel's once elegant dining room, either chattered amiably, or otherwise, to those positioned on a similar social rung. As Simon had studied the mandatory personal attributes necessary for entrance into the political arena, that included a good dose of self-opinionated arrogance, together with the expunging of any idiosyncrasy that may be misconstrued to resemble humility, morality or virtue, he was not surprised to see the Premier engaged in serious discussion with the only person in the room endowed with the similar intellectual attributes; deputy Premier, Mr Mason.

Neither Mason nor Buckmaster was quite sure why their presence at The Grovel had been demanded by the Minister for Police and the police commissioner who, having received advice from Chief Superintendent Paxton, believed there was the definite possibility an unlawful act had been perpetrated by an unnamed member, or members, of the lower house. Before the meeting had started, Simon had managed to raise the ire of the Premier and his deputy, both men being of similar mind; what the hell are we doing here, and what's it all about.

Irrespective of the mutual animosity Simon was able to provoke in politicians, he was a pragmatist with a job to be done, and if that meant placing the politician in an invidious position, so be it. Simon's last investigation ultimately culminated in a change of Premier and the disclosure of conduct unbecoming certain members elected by the community to represent them in parliament. To Simon's mind, politicians could never grasp the fact that because they claim not to have broken any criminal law, they may well be guilty of immoral or unethical conduct, especially when rorting the system's gravy train.

The "gravy train", as it is euphemistically known, is a fundamental and deep routed informal concession provided to politicians as a non-taxable fringe benefit in recognition of the arduous political and representational duties they are obliged to perform. However, while there is every expectation elected members should avail themselves of these concessions, there is also the implicit expectation that they exploit the system way beyond tolerable accountability and moral acceptability, provided it is done with a teeny bit of discretion and, needless to say, the perpetrator is not stupid enough to get caught. No, Simon's last investigation had left him a trifle disillusioned when it came to the integrity of the politician.

'Okay, lady and gentlemen, we have a great deal to get through, not the least being the murder of five victims, so if we can keep the discussion down to a dull roar, we will get on with it. While I take it you're all aware of the identity of the victims, there may be some of you who are of the belief that all five unfortunates were victims of exploits carried out by one diabolical homicidal maniac. However, we are now of the opinion a lone killer was not necessarily responsible for all the fatalities, but that each homicide was conducted independently by a number of people, all of whom had a common interest, that being the Glover family mansion at Elizabeth Bay and known as The Grovel. Strange as may seem, all five victims happened to share this same common interest, albeit for the own individual reasons, as their killers. As a consequence, we will approach each of the murders in consecutive order, although we will start with a living identity, Henry Haynes, who's currently in hospital battling to stay alive. Whether he's aware of it or not, his actions may have precipitated later events. Unfortunately, there appears to be no-one living who can confirm or refute my conjecture, so if I stray from someone else's solution, or theory, please feel free to voice your views.'

It was Ralph Glover who immediately interrupted Simon. 'Hang on, poor old Henry has no interest in the place, so you're wrong, right from the kick-off.'

Simon put his hands in his pockets and started to walk to and fro in front of the fire place. He suddenly stopped and abruptly turned to Ralph. 'Yes, you are correct on that point, Henry doesn't have any particular interest in The Grovel, save for the fact that he works for you, and you do, I mean have an interest in The Grovel. You sent him over to the jail to find out from Paul and Andrew Glover what they intended to do with the property once they had been released from prison. Unfortunately, we all know Henry is a bad-tempered bloke and not backward in displaying his arrogant and cranky qualities, qualities he no doubt used on his visit to see the incarcerated duo.

'Irrespective of what Paul and Andrew had in mind for the property, Henry, in his normal robust manner, conveyed your message that you intended to take over the property, as head of Glover Property Development, irrespective of whatever their future intentions might have been for The Grovel. Obviously, this didn't go down too well with either Paul or Andrew who believed they had council approval for the development of a townhouse complex on the property. Enraged by Henry's revelation of your intentions, Ralph, Paul sought to vent his anger against the one person who seemed to be literally usurping the ground from under his feet, Henry. Despite his vehement claims to the contrary while alive, it is our contention Paul Glover is guilty of attempted murder, if not the premeditated murder, of Henry Haynes should Henry not recover.

'You see, gentlemen, The Musgrave Solution to our over populated prisons made it quite easy for Paul to travel out to Bondi, give Henry the thrashing which resulted in Henry's hospitalization, then return to jail. It wasn't until much later Paul found out that, by being convicted of his brother's murder, his license to operate as a developer had been withdrawn. Needless to say, Stuart Boswell from the council had also thrown a spanner into the works to prevent Paul from following through with his plans. This spanner, of course, was the unpaid statutory fees levied by council which provided council the opportunity to relieve Paul of property ownership.

'Mind you, if Boswell hadn't upset Paul's plans, the Premier sure did by arranging for the dwelling to be heritage listed, effectively preventing the bulldozers from knocking down the place.' At this point Simon cast an eye over his captive audience to gauge any immediate response – which there wasn't. With failure to cast anyone still alive as a murderer, all Simon's hypothesis and speculation of events seemed to be generally accepted, so far. Who was alive to refute them?

Superintendent Fisher turned to his boss, Chief Superintendent Paxton, with raised eyebrows. 'Sounds feasible to me, and who's going to say he's wrong, unless someone steps up and admits to the assault.'

'Well, I don't know if Simon's right or wrong, but it sounds good enough for me to put the "Case Closed" stamp on Henry's file,' Paxton replied jovially.

Just as Simon was about to continue his spellbinding address relating to who gave Henry a hiding, a somewhat indignant Premier Buckmaster interjected. 'Now, just back up a bit, Chief Inspector. What's this all about the Musgrave Solution to prison overcrowding? I've never heard anything about overcrowding in our jails, and I certainly haven't any idea how we are dealing with it if, just on the off chance, a problem exists at all.'

Musgrave's face darkened, his look to Simon seeking an inferred non-verbal answer; will I deal with this, or will you? Simon nodded, the enlightenment of the Premier's obvious deplorable ignorance conveniently passed to Superintendent Musgrave who welcomed the opportunity to acquaint the Premier with reality. Musgrave then proceeded to address the Premier's lack of knowledge of the situation with a heart rendering account of the predicament confronted by the prison administrators, and the in-house scheme devised to cope with the prison's overcrowding problems.

'And you say my Minister for Correctional Services knows of the problem?' Premier Buckmaster asked, his already bellicose attitude in no way relieved by Musgrave's revelations.

'Of course he's aware of the problem; he just doesn't want to know, or do anything about it. To do anything would mean spending lots of money which would impact on the budget, and you wouldn't like that now, would you Mr Premier. Most of the jails we have were built in the colonial days when the entire population of the country was about what you'd expect to be able to fit into a telephone box. Irrespective of how few or how many criminals the judiciary sentences to incarceration, you can't expect us to be able to accommodate the mob we now have in our totally inadequate colonial jails.'

Premier Buckmaster sat unperturbed, fully aware that Musgrave was right. But what government, or any politician, wished to spend millions of dollars on building cushy prisons for the outlaws of society when the money could be far better spent on overseas fact-finding missions for themselves and their immediate, and not so immediate, families?

Simon nodded his head in appreciation of Superintendent Musgrave's attempt to defend his initiatives. 'Thank you, Superintendent, but before we go any further, I would like to stress that I may not necessarily agree with his courageous solution, which has become known as The Musgrave Solution, for want of a better title. Unfortunately, on this occasion it provided ample opportunity for a killing spree to be carried out when perhaps, with a different solution Andrew Glover might still be alive, Henry Haynes might be fit and well, and Paul Glover might still be alive and kicking. At least Paul would certainly not have had the opportunity to bash Henry within an inch of his life if the Musgrave Solution had not been implemented in the first place. While he has endeavoured to correct the inadequacies of the system, his appeals for recognition of the problem have obviously fallen on deaf ears. As a consequence, he's come up with the Musgrave Solution and, God knows, any solution is better than none.

'But this is neither the time nor the place for the night's little soiree to degenerate into some political debate on the spending of the state's budget or to discuss government policy relating to the housing of those in receipt of a custodial sentence. I would therefore remind you that this meeting has been convened by the police department, with the support of both the minister and the commissioner, the aim of which is to bring to closure a series of killings perpetrated within our city. Now, with your indulgence, we will move on.'

# CHAPTER 28

'$\mathcal{W}$ e have already established that the first victim in the series, Henry Haynes, who is valiantly hanging on to life and not out of the woods yet, was the target of Paul Glover's murderous intent. Next on the list of victims was Paul Glover's uncle, Andrew Glover, whose body was found floating in the harbour with all the indications of an underworld hit. Before we get into the "who did it" bit, let's seek a motive for doing away with a convicted murderer.

'At the time of Andrew's death, both Andrew and Paul Glover were unaware that their redevelopment scheme was hanging in the balance while awaiting the outcome of deliberations made by the council, namely Stuart Boswell. But while Paul believed Andrew had gone to see Boswell on the day he was murdered, Andrew's murder that is, Paul was unaware of the true nature of the visit.' Turning to face TBones, Simon asked, 'TBones, I believe you record the timings of visitors to the council members?'

'Yes, that's what I'm supposed to do, but you can't be in attendance at the counter all the time. I am obligated to avail myself of the union's hard-earned working conditions which include a mandatory half hour smoko break every hour. As I'm the only information officer, the desk is often unattended so there's a possibility people might come and go without being recorded in or out.'

'Yes, that's fine, but do you recall Mr Boswell having a visitor by the name of Andrew Glover?' Simon asked hopefully.

'Now, that bloke I remember,' TBones replied as he opened his diary to check the entry. 'He said he was in a hurry as he had to get back to jail where he was doing time for some petty misdemeanour. Ahh, yes, here it is. He called in late in the afternoon, which really peeved me because I would have to wait around until after he left, and that might be after knock off time.'

'And did he?'

'Did he what?'

'Leave after knock off time.'

'No, in fact he didn't stay long with Mr Boswell at all, about ten minutes, I'd say.'

'And you know nothing as to what transpired between the two?'

'Not a thing. That's not part of my job description; to know what goes on in the place, I mean.'

Simon paused, arms akimbo as he considered the situation. 'Gentlemen, and Cheryl, it is my contention that Andrew Glover went to see Boswell, who of course is now dead, for the specific purpose of determining the situation regarding The Grovel. Unbeknown to both the Glovers, Boswell himself was colluding with Paul Stack in furtherance of their own plans for the property. Whatever transpired between Andrew Glover and Stuart Boswell obviously caused Boswell some distress and sent the alarm bells ringing. It is my contention Andrew Glover told Boswell that the status quo could be maintained with Paul's redevelopment plan still on the agenda, but with GPD operating under Ralph's management. Boswell, certain in the knowledge that not only Stack but other contenders for the property would not be pleased with Andrew's idea, immediately phoned Paul Stack with the details of Andrew's proposition. I have no doubt it was Boswell's information that drove Stack into taking decisive action.'

Chief Superintendent Paxton shifted uncomfortably in his chair. 'Okay, but whatever upset Boswell just might have upset Stack a hell of a lot more; enough to go off and whack the poor bloke.'

'Who, Boswell?' Superintendent Fisher asked, not quite sure of whom Paxton was referring.'

Simon suppressed the sudden urge to fly off the deep end. 'Er, no Superintendent. If you recall, Boswell ended up number six on the list of victims. We are still stuck on victim number two, Andrew Glover.'

'Ahh, yes of course.'

Simon restarted his pacing after his little tete-a-tete with his boss. 'Boswell was aware neither of the Glovers could operate under the Glover Property Development banner, both having been convicted of murder. As a consequence, the Glovers, Paul and Andrew, once advised of the situation, turned to Ralph who, with Henry Haynes, had the necessary licence to trade as GPD, not that Ralph had ever agreed to the idea. Ralph, you can confirm that our two homicidal maniacs approached you with an offer to proceed with their development plans?'

Ralph pressed his lips together, raised his eyebrows, gave a small nod of the head and said, 'Yep, sure did. We had a bit of a problem regarding the profit-sharing aspects of the deal. Neither Paul nor Andrew could get it through their thick skulls that without me, any development idea had as much chance as a snowball in hell of coming to fruition. I must admit, the way things have turned out I wouldn't mind getting my hands on The Grovel for my private home, although I suppose Paul is still the owner, albeit, he's dead.'

'Thanks Ralph,' Simon acknowledged. 'Anyway, as far as

Boswell was concerned, Andrew's proposition was appalling to say the least, quite apart from the financial reward Boswell expected to receive from Stack for providing him the opportunity to purchase The Grovel well under market value. Boswell was fully conscious of the fact that if Stack didn't get what he wanted, the only return he could expect would probably be a bullet in the head.

'Now gentlemen, Stack was a very shrewd operator and, despite his garish dress, was not the flamboyant type preferring to maintain a low profile. While he may have displayed a degree of intelligence beyond that expected of the criminal mind, he certainly had no compunction in blowing someone's brains out if he thought the means justified the ends. No doubt he thought that in view of the circumstances, Andrew Glover was a complication he didn't need and suitable remedial action called for. Now, Stack liked novelties. Gally here has told us that Andrew was shot with a Walther P22 pistol, the type of weapon that would appeal to Stack, especially as it is a dainty little shooter and can be purchased in a pretty pink colour. Although it took us some time to find, the gun was finally recovered from Stack's office. It was then that Stack's real persona was uncovered; he had motive, means and opportunity to be identified as Andrew Glover's murderer.

'It is interesting to point out that during discussions with Stack, he said he believed Crawford would have been behind Andrew Glover's murder but would probably have had someone else pull the trigger. Stack was right on that score as it was Stack himself who pulled the trigger.

'In the meantime, Andy Crawford and the Premier were still prattling on with their own plan for a lavish casino. The Premier, in a moment of cerebral brilliance, took action to ensure Paul and Andrew's plan would never get off the ground by having the place heritage listed.' Simon ceased his pacing and folded his arms. 'And, that raises another point. We still don't know the outcome of Boswell's deliberations on ownership of The Grovel, so Paul might, or might not be the owner, even if he is dead. It seems that if you renege on paying your council bills, council can take pretty drastic action against you.'

Paxton scowled; Mason and Buckmaster appeared totally disinterested in proceedings; Cheryl wished she had bought along her knitting, and both TBones and Jacko seemed to be fascinated by the whole affair. 'Ahh, for goodness sake, there are nine of us here tonight who are either policemen, or connected to the force in some way, so let's cut the real estate garbage and get a move on to our bread and butter stuff,' Paxton directed angrily.

"Goodness sake"? And what was that, Simon, taken aback somewhat by Paxton's outburst of profanity, thought. I've heard him use expletives before, but I thought he would have shown a bit more respect for Cheryl and not have used such language in mixed company. 'Yes, sir, so the score so far is Henry hospitalised by Paul, and Andrew eliminated by Stack. The next in the chain of events was the demise of Paul Glover, not surprisingly, and not a pretty demise it was either. Even Gally here believes Paul would have suffered a long and agonizing death, not like his lucky uncle who just had his brains blown out; nice and quick. TBones, I see you have your diary handy, so can you please tell me who called on Mr Boswell around the first weeks of October, bearing in mind the names of people already mentioned?'

'Sure can, and the bloke you're after would be, now let's see, aah yes, Paul Glover. October eighth. He arrived at ten thirty and left at eleven fifteen, give or take a couple of minutes. I remember him 'cause I was about to take a smoko at ten thirty and he left just after I got back at eleven fifteen. Yeah, that's right, although he had visited Mr Boswell a couple of times before that date.'

'And wasn't it around that time Mr Glover was absent from where he should've been, and not bashing Ralph and myself senseless?' Cheryl asked.

Simon nodded his head in appreciation of a very good question as he was quite aware Paul should have been locked up in his cell. 'Good point, but in the misguided belief possession is nine tenths of the law, and Boswell seemingly indifferent to Paul's legal ownership, Paul had secretly set up camp in one of the old bedrooms of The Grovel. At the time I thought his presence at The Grovel, just when you and Ralph were having a look around, a tad coincidental. While absent from jail, Paul conveniently obliged Boswell by visiting the council on a number of occasions to see how the deliberations were proceeding. This provided Boswell the opportunity to provide Paul with ample cups of his invigorating coffee.

'Unfortunately for you and Ralph, Cheryl, Paul didn't stick around long enough for you to avenge the bashing he gave you both; he was dead. With countless cups of Boswell's coffee under his belt, I believe Paul would have already been well primed with small doses of ricin poison. It was the next cup of coffee Paul drank, subsequent to the attack on you, that broke the camel's back sending him running off to a nice warm bed in his jail cell where he finally conceded terminal defeat to the ricin.

'So, gentlemen, here we have two people with an interest in The Grovel, both of whom visited Boswell and ended up dead on the same day of the visit, Paul having partaken of Boswell's coffee, and Andrew, shot to death by Paul Stack following the tip-off by Boswell. According to Dave Gallymore, Paul Glover died of ricin poisoning and, although not here to defend himself, we believe the poisoner was Boswell. It was only after the death of Boswell that a recipe for ricin was found in his office which, while only circumstantial, enforces our belief Boswell cooked up the lethal doses on his stove at home. Many of us here in this room can attest to the fact that the coffee he served could conceal the taste of a roasted cane toad, not to mention the taste of castor oil from which ricin is derived.'

It was Cheryl who ventured to ask the obvious question. 'But why should Boswell become so involved as to start killing people? Sure, he might have been manipulative, but murder is a pretty big step to take.'

Simon dug his hands deep into his trouser pockets and gave a shrug. 'Oh, I think we can throw some light on Boswell's actions, Cheryl. Undoubtedly Boswell was in cahoots with Stack, as proven by the 'phone records and, although the content of the calls weren't recorded, there is sufficient circumstantial evidence to suggest they related to The Grovel. Around that time the death of Andrew Glover had no influence over Paul Glover's plans, except that it may have meant a little more work for Paul. In fact, Paul probably regarded Andrew's demise as somewhat serendipitous. Although Paul owns The Grovel, he needed Andrew's expertise to fulfil sub-contracting negotiations and act as project manager for the proposed townhouse development of the property.

'If, what Ralph tells us is correct and I have no reason to doubt him, the profits from the redeveloped property would have gone to Andrew and Paul, not GPD. Andrew's death doubled Paul's projected profits, if things had gone to plan and Paul had paid the council rates on time. Remember, when the Premier organized the recognition of The Grovel as a heritage listed building, Paul was totally checkmated. If Paul managed to retain title to the mansion, the only options available were to sell the place as is and at market value, rent it out, or live in it himself.

'Obviously the same motive for the murder of Andrew Glover applied to Paul Glover; the… I was going to say the ownership of The Grovel, but with Boswell apparently in charge of that decision, and with everyone else trying to get their hands on the property, who actually owned the place seemed of little concern. Boswell's main problem was that Paul Glover, if left alive, could appeal any decision he might make and still end up retaining ownership. If that was to happen, the plans of Crawford, Stack, Mason and the Premier would all go down the drain.

And who would be seen as the irresponsible moron to let that happen; Boswell.'

'Okay, but just who are the "everyone else" people you're referring to?' came a demanding interjection from Peter Mason.

'Well, not discounting those who have lost interest in The Grovel because they're dead, there's Ralph and Cheryl, Andy Crawford, Premier Buckmaster who, for a cut of the casino's profits, was providing the political support for Crawford's proposed scheme. Then there's Paul Glover, Andrew Glover, yourself, Mr Mason, as you have openly stated your desire for the place, while Paul Stack and Stuart Boswell are, or were, also involved. Now, out of those with an interest in the place and are still alive, there's only Ralph and Cheryl who can be considered implausible murderers having spent most of the time in hospital recuperating from the Paul Glover belting.'

Premier Buckmaster rested his elbows on the sides of his chair, clenched his fists together and took on a stern look. 'I take it from what you are insinuating, Peter and I are potential murderers, Chief Inspector Webster?'

'Sir, at this stage everyone is a potential murderer, and yes, that includes Mr Mason and yourself, despite you having been preoccupied for much of the time on your trade mission. However, if you will allow me to continue with our list of victims, I think you'll find it most interesting. Now, I believe the next one off the rank would be Andy Crawford himself. Yes, Andy wanted The Grovel to extend his casino business. He'd even approached Stack to come in on the deal, an approach Stack rejected for a number of reasons, not the least being that he and Crawford had had a falling out, probably due to the fact that Stack had decided the idea was a good one and wanted the place for himself. While we are aware Crawford had been in talks with the Premier seeking a little political support for the scheme, Stack had been in talks with Boswell, Mr Mason and, later, the Premier with the same idea.'

'And what would I want to talk to a seedy crim like Stack for?' came Mason's indignant question. 'I wanted the place to live in and make it the family home, not use it as some casino and bawdy bordello, which it would be under either the Stack or the Crawford scheme.'

'Well, I'm sorry, Mr Mason, but I find your statement a little incongruous seeing your wife has just run off and left you, and it's not as though you have a family to provide for. Putting that aside, you knew Crawford had been in talks with the Premier about the same piece of real estate you had your eye on. Stack, totally unaware of your own designs on The Grovel, had approached you for your support, which was a bit ironical in view of your discussions with Boswell with the aim of securing the property for yourself. Irrespective of what was going on around you, you believed Boswell would make good on his undertaking to provide you the opportunity to purchase The Grovel. In the meantime, Premier Buckmaster had already taken action to secure the future of the place for Crawford, and a nice little income for himself from the casino profits. Even blind Freddy could see that a fatal confrontation between Crawford and Stack was about to provide our forensic pathologist, Dave Gallymore, with yet another very dead victim. It was just a case of who would get rid of who first.

'Stack was well aware there were others actively pursuing ownership of the place, despite three contenders having already been eliminated. While Mason, Crawford and Ralph Glover were still in the hunt, Stack believed Crawford, being the most ruthless of the three, needed to be taken out of the equation before any decision Boswell might choose to make. Stack went over to The Red Ruby for a quiet tete-a-tete with Crawford, ostensibly to heal the rift between the two.

'It would seem the two men sat alone at the bar as both clientele and staff had left for the evening, it being after closing time of 3a.m. At some stage during their discussion, Stack drew his pretty little pea shooter, the same gun used to kill Andrew Glover, fatally shot Crawford and stashed his body in the cool-room until he decided what to do with it. Obviously, he needn't have bothered to give the problem any thought because he was soon to become the next victim.

'When you come to think of it, it's not so surprising Stack took the initiative and did away with Crawford, as Crawford had made it abundantly clear to Stack that anyone showing interest in The Grovel would be dealt with, permanently. Anyway, Stack, later that morning, made a point of contacting the casino's bar manager to advise him Crawford had a business-related meeting in Wollongong and would be away for a couple of days. This, he believed would give himself time to get rid of the body. Stack further advised the casino manager that Mr Crawford had decided to close the club during his absence and had given the employees time off on full pay.

'Now, Mr Mason, after Crawford's death, Stack went cold on your involvement, not that you were ever over enthusiastic with Stack's ambitions for the property you coveted. As Stack knew Mr Buckmaster was predisposed to a little wheeling and dealing, he jumped ship and entered into negotiations with the Premier rather than continue with whatever your support as deputy Premier could provide. Premier Buckmaster was ambivalent as to which gangster he was dealing with as both Crawford's and Stack's plans were virtually identical and, provided he got his share of the profits, he was happy.

# CHAPTER 29

'*N*ow, it would seem our illegal casino owner and gangster, Mr Stack, has a few questions to answer because he can be directly linked to the deaths of Andrew Glover and Andy Crawford. He had motive, means and opportunity, the motive we are all aware of, the weapon used to kill both victims was found in his office located in The Spinning Wheel casino, and he certainly had the opportunity to do away with the victims. Unfortunately, when the missing gun was found in Stack's office, so was Stack.

'Before we again enter the realms of the whys and where-fores of Stack's death, TBones, just how many visits do you recall Mr Stack made to see Mr Boswell?'

TBones immediately started to flip through the pages of his diary. 'Yes, he came out to see Mr Boswell a couple of times, the last time on October sixteenth. I think that must have been three days before his body was found.'

Noel, a bit confused with the ambiguity of TBones response, sought clarification. 'And exactly whose "body" are we referring to, Boswell's, or Stack's?'

'Oh, sorry,' TBones apologised. 'The "body", as I put it,

referred to Mr Stack's. We're not up to Mr Boswell's body yet, are we?'

'That's right, we're dealing with the dead in chronological order and we're up to Mr Stack,' Simon replied with a touch of impatience.

'Yeah, okay. Mr Stack came out a couple of times over a three day period. I haven't a clue what they talked about because knowing what they talked about isn't in my job description,' TBones volunteered, nullifying Simon's next question.

'So, the last time he came out was a few days before you learnt of Mr. Stack's untimely death?' Simon asked.

'Yes, that's about right, Chief Inspector Webster.'

Turning to Jacko, Simon asked, 'Jacko, you were the person to find Mr Stack dead in his office. Could you tell us what happened?'

'Sure thing, boss. I opened the door and he was slumped back in his seat dead to the world. He still had an unlit cigar in his hand,' Jacko replied enthusiastically.

'Yes, but did he complain of feeling sick or anything like that?'

'No, he was dead.'

'No Jacko, I mean before that.'

'Ooh yeah, I see what you mean. He said he hadn't been feelin' too well for a number of days but I put that down to worry. He seemed to have somethin' on his mind recently.'

'Okay, Gally, can you give us your slant on the victim?'

Dave Gallymore sat back on his chair and nodded. 'Yes, there was no doubt Stack had been poisoned, similar to Paul's death. He had received several small doses of ricin, lethal over a period of time with death varying anything up to five days after ingestion, although those five days would not be pleasant.'

'Yeah, well Boswell's coffee would probably kill you in five minutes without the ricin,' Noel remarked.

Chief Superintendent Paxton held his face with one hand, the elbow resting on the knee with the other hand on his hip. After staring absently at the floor for some time he finally aroused himself from his apparent reverie, sat back into his chair and adopted a more purposeful disposition. 'DCI Webster, so far we have dealt with four homicide victims that can be accounted for, two attributed to Mr Stack before he became a victim, and two attributed to Mr Boswell who also happened to become a victim. The odd one out, so far, is Henry Haynes who was brutally bashed by Paul Glover, who just happened to become another victim. If you think for one minute you expect anyone to be able to believe, or understand, who did what to who and the reasons, you're nuts. And you haven't told us why Stack had to go.'

'Yes, sir, I was coming to that. Boswell poisoned Stack because he knew that unless Stack was given the opportunity to buy The Grovel, things might get a bit sticky for himself. As we know, Mr Mason had been in discussions with Boswell with an aim of procuring the mansion for his own personal use. But Boswell was real smart. He had used the old three card trick by playing Crawford, Stack and Mason off against each other with the highest bidder getting the nod.

'However, there was one major hurdle for Boswell. While he may have been able to legally dispossess the current title holder, Paul Glover, of The Grovel, irrespective of whether he was alive or dead, any decision as to who the new owner might be stood to be contested with a possible legal appeal by the sole remaining Glover, Ralph. As Paul died intestate, any legal suit brought by Ralph could well be looked upon favourably.'

Ralph's eyes lit up as he gave a "that's interesting" look to Cheryl. 'Now, that's a very good point, Mr Webster. It's such a good point I'm surprised I didn't think of it.'

'Well, don't forget that a lot of what I have said is pure speculation, but it does have a ring of truth, at least to Noel, Ron and myself,' Simon said before continuing with his off the cuff delivery of events. 'Boswell, in his attempt to line his own pockets, had worked himself into an invidious position as he finally realised that a good decision for one person might be a terminal decision for himself as far as the other contenders were concerned. Thankfully, Stack came along and blew the tripe out of Crawford which effectively put an end to the swanky casino ideas of Crawford and the Premier, thus leaving Stack and Mason the only contenders.

'Mason had paid Boswell a substantial incentive for his favourable decision whereas Stack didn't have to offer Boswell any inducement to provide him the opportunity to purchase the place. All Stack had to offer Boswell was a vindictive bullet in the back of the head if The Grovel didn't come his way. With the realization that Ralph Glover may have a legitimate claim to The Grovel, Boswell suddenly saw the danger both Ralph and Stack presented.

'Boswell knew very well that if Stack wasn't happy with the outcome of events, he would have grave difficulty in spending the kickbacks already invested by several of the intrepid would-be real estate entrepreneurs; he'd be dead. Of the two, Boswell regarded Ralph as posing no direct physical threat, whereas Stack was another matter. Having poisoned Paul Glover with ricin, Boswell started feeding it to Stack in the hope he would be able to kill him off before Stack had the chance to kill him. Obviously, Boswell's coffee had the desired effect and provided Gally with yet another cadaver; this time Stack's.

'For Boswell, the field was rapidly dwindling with only Ralph Glover and Peter Mason the only contenders left. Mr Mason had, as opposed to Ralph, already paid Boswell a heap of money, as had others in the race for the place, but they were now all dead. Ralph, on the other hand, had no intention of paying anybody anything as he was happy to let events take their course. Obviously, an appeal to the Family Law Court would probably see Ralph end up with The Grovel without any inducement having to be paid to anyone, although it appears Ralph hadn't considered that option.

'Boswell's total lack of forethought in regards to the legal action Ralph could pursue, and the fact that Mr Mason had already paid money to Boswell, the next logical victim, so one would have thought, would have been Mr Mason. Such an event would have brought the Grovelgate proceedings to a close with Ralph becoming the owner and Boswell walking away with a stack of Mr Mason's money, along with the hard-earned cash of all the others who had paid Boswell. Needless to say, it came as some surprise when it was Boswell himself who turned up his toes. Discounting Premier Buckmaster, who was anxious to play the silent partner in any skullduggery dreamt up by either Crawford or Stack, it was Ralph Glover and Mr Mason who were the only people we considered as suspects in the demise of Mr Boswell.'

At that point of the monologue, Simon stood still in front of the fireplace, hands in his pockets, his eyes surveying the results of his exposition. Everyone sat motionless, staring at nothing, the enormity of the long-winded revelation appearing to have been too much to digest. It was Chief Superintendent Paxton who was the first to shake himself back to reality and, after scratching an unitchy earlobe, looked at Simon with an air of hostility.

'Okay, Simon,' remonstrated Chief Superintendent Paxton, 'so that lets Premier Buckmaster off the hook, and he won't have to declare his pecuniary interest in a high-class house of ill repute to the other members of Parliament, which would have gone over like a lead balloon. I'm sure his intervention into the heritage thing can be fudged over to make it look like a routine government decision. Good grief, the mansion looks like it should've been heritage listed years ago, and if not listed, demolished.'

Simon nodded his head in agreement. 'Yes, sir, but that does not exonerate the Premier from conspiracy to murder, accessory to murder, both before and after the fact, conspiracy to gain a financial advantage through illicit means, and a host of other charges that, if not illegal, are certainly inconsistent with the moral integrity expected from the leader of the state. But that's a problem for greater minds than a humble DCI. We still have one murder left, and that's of Boswell.'

# CHAPTER 30

*D*etective Superintendent Nigel Fisher scowled. He appreciated the fact that Detective Chief Inspector Simon Webster had, at least on face value, brought to finality four brutal murders without one arrest having been made, apparently a record in the annals of Sydney policing. Now, with only one more case to be scrutinized, Nigel was aware there was a good chance that that record was about to be extended to equal Jack the Ripper's tally of victims. While not of cataclysmic magnitude, it was an irritation the superintendent could well do without, especially as the press was bound to have a field day once it became known the police had, so far, solved four murders, but were incapable of making any arrest. In keeping with the journalistic creed of never letting the truth get in the way of a good story, the fact that the murderers had themselves been murdered before they could be arrested would be a journalistic scoop to be seized upon by a press out for a little sensationalism. Aah, what the heck; I can live with that.

'Right, moving right along,' Simon declared. 'Last on our list of deceased potential real estate tycoons comes that doyen of public service ineptitude, Stuart Boswell. While not wishing to speak ill of the dead, I find it difficult to speak of him in any other manner. Mr Boswell, unfortunately, failed to recognize that he had been promoted way above the level of his capabilities. With boundless zeal and stamina, he had set himself an exceptionally high standard of bureaucratic incompetence and, without any assistance, managed to attain that standard in spectacular fashion. Unfortunately, for the council's personal administration staff, Boswell had been offered the luxury of a permanent position which meant he had become virtually unsackable, much to the chagrin of his associates.

'In keeping with bureaucratic doctrine, if you can't sack someone, you promote them to another position. In this case, Boswell was shunted into a job that sounded important, and had an office to go with it. Aided by his rocketing ego, Boswell believed he was the all singing, dancing wonder kid of the council. Now, as I have finally made known my profound enmity towards our Mr Boswell, I'll continue with the saga of Grovelgate.

'Yes, there is provision for council to seize property under certain circumstances, and non-payment of statutory fees is one of those circumstances. However, usually such a decision is not made by one person, but by a board of executives within council and is only applied when all other avenues have been exhausted. Unfortunately, due to clerical ineptitude, Boswell was handed the task of making serious determinations and decisions, an exercise in cerebral dexterity alien to, and beyond the capability of many bureaucrats, even at the highest echelons of government employment. After speaking to Boswell several times, we found it odd that one person should wield so much apparent power. But Boswell was revelling in his own success and, with so many people approaching him for his decision on The Grovel, he felt he had reached the ultimate goal of the public servant; absolute power over the plebs.

'Sadly, for Boswell, he failed to recognize the true nature of those with whom he was now dealing; developers, gangsters and the most perfidious egomaniacs on the planet, the politician. It is not unrealistic to believe the character of some of those involved had the potential to eliminate anyone who stood in their way, as many found out to their terminal misfortune. Gullible as he was in dealing with such people, Boswell saw the opportunity to make some easy money by playing off those interested in acquiring the property against each other. However, when the killings started, Boswell realised the game was getting rough and was a little out of his depth.

'It was following the death of Andrew Glover, and the manner of his death, that Boswell realised the situation had become desperate as any decision he made was going to be, in someone's eyes, the wrong decision. Our poor Mr. Boswell, having suddenly realized that he couldn't please all the people all the time, saw that his chances of survival on planet Earth were rapidly decreasing. We have already dealt with the death of Paul Glover and Mr Stack, both of whom were poisoned by Mr Boswell in an effort to increase his own chances of reaching retirement. When Stack murdered Andy Crawford, Boswell was absolutely delighted, for obvious reasons. In fact, at that stage Boswell believed he had only one claimant to the property and that was deputy Premier Mason, clearly a trustworthy and honourable person who would never stoop to murder.

'However, lurking in the background and keeping a low profile was the sole remaining member of the Glover family, Ralph. He had shown his hand early in the piece when he had Henry make a call on Paul and Andrew Glover during their incarceration in the City Jail.'

'And what's so wrong with that?' Ralph piped up. 'The Grovel has excellent development potential and I am not averse to taking an opportunity when presented. I sent Henry over to find out what Paul and Andrew were planning. Hell, even when it got to the stage where the Premier had the place heritage listed, a fortune could still be made with a few internal renovations and a bit of landscaping. Cripes, you only have to take a look around this room and you can see the obvious potential,' Ralph entreated with a wave of the hand, 'not that I think there's any chance of realizing that potential for myself, now.'

Simon clasped his hands behind his back and started the stroll back and forward in front of the fireplace. He finally stopped his wandering and turned to face Ralph. 'Yes, Ralph, and you were quite content to sit on the sideline and watch the mayhem being carried out by others wanting to get their grubby little fingers on The Grovel. In fact, as you wanted the place for yourself, you couldn't give a toss what was going on around you with each murder increasing the odds of you gaining the property.

'It wasn't until Boswell started to see the possible ramifications of his pending decision regarding ownership that things started to go wrong. While in the process of playing each contender off against each other, people started to get themselves murdered. When it got to the stage where there was only one other person left alive who wanted the place, that being Mr Mason, apart from yourself, you had to make sure Mr Boswell made the correct decision, and that was to leave the place to the current and legal owner, Paul Glover, even though he was dead. As the only remaining member of the Glover family, irrespective of whether Paul had made a will or not, you had a legitimate claim on Paul's estate.'

'So, you think I strutted over to Bondi Junction and stuck a letter opener into Boswell. How very convenient for Mr Mason then,' snarled Ralph as he clasped Cheryl's hand, waking her from her slumber.

Simon shook his head in a display of disappointment. 'Ralph, you had motive in your belief Boswell was going to virtually hand the place to Mr Mason on a silver platter. The means to kill

Boswell was readily available and provided by Boswell himself with a metal letter opener in the form of King Arthur's Excalibur there on his desk. The opportunity was readily available as TBones was rarely at the information counter and you could have walked in at any time. You didn't have to have TBones around to show you where Boswell's office was, you knew exactly where it was from your previous visits.'

Ralph let go of Cheryl's hand and jumped to his feet. 'Look, you, you...Sure I wanted the place, but after Henry's near-death incident, I certainly wasn't going to go around murdering people to get it. I feel guilty for what happened to Henry as I have always believed his attack had something to do with The Grovel. But the way these other brain-dead lunatics were acting, I didn't have to murder anyone; they were doing it for me. Quite apart from all the in-fighting and murdering, after some thought I decided the game was getting too rough for me. Sure, I wouldn't mind owning The Grovel, but not for some witless money-making scheme. If per chance the place did come my way, I would hope Cheryl and I would make it our home, permanently.'

'Okay, okay, just take it easy, Ralph, relax. I know you didn't kill Boswell, or any other person, but I had to cover all possibilities,' Simon said, placating Ralph's obvious indignation.

The majority of those sitting in the lounge room of The Grovel were now listening in rapt attention to Simon's outpouring of speculation, guesswork and theories. Premier Buckmaster, however, was showing some concern that the killer of Boswell had been whittled down to his deputy, Peter Mason. Buckmaster was of the firm belief Mason was a pillar of virtue and integrity, a belief the majority of voters out in the electorate might claim to be an oxymoron.

While Premier Buckmaster was somewhat tetchy with the

direction Simon's revelations had taken, deputy Premier Mason sat seemingly bemused by the situation. With all the arrogance only a politician can convoke, Mason sneered, 'So, DCI Webster, it appears I am the last person here to undergo your judgment unless, of course, you have other contenders for Boswell's murder hidden away somewhere. All your previous revelations have been based on pure guesswork, and I'm inclined to think you haven't a clue in the world as to who killed Boswell, or anybody else for that matter.'

'Careful, Peter, you will need to be very cautious with what you say as I can guarantee your future career is hanging in the basket,' quipped Buckmaster.

The closest thing to a basket around here is you, who's a basket case; the word is balance, you moron, Simon thought. With a shrug and a pout of the lips, he raised both his hands, palms upward in a gesture of acceptance and addressed the Premier. 'I'm sorry, sir, but I can only relate it as I see it. But before you come to any conclusion, you might like to know that Mr Mason was prepared to undermine your position should your joint venture with Andy Crawford or Paul Stack have come to fruition. Firstly, Mr Mason has copies of all the paperwork in regard to your little two-man trade delegation to New York with your secretary, including trips to Broadway shows and baseball games, all at public expense. Okay, let's make that politically correct; a two-person trade delegation to The States.

'Then there is the matter of the disclosure of pecuniary interests which Mr Mason was itching to provide parliament, if you failed to do so after you started to take your share from the casino profits. Obviously, as a silent partner, all monetary returns from the casino would be squirreled away in some overseas tax haven. While Mr Mason was waiting for the opportunity to stab you in the back, you, Mr Premier, weren't covering yourself in deeds of distinction and probity by blackmailing your minister for the environment into having The Grovel declared a heritage listed dwelling without departmental consultation. And all this so you could partake, no, let's make that so you could invest in the setting up of an illegal gambling casino and bordello.

'When taken into context of how you came to power following the debacle of the previous premier's gravy train rorting, there is bound to be speculation that your position as Premier is on pretty shaky ground, to say the least. While you have shown admirable qualities in supporting your deputy, I doubt such qualities would be reciprocated should the circumstances arise, or when they arise, especially when the backbenches get to hear of events.'

'Oh, for heaven's sake, get on with it,' the irritable outburst emanating from Superintendent Musgrave. 'So, Boswell was the venal flee who poisoned two victims and someone had the sense to do him in before he knocked anybody else off the planet. Whoever it was deserves a medal.'

Simon, his arms folded in a fair indication of an adopted defensive posture, started his walk to and fro in front of the fire place. 'I apologise for what may seem a waste of time, but I believe it necessary to paint the whole picture as there are very few people around to refute or take exception to what I believe is the sequence of events leading up to Boswell's death. TBones, you have recorded the name of the last person to have visited Mr Boswell?'

'Yes, Mr Webster, that would have been Mr Mason. I have him recorded in around eleven, but as he's not recorded out, he must have left while I was either at lunch or on a smoko break. I thought Mr Boswell must have gone out himself as a couple of people came in to see him during the afternoon. As he never answered his phone, I took that to mean he was either out or just wasn't available to see anybody.'

'So, Mr Mason, at what time did you leave Boswell's office?' Simon asked.

The deputy Premier shifted uncomfortably on his chair. 'Yes, well I wasn't there for very long. I'd gone in to ask what the position was regarding The Grovel in light of the number of people who had lost interest in the place.'

'Yes, one does tend to lose interest in a lot of things when they're dead. And?'

'The little pipsqueak had reneged on the whole deal. It seemed Paul Glover was still the owner, despite the ducks and drakes Boswell had been playing. The rotten sod had no council authority to foreclose on the coffee fund, let alone a mansion worth millions. The question of ownership of The Grovel was never in doubt. Boswell had previously assured me that in light of the way things were going, and my payment of a sizeable amount of money, I would be able to buy the place way under market value, which is exactly what I wanted. Even the Premier's action relating to the place being heritage listed didn't present any problems as I didn't want to have a bulldozer come and knock down the place.'

'And did Boswell ever offer you a cup of coffee?'

'Yes he did, but I declined as I'm a tea drinker and he didn't make tea.'

'And you left after that little discussion?'

'Yes.'

Simon turned to Inspector Ian Francis. 'Ian, although the murder of Boswell happened in your bailiwick, the potential for his murder to have been influenced by previous circumstances, including the Henry Hayes incident, seems too much of a coincidence. As a consequence, and as those circumstances are under investigation by Day Street, we have incorporated his murder into the chain of events now referred to by a few of us as Grovelgate.'

'And we over at Waverly were very glad of that as Boswell was the fifth victim in the saga, with only his elimination, along with the Haynes incident, committed in our Local Area

Command,' Francis replied. 'Although you conducted the investigation into the murder, we maintained an obvious interest as to what was going on. I remember the call-out we had when Boswell was finally found in his office with a letter opener stuck in his chest. At least we had no problems in finding the murder weapon. We also found a recipe for concocting a dose of ricin, which is not difficult to make.'

Simon looked at Mason dubiously and raised his eyebrows, an action that evoked a profound effect on the politician. 'And you think I murdered the little weasel who we all know just happened to be some psychopathic poisoner,' Mason angrily responded, his face taking on a frightening shade of crimson. Simon and Mason were now in the throes of a serious confrontation, usually the time when the famous literary detective springs the trap and makes the correct accusation against some nondescript individual no-one had ever suspected. The remaining visitors to the little soiree tensed and waited in expectation.

'You know, Mr Mason, during the course of the investigation into the death of your political associate, Robert Porter, we recorded the finger prints of all members of parliament involved in the case, some by consent, others…' Simon gave a condescending shrug. 'It just so happens that forensics has matched your prints with those found in Boswell's office…'

'Of course they would've. I've already admitted I went there to see him,' roared Mason.

'And you just happened to play around with his Excalibur letter opener and it, somehow, just got stuck in Boswell's chest with your prints on the thing?'

'Aah, come on. Who'd be so bloody stupid as to dirk a bloke and leave the murder weapon sticking out of the victim's chest with their prints all over it?' Mason scornfully responded. 'You've only to watch one of those Miss Marple movies to know how the killer does it, and I didn't.'

Simon slowly shook his head in wonderment. 'I'm sorry, Mr Buckmaster, while I do not wish to cast aspersions on the integrity or wisdom of any particular politician, I can only say that, in this case, it was a particular politician that was so bloody stupid as to leave his finger prints all over the murder weapon. Mr Mason, I put it to you that you went to see Boswell about The Grovel and when told of the situation, which was totally contrary to your expectations, you fell off your perch, withdrew Excalibur from King Arthur and, in a fit of rage, did maliciously stab Stuart Boswell to death.

'Without withdrawing the weapon from Boswell's body, or cleaning it of fingerprints, you engaged the internal Yale dead-lock to the door and, as you left, you pulled the door closed leaving your finger prints on the door knob. Fortunately for you, TBones was not at the information counter when you left the building, which comes as no great surprise as he is obligated to partake of the onerous smoko provisions. The one thing it does explain is the failure of TBones to be able to contact Mr Boswell after lunch because, by that time, Mr Boswell was dead.

'It wasn't until the cleaner, a Mrs Henniker, was in the process of doing her rounds that Boswell's body was found. As there was no response to her knocking, and believing the office to be unoccupied, she used her key to open the door, as per the usual routine in such cases. The door is fitted with a Yale type lock and a door knob that has no locking function. Mrs Henniker opened the inward opening door using her key without touching the knob, as one does when using a key. The fingerprints found on the door knob were left by the last person to have pulled the door shut as they left the office. That person was you, Mr Mason, and the fingerprints have been confirmed as yours.'

Premier Buckmaster's head dropped as he slouched forward and held his face in his hands. 'So, you're saying my deputy would stoop to murder, Chief Inspector Webster, or are you just casting aspersions on politicians in general?' he finally asked.

'Mr Premier, I'm not saying Mr Mason would, or could, stoop to murder; I'm saying Mr Mason did stoop to murder. Due to the cumulative effect of adverse circumstances, Mr Boswell provided the last piece of straw needed to break the camel's back. Mrs Mason had just walked out on Mr Mason and gone off to Europe with the previous deputy Premier, Wally Ackerman, in hot pursuit. On top of that, Mrs Mason currently owns the house over at Kogarah, and you can bet the Masons will not be residing together in matrimonial bliss at that address, or any other address for that matter. All it took was Boswell to provide another bit of bad news for Mr Mason to do his nana and stick Boswell to death.'

The audience remained seated while an uncomfortable silence prevailed over the room. Simon stood in contemplative reflection, waiting. Contrary to his expectations, the howls of dissent expected from DS Fisher and Chief Superintendent Paxton failed to materialise. Fisher was whispering intently to Paxton, while Dave Harris, Ian Francis and Dave Gallymore had organised themselves into a huddle and were discussing the pros and cons of Simon's deliberations. It fell to Jacko and TBones to be the first to return to planet Earth and were in deep and meaningful analysis of the recently decided football grand final. Ron and Noel now stood together mulling over a half empty bottle of Glenfidditch, the sole surviving vestige of a once extensively stocked cocktail cabinet. Aah, what the heck, who'll notice, and at least we'll appreciate it, Noel concluded.

Superintendent Musgrave sat alone, a look of sheer despondency etched across his face. Okay, so he had implemented a courageous decision to overcome a problem no politician wanted a bar of. He was well aware there were bound to be those who believed he was directly, or at best indirectly, responsible for the abhorrent massacre perpetrated by a bunch of troglodytes all striving to take control of a piece of real estate; and none of this would have happened if he hadn't adopted such a radical prison plan.

Simon gave a single clap of his hands to draw the guest's attention back to the revelation he had so painstakingly unveiled. 'And there, Superintendent Fisher,' Simon announced to his superior officer, 'is the outline of the case we will be presenting to the DPP at the preliminary hearing of Mr Mason for the murder of Stuart Boswell. Noel, read Mr Mason his rights.'

'Hey, hang on to your horses a second,' yelled Premier Buckmaster. 'You mean you're actually going to charge Peter, a minister of the crown, with murder. Have you no idea what the repercussions of such an action will have?'

Simon shrugged and raised his hands in the universal gesture; "c'est la vie". 'Regrettably, Mr Premier, it is not my job to consider the repercussions of putting some harebrained homicidal half-wit behind bars. However, with the judiciary being what the judiciary is, and the current sentences being handed down, I would say that for a straight forward murder, the guilty party could probably expect about six months community service, or even a suspended sentence, depending on the vacancy availability in Superintendent Musgrave's jail.

'And that in itself raises a question. In view of Superintendent Musgrave's open prison plan, if Mr Mason should be found guilty of Boswell's murder, the judge might not be able to hand down a custodial sentence due to a "Jail Full" sign. Such a situation may not preclude Mr Mason from continuing on as a politician. Now your position, Mr Premier, might be a totally different question. We plebs out in the electorate may view your situation differently and decide to call for your resignation leaving the deputy Premier who, at least for the moment, would be Mr Mason in charge of the state. Now that would be something.'

It was Chief Superintendent Paxton whose patients finally ran out. 'Look Simon, Superintendent Fisher and I have had a quiet word with DI Harris and DI Francis and we are all of the opinion your assessment of the situation is probably correct, and we're not too concerned if it's not. In view of the lack of witnesses available to refute your claims, we are happy to go along with your conclusions and can see no reason why Mr Mason should not be charged with murder. So, DS Elliott, please proceed with the caution; I vote for the other mob in any case.'

'They tell me you've been having a hard time,' the tall, lean, sun tanned gentleman with collar-length black hair commented, more as a statement than a question.

Simon heaved a sigh, cast a knowing glance at Noel then paused for a moment of reflection before replying to his guest. 'Yes, one might say things started to get a little out of hand. Five homicides perpetrated by three murderers with only one arrest, and that's not counting an apparent murder next-door. For all the opportunities you had to leave country, you really picked the most inappropriate time. As nearly everything that happened related to your area of business interest, we'd have really appreciated a little bit of your assistance, especially as you knew Stack and Crawford pretty well.'

There is no doubt the Grovelgate investigation could well have done with some help from Graham Lee who, as the owner of the exclusive but illegal Taipan Club, had both an interest in, and an extensive awareness of, events pertaining to Sydney's other illegal gambling casinos. 'Yeah well, much as I would have liked to have helped, Simon, I doubt Louisa would have been too pleased to cancel the wedding and honeymoon arrangements just so I could go and play cops and robbers,' Graham declared as Louisa accepted his proffered hand with a squeeze.

The backyard lawn of 24 West Bank Lane was, again, the venue for a convivial afternoon get together. However, on this occasion there were slightly more visitors than usual indulging in the hospitality provided by their hosts, Simon and Georgie Webster. The customary number of friends relaxing on director chairs had been augmented by the presence of Graham Lee and Louisa Porter or, more correctly, Louisa Lee, following their wedding and honeymoon to some exotic and expensive secluded resort.

'Anyway, from what I hear, both Mr Crawford and Mr Stack are no longer providing any opposition to The Taipan Club which means there's another three people who have turned up their toes. Mind if you précis a rundown of events?' Graham enquired as he filled Louisa's glass and then his own with a delicate, unpretentious but titillating drop of Moet.

The amiable chitchat around the circle came to a sudden and expectant halt. While Noel and Ron had the general gist of events, the girls had only managed to glean fragmentary pieces of information from their unresponsive spouses. As a result, they were eager to hear just who had eliminated who, and the reason behind the expunging of candidates in competition for The Grovel. Before he started his explanation, Simon finished off his beer, tossed the empty can into the garbage bin and replaced it with another from the ice filled Esky.

After an hour of explanation and précising down the murders to the nitty-gritty, Simon completed his narration of events, as he believed they were. 'Yeah, so everyone who wanted The Grovel were walking around with a target on their back while, at the same time, quite prepared to assassinate all opposition,' Judy said before her facial expression broadcast the inevitable "but" was on the way, which it was. 'But who actually ended up with the place?'

'Well, it didn't come as any great surprise. Seems like the Family Law Court was on Ralph's side and, as he was the last Glover standing, The Grovel passed to him. Needless to say, I expect Cheryl Drake, who will undoubtedly become the next Mrs Glover, will have a say in the fixing up of the place.'

'And what about Henry Haynes?' Sue asked.

Simon nodded and smiled in acknowledgement. 'The good news is Henry's okay and will be out of hospital within a day or two. He's going up to the Sunshine Coast to recuperate for a few weeks before coming back and taking up a position within GPD with Ralph.'

Sue turned to Graham with a quizzical look. 'And with The Spinning Wheel and The Red Ruby pretty well put to the sword, have you any plans for The Taipan Club?'

Graham Lee smiled and nodded his head. 'Despite whatever Paul Stack or Andy Crawford may have said about their respective concerns, both their premises were rented. That in itself comes as no great surprise as illegal casinos are prone to be raided by the police's vice squad. Obviously, renting premises provides the flexibility to shut up shop and open up somewhere else as quickly as possible. Stupid part is they usually pack up their bongos and move to a new location, blissfully unaware that the police probably know exactly where they've gone. On the other hand, I own The Taipan Club and the property that goes with it. Although subject to the same police threat as Stack and Crawford did, I always make a point of keeping the police on side. I provide them with information regarding underworld activities which they would never receive if there wasn't that rapport in the first place.'

Graham paused and, after some deliberation, returned to Sue's initial question. 'There is no future for The Taipan Club and I have already received quite a substantial offer from a developer who wants the property for a high-rise residential development. While I have a secure future in the legal casino business, I do have other options open to me. Who knows? I might even try my hand at politics.'

Ron, in the middle of downing a mouthful of beer, immediately went into a convulsion and choked. After regaining his senses, he quite bemusedly, asked, 'You're kidding? People go into politics and become corrupted. You'd be putting the cart before the horse; you're corrupt before you even get there.'

'And that's the angle,' Graham returned. 'I'm aware of most of the tricks politicians pull, especially having worked with Simon and Noel. While I can freely admit I haven't been the sole of discretion, I'm fully aware that politicians are so bound up in their own importance that they fail to recognize their own dishonesty. Unfortunately, they dribble on with diatribe in an effort to justify shonky activities, and they certainly cannot recognise the difference between something being legally corrupt and something being morally corrupt.'

Sue passed Noel a look that said it all; cripes, sorry I asked. Having been married to a politician who happened to get himself murdered to death, Louisa decided to intervene. 'Look, Graham has embarked on a totally new life. He now has me to consider and we have his lovely boat "Gemini" for a bit of relaxation. While we don't propose to go overboard and become completely hedonistic about life, I applaud his intentions and he has my support, so there!'

'Goodness, no malice intended, Louisa,' Sue appealed, 'I'd vote for Graham any day in preference to the idiots we currently have. But getting right off the subject, what in the world is happening, or has happened next-door? Simon, you say a murder has been committed but you haven't given us any details. Who's murdered who, how, and why?'

Simon looked to Georgie for support in answering the question but, as Georgie knew as little as Simon, the expected support was not forthcoming. All Detective Inspector Spring-Brown had advised on his previous visit to Collaroy was that a body, believed to have originated from Collaroy, had been recovered for the Manly municipal garbage tip. While not wishing to cast aspersions, Spring-Brown suggested the marital record of Moira Sampson may give rise to speculation that the little old lady is either cursed in her efforts to find a partner to accompany her in her dotage or, if nothing else, she is a maniacal, scheming serial killer.

Fortunately for everyone concerned, the afternoon's discussion was interrupted by the sound of the side gate being opened and closed heralding the arrival of an unexpected visitor who, on rounding the corner of the house, was immediately identified as Detective Inspector Spring-Brown.

'Well, speak of the devil, if it's not DI Spring-Brown himself. We were just talking about you and the mystery of the manor next-door,' Simon exclaimed. 'Pull up a pew and have a beer. I take it you're not on duty?'

'Thanks, Chief, I'd really love one but, unfortunately I am, well, sort of. Sergeant Gaskill and a couple of constables are next-door arresting Moira,' the DI replied as he uncollapsed a director's chair.

'Arrested her for murder? Ooh, how exciting,' Judy declared with unfettered excitement.

'I'm not so sure Moira would regard it as exciting,' Ron interjected. 'Anyway, let's have it; the how, when, where and why.'

As it was a warm, nudging a hot afternoon, DI Spring-Brown's eyes were inexorably drawn to the ice filled Esky containing an assortment of amber beverages. 'Ah hell, the boys can take her back in the van so I'll limit myself to one coldy, purely for medicinal purposes, if you don't mind, Simon?'

'No, no problems. Help yourself,' Simon replied congenially, 'but only if you tell us all there is about the little old lady, Moira.'

The DI settled himself back on his chair, opened his can of

beer and took a thirst-quenching swig. With an eager audience full of anticipation, he commenced his disclosure of events. 'Yes, the wonderful but morbid Moira. First off, let me stress we have not charged Moira with murder; manslaughter yes, and obviously that is yet to be proven. As you know, Eric Tindale was husband number three for Moira, the first two cremated in what could be considered disrespectful haste soon after they were deceased. Come to think of it, it would have been a poor show if they had been cremated before they were deceased. But fortunately we were lucky with Eric, not that he probably thought so, but with him we at least had a body on which an autopsy could be performed.

'Now, it appears Moira was an enthusiastic gardener which presented us with a bit of a problem. Either Moira doesn't know her avocado from her azalea, or she has a good grasp of toxic plants and their fatal effects on humans. The autopsy carried out on Teddy found he had levels of the poison andromedotoxin in his body, a poison derived from the azalea plant. Georgie, can you confirm Moira was a coffee drinker and didn't partake of tea?'

'Yes, that's what she told me. She said she didn't like tea although she didn't mind making it for other people,' Georgie replied.

DI Spring-Brown nodded. 'Yes, I thought that's what you told me earlier. Anyway, as soon as we had the autopsy report, we checked Moira's kitchen and took possession of a tea pot which, following forensic tests, indicated traces of andromedo-toxin. And this is where we have a slight problem. We know Moira was intrigued with the gum tree leaf in the billycan trick used by the outback drovers when making a brew of tea. Moira doesn't deny the fact she always puts part of the azalea, or any other plant such as the poinsettia or oleander, in her husband's teapot. Her reasoning behind this little peculiarity stems from the fact that if a gum leaf can make tea taste better, a part of a pretty flower must make it taste much better.'

'Yeah, well that's all very good,' Noel declared. 'You've established the means and obviously the opportunity was there. You say her previous husbands, or partners, or whatever they were, left her all their assets including bundles of cash. Now, just because we can see a very strong motive doesn't mean she sees it that way. Such a thought may never have crossed her mind.'

'And there's the rub. We can satisfy the actus reus part of the case but the mens rea will present all sorts of problems for the prosecutor. Can we prove that by giving her partners a cutting from a pretty flower in their tea she knew she was providing them with a lethal dose of poison? I've no doubt most people out in suburbia believe the only lethal plant in the garden is a triffid. And Noel, you're absolutely right, motive is very subjective. Although we might see a patently obvious motive, Moira may consider the idea of deliberately poisoning her better half for a financial windfall as totally preposterous. And the fact that she had Body One and Two cremated soon after their death doesn't tell us anything either. The disposal of Body Three, or Eric, is a bit different, but if Moira is a tad potty then she probably had her own good reason for stuffing Eric in the garbage can. And therein lies another unanswered question; how did she ever manage to wheel her bin up to the roadway for collection. She's not the strongest of little old ladies and Eric must have been around fifty to sixty kilos.'

Georgie, who was sitting next to Simon, put a steadying hand on his shoulder as a shiver ran through her body. Ooh no, I couldn't possibly have, she thought. Did I tell Simon? Yes I did, but he won't remember as he had other things on his mind. Crikey, this is another pickle you've got yourself into, Georgie.

It seemed DI Spring-Brown had nothing more to add to his version of events and, after thanking his hosts for their hospitality and nodding a farewell to the others, headed up the driveway to his car for the trip back to Manly. A silence descended over the remaining eight people sitting in the circle of Simon's back lawn as they digested the contents of the DI's revelations. Moira must either be nutty as a fruit cake or a very proficient poisoner and master criminal.

Judy, having somewhat of a mercenary nature, broke the silence. 'Damn and blast, that leaves the place empty again and no rent coming in. And this time I'm going to smudge the place and get rid of all the bad karma and spirits before I do anything else'

'Smudge'? queried Ron. 'Never head of that one. I thought it was exercise.'

Judy, her face contorted in a brutish scowl, shook her head in wonderment. 'Exorcise, you dunderhead, spelt with an "o", not an "e". What you'd expect me to do, take the house for a walk?'

Totally preoccupied with another thought, Simon turned to Georgie. 'Georgie, didn't you mention you had taken Moira's wheelie bin up to the roadway the other day?'

Knowing an untruth would most likely result in diabolical consequences, Georgie's head fell in abject despondency before slowly nodding assent. 'Well, how was I to know what was in it? You don't usually look in other people's garbage, at least I don't.'

Strangely, there wasn't a person sitting in the circle who didn't have a smile on their face. Georgie was quickly becoming quite renowned for her accidental, or inadvertent, involvement in murders and mayhem associated with Number 26 West Bank Lane. But, while Louisa Lee had, moments earlier, proclaimed Graham's undying solicitude, Detective Chief Inspector Simon Webster, in spite of his forbearance and patience, had Georgie, along with her growing portentous reputation to look after. However, there were times…

# ABOUT THE AUTHOR

John Henderson was born in Singleton in the state of New South Wales, Australia. The family moved to the town of Yass soon afterwards where he spent his younger days before a move to Sydney. John went to Manly Boys' High School, represented the district in cricket and spent a lot of time surfing. He joined the Army in 1968 and toured South Vietnam in 1969-70.

Following his discharge from the Army and a brief stint in the Commonwealth Public Service, John chose to write crime satire. With his dry, cynical sense of humour, The Simon Webster Fiasco series represents an amusing and sceptical view of life and bureaucratic nonsense, as viewed by the author.

John now lives in Canberra with his wife, and cat, Fergus.

**Connection with me on-line**
http://www.twitter.com/JohnHenderson07
http://www.amazon.com/author/johnhenderson7